Castle Ruins

Peter R Sherratt ©2019

Other books by Peter R Sherratt

Cornish Princess
Girl in a Tree
River Song
Imperial Measurements for Crumblies

Thanks to:
Peter and Ann Walker for help with farming issues
Alwyn Marriage for her work on editing the script
Andrew Harris (assisted by Joanne) for advice on 'mending' castles
and to Paul for notes on the Seychelles

www.psherratt.uk

*Frontispiece: Orford Castle, Suffolk – a magnificent keep and definitely **not** a ruin*

For Paul, Adam and Mark

Chapter 1

The corridors of the Estuary View Care home in Grange-over-Sands were in almost complete darkness, hiding the scrapes, scratches and dents of numerous wheelchairs and trolleys on the dingy, dark green and brown paintwork of the walls. The only light came from a crack in the door at the far end where the night carer lay fast asleep, despite the blaring of the television in her room. The noise was a boon. It drowned out the sounds emanating from each room on the corridor; heavy sonorous snoring from number six, whimpering from number ten, screaming from twelve

There was no sound from number fourteen where a huge giant of a man lay dying. He was not aware of it but the doctor had visited earlier in the day and pronounced that he had double pneumonia and would probably not last until morning. He had no memory of today, nor yesterday, nor any of the yesterdays of his entire life but there were occasional, nameless goblins from things past, which still came to haunt him although he had long-since forgotten why. Had he been aware of the doctor's prognosis, the old man would not have cared. He was more than ready to die and would have welcomed the 'old man's friend'. He was eighty-nine years old and had no reason or wish to cling to life.

He had been admitted to the care home fourteen years earlier on the recommendation of a consultant when he been diagnosed as suffering from advancing Alzheimer's disease. He had never married and had no living relatives and had entered the care home because he knew that he could no longer cope with even the most minor of day-to-day decisions and was desperate to escape from them. In the early days at the home he had enjoyed being able to wander about the corridors without a care in the world and would spend hours gazing out of the windows at the view across the sands of Morecombe Bay. He could see right across the estuary to the Heysham power station and, on an exceptionally clear day, could even see down as far as Blackpool Tower.

His huge frame lumbered happily about the care home and his every need was pampered to; his meals, his cleaning, his washing, clean sheets on the bed and every other requirement. He was totally unaware of when his Alzheimer's developed into full-blown dementia and he lost all contact with reality; his shock of vivid red hair and his beard started to turn grey at the edges.

When he had first arrived at the home, the staff had been deferential and had accorded him his proper titles but there was a huge turnover of staff; they rarely lasted more than a few months, a year at most, and his identity was quickly forgotten. The current manager had been in place for less than a week.

He had ceased to care about or have any interest in his appearance or personal hygiene and rarely submitted to having his hair cut: one nurse had christened him 'curly' on account of his great mass of curls. The name stuck and everyone now referred to him as 'Curly'. It was not important; he had long since forgotten who he was or who he had been.

Occasionally, over the years, staff would hear snatches of one-sided conversations from his room as they passed on their rounds and heard the random exchanges with the ghosts of his subconscious mind. "I didn't mean to hurt her. The fire wasn't really my fault, I was just trying to get rid of the demons, I need to get to the House for the vote." They thought little of it; there were bizarre rantings from most of the rooms.

Just before dawn, Curly's lungs finally gave up the struggle and he breathed his last and lay still on the bed.

An hour or so later the night carer awoke from her orgy of sleep and television and, belatedly, did her round of the rooms. She peered briefly into Curly's room and concluded that he was sleeping peacefully. She was just about to leave when something prompted her to take a closer look. Curly had gone to join his maker.

Matron arrived just after eight o'clock and the girl relayed the departure of Curly from room fourteen. She had already left a message with the doctor requesting a visit to certify the death. Matron unlocked the drawer which held the personal files on every patient, pulled out Curly's file and started to read. It was the first time she had had occasion to read the file and her eyebrows expressed her surprise as she perused the details. There were no next of kin and she was instructed to notify a Carlisle firm of solicitors, in the event of his death.

That afternoon she closed her office door and sat down to compose a letter to Messrs Downham and Sparrow in Carlisle.

> *"I beg to inform you that Lord Frederick Mountjoy, 12th Duke of Dunkield passed away in the early hours of this morning after a brief bout of pneumonia. His personal file notes that there are no living relatives and I am instructed to advise you of his passing. His papers include a request to be buried at Dunkield Castle and I have asked the undertaker to make the necessary arrangements."*

Chapter 2

Five years later and nearly three hundred miles to the south, the wind was howling through the arches under Charing Cross Station. One tiny corner of the arch provided some limited protection from the snow which drove in on the gale and five people were huddled together there for mutual warmth and protection in unbelievable filth and squalor; the dregs of society.

They were an eclectic bunch. At one end of the scale was Big Lizzie and she was big and she smelt awful; she had not had a bath or even a proper wash in years. Twenty-nine stone of blubber and fat. She heaved her massive weight off the ground, went to the far end of the archway, hitched up her skirts, squatted in the corner and peed just far enough away to avoid the stream of urine running back towards them all. She was gross.

At the other end of the scale was Wee Willie, a seven stone weakling in the advanced stages of untreated Tuberculosis. The team had adopted him and did all they could to help the lad but it was clear that he was on a downward spiral as he spent hours coughing his heart out and, increasingly, bringing up blood.

Pretty Polly was a young fourteen-year-old girl who had run away to London on finding that she was pregnant. She had no plan for her future and was a liability but the others had also adopted her and they shared whatever little they had. She was likely to end up walking the streets as a prostitute. For the moment, however, the others vied with each other to accompany her as they begged on the streets in the daytime. The sight of this diminutive waif often helped to loosen the purse-strings of passers-by.

Boots was the finder and earned his name from the magnificent pair of boots he wore; they never discovered where he had stolen them from. He was an argumentative little beggar and would happily pick a fight with anyone in his way. His strength was that he was superb at finding food sources. At lunch time he had led them all to a church soup-kitchen where they were able to satisfy their hunger. This evening there was a children's party at a nearby burger bar and they made their way there to scavenge the bins for the left-over food. and had a good feast on the kids rejects. Just as they got back to the arch, the police turned up for their nightly ritual of harassment and moved them on. As on every other evening, they went around the corner for ten minutes and came back to the arch as soon as the police had gone.

The fifth member of this motley little band was something of an enigma. Jim stood more than six and a half feet tall, towering over the others and was from a different mould. The tangles in his overgrown beard and his untidy shock of red hair made him look much older than his twenty-seven years. His eyes were bright and intelligent as he surveyed and appraised his compatriots. Even the most dismissive stranger was forced to wonder what he was doing in this company.

Jim had graduated from Cambridge with a first-class honours' degree in Economics and Business Management. After university, he had bumbled round Europe with friends, drifting from one holiday spot to another: Ibiza, Tenerife, Benidorm and so forth, living on a pittance in a kibbutz-like existence where everything was shared. The parties started with spirits and wine but degenerated with diminishing funds into a search for strong cider and meths, with the occasional drugs when they could afford them. Returning eventually to England, he had continued the same life-style and felt no need to change although, in his more sober moments, he hated what he had become.

Had he chosen to do so, Jim could have smartened himself up, got a good job in the city and re-joined the human race. Instead, he had deliberately chosen this life to avoid responsibility, decisions, commitments and work. The others had not; they were truly homeless. They had nowhere to go to, no one to care for them. Being truly homeless brought its own raft of problems, not least was that, without a permanent address, they could not even claim unemployment benefits. They scraped by on what they could beg or steal. They appeared on no one's lists or registers; they were invisible to society.

Underneath Charing Cross station that night they shared out the cardboard boxes to sleep in and the few remnants of blankets they still had between them and the old newspapers to cover themselves and keep them warm. The boxes were huddled into a close formation to try to maximise the little warmth each had and they settled down to sleep another night in the blistering cold.

The conditions were too harsh for Wee Willie and he died in the night. They told a policeman in the morning and he organised for the body to be carted away. They were all a little sad to see him gone.

Jim had other problems, however. The food he had eaten must have been contaminated and he had violent diarrhoea. If there is any good place to have the runs, it is certainly not a railway arch under Charing Cross station and the whole area stank. Even Big Lizzie objected to the stench which was pretty rich, coming from her. By the third day, Jim was in a really bad way with food poisoning. He was writhing in agony from violent stomach pains and knew that he needed help. The quickest way to get to hospital was to stagger up to the Strand and collapse in the middle of the road, preferably within sight of a policeman who could radio for help and an ambulance. It worked brilliantly and, just a few hours later, Jim had been bathed and treated and was in a comfortable bed, in a warm nightshirt, on a saline drip. The food poisoning was severe and he was still hospitalised over a week later.

The doctor who came to discharge him had previously chatted with him about his life-style on several occasions throughout his stay.

"I'm discharging you today because the poison is mostly out of your system. However, you are still very weak and it really would not make much sense for you to go straight back on the streets in your condition. You need some TLC for the next few weeks: is there anywhere you can stay whilst you complete your recovery?"

Jim was about to say there was no one when he thought of his sister.

"I've got a sister who lives in Bromley. She would probably not be thrilled to see me but I do still feel incredibly weak. I could try her."

His badly soiled clothes had been unceremoniously incinerated on his arrival at the hospital but they did have a small charity store and fund and managed to find him some replacement togs although that was a bit of a challenge, given his size. He was also handed a travel warrant to take him to Bromley.

The train for Bromley departed from Victoria station and he intended to pop down to see his old friends under the arches at Charing Cross, before he left. However, he found that the next train was due to leave Victoria shortly and the one after that was nearly two hours later so he made his way to Victoria and jumped on the train.

It took him about twelve minutes to walk from Bromley station to his old home. It had been their family home and he had walked that way a thousand times on his way to school. Their mother had died when both he and Susan were quite young and father had died in an accident at work, just before Jim graduated. Although he would not have admitted it, the shock of his father's death was part of the reason that Jim had cut loose after his final examinations and gone wild around Europe.

Susan had chosen to continue to live in the family home and, he realised as he approached, that it was several years since he had been in touch. This return to suburban normality was not going to be easy.

But, as Susan opened the door, a huge smile spread across her face.

"Jim, how lovely to see you. Come on in." and she led him through to the kitchen. "I was just about to make some dinner for myself. Will you join me?"

"Thanks, I'd love to. I've been a little unwell and the hospital only let me out on the understanding that there was somewhere I could go for a couple of weeks for some TLC while I recover. The only person I could think of who might tolerate me, was you."

"Well, I'm delighted to be of service; but come on, I think you'd better tell me the whole story and all your news."

They spent a delightful evening together exchanging news and Susan cooked him what was almost certainly the best meal he had had in a long time. At one point, Jim summonsed up the courage to ask her about her love life. "You're a pretty lass, Sue, and a catch for any man. How come you've not been snatched up?"

"Well," she confessed. "I have had a long term on/off affair. A guy called Adam Davies."

"So, What's the problem?" Jim asked.

"He's a drop-out. He dropped out of school, has no qualifications, no proper job and no prospects. I love him to bits. He's absolutely brilliant with his hands, and I don't just mean in bed," she added as she saw the grin spread across Jim's face. "He can make or mend anything. He's one of those guys who can take three bits of Lego and an elastic band and make a Rolls Royce. He's done all sorts of jobs for me around the house. But I can't see our relationship going anywhere."

"My advice would be 'take happiness where you find it'," was Jim's view.

Towards the end of the evening she went upstairs and made up the bed in the room which had been his for so many years. As he got up to go to bed, he was filled with gratitude for the way she had received him. "Sue, I was quite worried about coming here today and wondering what reception you would give me. Thank you!" And he gave her a brotherly peck on the cheek.

"Get to bed, you great idle lump," was her response. But she was genuinely pleased to see him.

Chapter 3

The following morning, Susan was waving two envelopes in her hand when she came down to breakfast. "I forgot to tell you last night, you've got fan mail. The first letter came about two years ago; the latest was two or three months ago. They looked rather official and, as I'm never quite sure what you've been up to, I decided not to open them."
She put them on the table beside him and he slit them open with the back of his teaspoon. He removed the first letter from the envelope and read it.

It was from Messrs Downham and Sparrow, solicitors, of Carlisle and was addressed to Mr James Mountjoy.

> *"We are executors for the estate of the late Lord Frederick Mountjoy, 12th Duke of Dunkield in Cumbria. We write to inform you that you may be a beneficiary of his estate. In order that we can progress the matter we would be grateful if you would kindly supply us with a photocopy of your birth certificate and some additional identification, at your earliest convenience.*
> *Yours sincerely*
> *Jonathan Downham (Junior)"*

He slid the letter across to Susan and opened the second one which contained a similar message, but with greater urgency.
"Wow!" said Susan, when she had read the first one. "Dad always used to maintain that we had blue blood, somewhere in our past, but I'm not sure that I ever believed him. What are you going to do?"
"I'll get in touch with them, of course. I'm pretty certain that my birth certificate will be up with all the other family papers Dad kept in his desk. Then I'd better go and get some new clothes to replace these hospital rejects."
"Are you OK for money?"

"I've got a savings account somewhere that I've never touched. I think there's quite a bit in there and this seems like the right time to plunder it."

"OK, I'm off to work. There's a spare house key in the kitchen drawer. Have a great day. Bye!"

Jim washed up the breakfast things and made sure the place was clean and tidy and then went up to his father's family drawer. He found his birth certificate easily and also the pass-book for of his savings account but he was stuck trying to find any other form of identification. He wandered through to his bedroom to see if he could find anything there and was about to give up when his eyes fell on the discharge papers from the hospital which he had left on the dressing table. Well, they may not be comprehensive but they did have his name on them.

At ten o'clock he telephoned Messrs Downham and Sparrow and asked to speak to Mr Downham junior who sounded like a very senior junior and had a slow and ponderous Scottish accent. Jim explained who he was and Mr Downham exclaimed "My, you're an elusive laddie and no mistake. I've been trying to trace you for over three years, at least."

Jim was not yet ready to share all his secrets with someone he had never met and simply told him that he had been 'travelling'.

"When can you come to my office?" Downham enquired.

"Could you make it next Monday?"

Jim would have liked to have asked a thousand questions but that seemed to bring the conversation to a close and, after agreeing a time, he rang off.

He picked up the house key from the kitchen drawer and set off for the shops. His first call was at the bank. The passbook was brought up to date and the balance on the account was even more substantial than he had remembered. He withdrew the maximum allowed in one day and then arranged to have the balance converted into a current account and made the necessary application for a credit card to give him greater flexibility for the future.

He then spent several hours browsing the clothes shops and kitted himself with a couple of complete changes of clothes as well as underwear and shoes. Before leaving the shops, he bought a large rucksack to carry his purchases in, rather than a suitcase. Finally, he went on a hunt for a mobile 'phone. He had avoided a mobile for several years but felt that he was about to enter a new phase in his life which could well require communications. He was not prepared to pay the crazy prices for an Apple phone but picked up an excellent 4G mobile for a fraction of the price.

He arrived back home almost simultaneously with Susan and she was anxious to learn what he had discovered about the mysterious letters.

"Almost nothing, except that they appear pretty anxious to meet me in person and I've arranged to be in Carlisle on Monday."

"I've been thinking," Susan told him. "I'm sure Dad did some work on the family tree when we were little. I've no idea how far he got but it might be helpful. I'll have a look and see if I can find his notes, after we've had dinner this evening."

While she prepared dinner, Jim settled down to look up travel possibilities on his new mobile. The train was the obvious first choice. It was fast and frequent but the prices were off the Richter scale. He looked up National Express Coaches and found that the prices were far more reasonable. There was a coach leaving Victoria Coach Station just before midnight on Sunday evening, arriving in Carlisle at breakfast time on Monday morning meaning that as a bonus, he could sleep on the coach and would not have to fork-out on overnight accommodation. Perfect!

Susan had taken to heart his need for tender, loving care and produced a delightful dinner for the two of them and they continued chatting as they ate. At the end of the meal Jim told her that he would do the clearing-up while she went to see if she could find their father's papers on the family tree. He was just completing his side of the bargain, half an hour later, when she emerged, triumphantly waving a batch of papers and they settled down at the table to study them together.

It was not easy to follow the notes; for the most part they were scribbled jottings, and seemed unrelated to each other but, in later pages, a pattern did start to emerge.

"All the wives are listed," Susan observed. "But we are obviously trying to follow the male line so we can ignore those for the moment."

Jim turned over a couple more sheets and picked up the dialogue. "Here, this is starting to make a bit more sense. Here's me, James and here is father, Peter Mountjoy, born 1960. Then there is Grandfather, Anthony Mountjoy, born in 1920. He died the year I was born so I never met him. Then we have a Harold Mountjoy who must have been our great-grandfather, born 1879, died 1961. There's nothing more before that."

"Well, it's more than we knew before. It might be worth you copying that out neatly so that you have some background information, if asked."

The next few days were a mangled web of speculation as they both came up with possible alternative scenarios to match the phrase "you may be a beneficiary of the estate". These ranged from the sublime to the ridiculous but Jim's favourite was that he was to inherit the Duke's second-best suit of armour. He wasn't sure that would justify his trip to Carlisle but the whole process was fascinating and captured their imagination.

Jim set off for London, early evening on Sunday. He was already feeling much better and, on arrival, visited one of the late-night shops. He bought a whole basket full of nutritious and filling food and then added a bottle of whisky and some cans of cider and carried his purchases down to the archway underneath Charing Cross station.

The usual suspects were there. Wee Willie had died but Big Lizzie was there and eyed his carrier bags hungrily; Boots helped him unload them and handed the contents around; Pretty Polly was there looking thinner than ever and a couple more vagrants had come to join them.

"Blimey!" said Lizzie. "You robbed a bleedin' shop, Jim?"

"No!" Jim replied. "Every time they let you out of hospital, they give you a great bag of goodies to keep you going until next time."

"Well, it don't look like it's done you no harm, Jim. You coming back to join us, mate?"

"Not just at the moment, Lizzie. I had my fortune read by Gipsy Rose Lee and she told me that I had to go on a long journey. Possibly after that."

He made his farewells and left them happily partying on the victuals he had provided.

He walked back to Victoria Coach station along the Thames, past Big Ben and Westminster Abbey and along Victoria Street. He arrived over an hour before the coach departure time and settled down in the waiting room. Susan had judiciously provided him with ample food for his journey and he ate a hearty supper, intending to spend his time on the coach, sleeping. When the coach was announced, he was one of the first on and grabbed a double seat towards the back of the vehicle and settled himself in the corner beside the window, using his rucksack to maintain his claim to the remainder of the seat. He need not have worried; the coach was less than half full and he did not have to defend his territory.

The journey was interminable; a tortuous nightmare kaleidoscope of flashing lights, stops, flashing lights, stops and more flashing lights, for ever. He dozed spasmodically but spent as much time awake as asleep and, by four in the morning, recognised that this was not going to be his best night's sleep ever. It was almost a relief when the coach arrived in Carlisle at breakfast time and he was able to climb out into the clean morning air. There was a supermarket close by and he made use of their washroom facilities for a clean-up before sitting himself in their restaurant area and ordering breakfast. It was a luxury to be savoured, and he savoured it. He took full advantage of the free coffee refills and took his time over his meal, finally visiting the washrooms again to smarten himself up before making his way out and following the instructions on his mobile's satnav to reach the offices of Messrs Downham and Sparrow.

Chapter 4

The offices were in an impressive, Regency Period building in an older part of town which had probably been a fashionable district in its day. He entered the huge front door, approached the receptionist and announced himself. She gave him the oddest of looks and then showed him into a reception room, saying that she would inform Mr Downham Junior.

Mr Downham junior entered in a wheelchair. He must have been well into his seventies. He paused by the open door and looked at Jim but, instead of addressing him, simply said "Good heavens!"

He reversed his chair out of the door and beckoned Jim to follow him into the next room. There was a painting on the wall and Jim found himself staring at a mirror image of himself, complete with red beard and a huge mop of red hair. It was uncanny, almost frightening.

"That is a painting of the 12th Duke at roughly the same age that you are now. I think that we can probably dispense with some of the niceties of proving your identity. Come on back in the other room."

"Do you know anything of your family tree?" Downham enquired.

"I recently found some research my father had done," Jim replied. "I'm James Mountjoy; my father was Peter, his father was Anthony and his father, born in 1879, was Harold Mountjoy. That is all I have been able to establish."

"Well done, but I am about to add over seven hundred years to your family tree," Downham told him. Your great-grandfather, Harold, was the second son of the 9th Duke, Lord Edward Mountjoy. His first son, Simon, inherited the title as the 10th Duke and, as the second son, your great grandfather, poor old Harold, inherited nothing and went to join the army and then made his own way in life. Simon had only one son, James, who became the 11th Duke and James had only one son, Frederick who became the 12th Duke on the death of his father. Frederick never married and he passed away about five years ago, leaving no heir. Therefore James, it appears that you are the only surviving male relative to the title and the estate."

Jim's mind was in a whirl. His mouth opened and closed but no sound came out.

"Don't try to thank me too quickly, James. Are you sure you want to be a Duke? Every silver lining has a cloud, and this one has a massive cumulonimbus," Downham concluded and he called for coffee for them both.

As they drank their coffee, Downham continued.

"Let me tell you something of the history of the Mountjoy's to help you understand their background. They can trace their lineage back to the time of the Norman conquest when they came to England with William the Conqueror. Their service to William may have been unremarkable as their reward of land in a remote area of Cumberland, south of Carlisle was probably not one of the star prizes. None-the-less, they settled down, built a heavily fortified, three storey tower, surrounded it with a stone walled barmkin to keep the livestock in and protected, and prospered over the next couple of hundred years. "

"Towards the end of the thirteenth century, a new threat arose in the form of the Border Reivers, or border raiders. For the next four hundred years, scores of families from both sides of the border formed themselves into little tribes of brigands and made regular raids backwards and forwards across the border and, even within their own country. It wasn't just local to here; the raiders went well down into what was then Cumberland and into Westmorland and you can still see heavily fortified farms throughout Cumbria. At the beginning of the fourteenth century, Scottish raiders twice raided as far south as Cartmel, which was then in Lancashire, and damaged the Priory which was then still under construction. However, the raider's main target was stealing cattle but they would happily kill or take hostages if it suited them, especially if there was some old score to settle.

It was a period of complete lawlessness with incessant raids and killings. In 1525, the Archbishop of Glasgow issued an interdict against the border raiders which was read from every pulpit, excommunicating them. It was a terrible curse. If you ever have occasion to visit Carlisle Museum you can see the Bishop's stone or the 'cursing stone' as it is sometimes called. It stands seven feet high and part of the curse is chiselled into its face. A totally frightening curse but it did not produce the desired effect and the raids continued.

"There were literally dozens of Acts of Parliament on both side of the border designed to forbid such raids and introduce punishments but they were all ineffective in this isolated corner of England. Safe in their fortified tower, the Mountjoys maintained that they took no part in this incessant warfare although it is probable that they happily accepted any benefits which fell their way from time to time. "

"In the time of Elizabeth, the Mountjoy's were appointed 'March Wardens' with the task of discouraging cross-border raiding and keeping the peace. When James (VI) of Scotland became James (I) of England following Elizabeth's death, he introduced new legislation in 1606, further discouraging the activities of the Border Reivers and, at the same time, rewarded Mountjoy with the Dukedom of Dunkield. The family became 'respectable' and continued as such right up to the time of the late 12th Duke, Frederick.

"Frederick spent the first fifty years of his life travelling the world as a playboy and squandering the family fortune until he finally succeeded to the Dukedom in 1975, on the death of his father, James Mountjoy, the 11th Duke. My firm has acted as advisors to the Mountjoy family for many generations and I have personally known Frederick since well before his accession. It is not in my nature to be disloyal but Frederick would have been the first to say that he was not cut out to manage a huge estate. He tried to continued his life as a playboy and squandered more money. His Estate Manager died in about 1985 and his clerk died just a few years later. He did not replace them and the estate quickly fell into decline. At the time of the millennium he realised that he had progressive Alzheimer's Disease and could not cope; he booked himself into a care home in Grange-over-Sands where he died fourteen years later. So, you see, the estate has been largely unmanaged for the past thirty to forty years. It is some years since I was able to visit the estate," Downham concluded, gesturing towards his wheelchair.

"My colleague, Jeremy Sparrow, acted as executor to the estate. He agreed the probate valuation and paid expenses as they arose and also paid the farm workers until they became entitled to their state pensions. He was not a farmer and made no attempt to actively manage ongoing activity at the farm. Jeremy died, very suddenly, about six months ago and I have been struggling to try to catch up with where he had got to, ever since.

"But, at the time of Frederick's demise, Jeremy went out to make an appraisal of the estate. For some reason, a copy of his report is not on the file. However, if I remember correctly, his summary was that the estate is in a bad state of decline."

"At the time of the 11th Duke's death in 1975, the estate was wealthy and profitable. On the death of your namesake, Lord James, probate was prepared in line with the Royal Institute of Chartered Surveyors Red Book recommendations and there was an enormous bill for death duties. Foot and mouth disease wiped out all the animals on the farm in 2001 and there has been no attempt to re-start farming activities since then so there has been no subsequent income from that source. Although there was some level of Government compensation for the animals destroyed, this and most of the rest of the estate wealth was gradually used to pay Frederick's care-home costs. Finally, on Frederick's death, a further valuation was prepared for death duties.

"This valuation reflected the calamitous decline in the fortunes of the estate since his accession and, on this occasion, the charge was significantly lower than on the death of the 11th Duke. Sadly, however, it was still sufficient to wipe out all of the remaining wealth of the estate to the extent that it is now virtually bankrupt."

"I see what you meant about every silver lining having a cloud," Jim interposed. "What are my options?"

"In essence, they are simple. If you wish to succeed to the Dukedom, it is yours for the asking; otherwise the title will lapse, permanently. If you wish to succeed to the estate, likewise it is yours, otherwise the estate will revert to the Crown. What I am going to suggest is that you spend the next couple of days here in these offices with complete access to all the history and documentation in our possession. You can have copies of anything you wish, including bank accounts and deeds but I would ask that you don't remove any original papers. If you need guidance in any area or on any subject, I shall be at your disposal and will do all I can to help. Afterwards, it would make sense for you to pay a visit to the estate to see things on the ground and make your own assessment. After that, it will be up to you to decide what you want to do."

With that, he whirled his chair around and headed for the door. "Come this way." He led Jim down a long corridor to a door at the far end and entered. "This is known as the Mountjoy library. I've no idea who started it or why but it contains all our dealings with the estate over the years, as well as inherited documents from earlier periods. Have a seat and help yourself. Our receptionist, Melanie, will be popping out for some sandwiches, shortly. I'll ask her to check what you would like. Anything else you need, I'm in the room next door."

Jim was still sitting there dazed when Melanie came in a few minutes later to enquire about lunch and he managed to focus sufficiently to order a couple of sandwiches. She returned with them a few minutes later and he munched them, trying to work out where to start.

If he wanted the title, he was the 13th Duke of Dunkield. That was fact and there was little point in thinking about that at this stage. The real question was how bad things were with the estate so that he could make an informed decision on whether that was a good idea or a poisoned chalice.

He thought back to his studies in Cambridge. Right, this is a project, let's think about how to approach it, what do I need to know? He spent a few minutes going around the shelves and drawers, learning where everything was and decided his first priority was finances; how much was in the estate accounts, where did it come from and where did it go?

There were several different bank accounts. Most had only tiny amounts in them but one had a very sizeable balance and he made a note to ask Downham if that was for any particular purpose. Next, he looked at the income and analysed this over the past three years; it was mostly rental on estate cottages. On impulse, he pulled out the probate report file prepared on the death of the 11th Duke in 1975, the year Frederick inherited the estate, and looked at the income at that time.

He analysed out the sales of cattle and corn and found that the rental income for that year was five times higher than currently. There may be some other logical explanations and some of the cottages could have been sold off but it was possible that some rentals were simply not being received; another question for Downham. He made a list of the cottages and occupants in the 1975 list and annotated those still in the current list.

Next, he turned his attention to payments from the accounts. Most were small and fairly obvious but there were few which made him pause. There was a standing order for lift maintenance and another for photocopier rental. He had not seen the place so far but those did not seem to align with Downham's description of the estate. There were quite a number of other items which he found questionable and he made a list to enquire about. In total, they came to nearly twenty thousand pounds each year.

He wanted to get a handle on the size of the estate and found an excellent study and report prepared for his namesake, Lord James Mountjoy, the 11th Duke, in 1950. It was a highly detailed paper of over an hundred pages covering every aspect of the estate, including maps. It was exactly what he needed and he went to find Melanie.

"I apologise for putting on you but I wondered if you could possibly photocopy this report for me. It's exactly what I need to get my mind around the detail of the Dunkield estate." Melanie was perfectly happy to oblige and gave him a most beguiling smile. She returned half an hour later with the photocopy beautifully bound and he thanked her profusely and returned the original to its proper place.

Whilst she was there, he asked her where he might find a bed for the night, half hoping that she might say he could share hers. She didn't, which was a pity, but she did suggest a number of places to try. Just after four o'clock he knocked on Jonathan Downham's door and told him he was going to look for accommodation for the night. He had taken a photocopy of the 1950 Estate Report to study overnight. He had various questions but nothing which couldn't wait until the morning.

He tried a couple of the hotels Melanie had suggested and the second one turned out to be ideal. It was small and clean and the price was reasonable. He booked in for two nights, had a good wash and went out to explore the town. He wandered around for some time then, when he judged that Susan would be home from work, gave her a call.

"Jim," she said "I was…."

"Excuse me, little sister" he interrupted. "Will you please address me correctly. This is Lord James Mountjoy, 13th Duke of Dunkield speaking."

"What? You're kidding me! Oh Jim, that's fabulous; is it really true?"

"Well, it's up to me. It's a great thought but the estate is beset with a million problems and I'm going to spend the next few days trying to decide if I'm prepared to take on the burden."

"Would it mean that I get to be a lady?"

"You've always been a lady, Sue."

"Smoothie! But why is it so difficult to decide?"

"Well, it's a bit like being asked to build a mountain using just a teaspoon.

"Hey! Come on Bro. You're up near Hadrian's Wall and the Roman's built that without a single JCB. Go for it."

"I'll let you know how things progress. Bye for now."

He wandered around the town, found a restaurant which took his fancy and had an excellent meal, fit for a Duke. Back at his hotel he settled down into an easy chair and started to read the Estate Report, it contained precisely the information he needed. It listed every building, its purpose, the occupant, the annual rental and history and recent maintenance. It listed every field, its size, soil condition, use and rotation, if appropriate. It listed every stream and waterway, every pathway, bridleway and road. The accompanying maps were a boon and gave him a clear picture of the estate. It included an excellent line drawing of the Castle, the Elizabethan manor and the surrounding farm buildings and a smart stable block. The Castle was rather like a Peel Tower and reminded him of Orford Castle which he had once seen on a school visit to Suffolk. It had similar imposing lines, was from the same period and looked highly defensible. It looked good. The report was fully comprehensive and he climbed into bed, confident that he was starting to get his mind around Dunkield Estate.

As he walked to the offices of Messrs Downham and Sparrow the following morning, he glanced in the window of a second hand shop as he passed. There was an old bone-shaker bicycle for sale and it triggered a thought in his mind. He had already realised that he was going to need some form of transport. This could be the answer.

He arrived at the offices and found that Jonathan Downham was already there and was happy to come and answer his questions.

"I found the 1950 Estate Report tremendously helpful and I'd like to use that as my starting point," he told Downham. "What significant changes have there been since then? Have there been any sales of land or buildings?"

Downham wheeled himself over to a filing cabinet and spent a few minutes going through some of the files. Finally, he said "No! Nothing at all."

"And what about individual cottages? Have any tenants bought their cottages from the estate?"

"Again, the answer is no. It has never been estate policy to sell off the stock of properties. Although I would add that it is possible that some may have fallen down over that period."

"Thanks for that," Jim said. "Do you think you could prepare me a brief note on what I can and what I cannot do to pursue unpaid rents, the eviction process, if appropriate and also the process I would need to go through to increase rents in line with inflation." Downham agreed.

"There's a huge discrepancy between the current income and that when Frederick took over the estate and I think most of it will be down to unpaid rents."

"On the expenditure side, there are some really strange disbursements. For example, do you know if the estate has any lifts or rents photocopiers?"

"No, not that I'm aware of." Jonathan told him. "The accountant here simply makes a note in the cash book of all the payments which go through the bank."

"Well, I've listed payments of about twenty thousand per annum which look questionable. Please would you get your accounts department to check them out and, if they are fraudulent, use the full power of your legal status to recover them for however many years you can.

"Well," said Jonathan. "It certainly looks as though you are getting your mind around the details. Does that mean that you have decided to take on the burden of the estate?"

"Not yet," Jim told him. "As you suggested, I plan to go out there tomorrow to have a look around. In the meantime, one other question. One of the bank accounts has a sizeable balance on it but does not seem to be used. What's the background?"

"Aaah! Inevitable that you should come upon that one. The answer is that I really don't know because, for some unknown reason, Frederick would never come clean on that. So far as I have been able to guess over the years, I have always suspected that it was set up as some kind of hush money, slush fund about twenty years ago although I don't know what for and I don't recall that it has ever been used in all that time."

Jim thanked him for his help and settled down to study more files and learn more about the estate.

At lunchtime he asked Melanie to get him some sandwiches again and then popped out to the second hand shop. They wanted £35 for the bicycle but he bartered hard and eventually settled on £20 and rode it back to the offices.

The history of the estate was fascinating but was not the thing that was going to influence his decision on whether to proceed. He was an economist and the decision would rest on the economics.

He spent the afternoon gleaning everything he could which could help him to identify possibilities for improving the viability of the estate. At the end of the afternoon he had a few more questions which Jonathan was able to help him with and then rode his new second-hand bicycle back to his hotel.

He ate at the same restaurant again that night and then spent the evening making notes of the things he wanted to look at and check up on the Estate.

Chapter 5

His ride out of Carlisle the following morning was really enjoyable.

Coming from London, he was tremendously aware of the openness of the countryside around him as he left the confines of the city behind him. He passed beside neat fields full of animals or early crops, surrounded by well-maintained dry-stone walls. Everywhere there were trees although most were not yet in leaf and he passed pretty cottages and small farms along the way.

Despite still being early in the year, it was a reasonably warm, sunny morning and his route took him along increasingly narrow country lanes. He came to a cattle grid and wheeled his bike through the gate at the side of it. Beyond there, he was into open moorland with gentle rolling hills as far as the eye could see. Sheep grazed happily on the grass growing through the tarmac in the middle of the road, totally unimpressed at his approach and unwilling to budge, despite his bell.

He passed through charming little villages and hamlets, including a village which had a pub, a post office and a shop and café. That could be useful. He was thoroughly enjoying the ride although it gradually dawned on him that some long-unused muscles were starting to complain. He passed a static caravan park and then the road started to rise steeply uphill. His bike had no gears and he eventually chickened out and pushed the bike for the remainder of the journey.

The entrance to the estate was marked by huge, imposing gateposts although, sadly, the gates were damaged and hung from them at haphazard angles and it would be a long time since they were last able to close. Beyond this point, the road was a private drive, not maintained by the council. It was pitted with potholes and the edges had collapsed in many places. Half-way along, there was a massive fallen oak tree completely blocking the road. It had probably been dead for twenty years or more and it was necessary to swerve onto the wide grass verge, to drive round it. Not a great introduction to the Dunkield Estate.

He could see that most of the estate cottages he passed were dilapidated and in a poor state of repair and he ticked them off in his mind against the lists he had prepared.

Even his amateur eye could see that the fields were in a sad state in total contrast to those he had passed earlier in his journey. There was no livestock in them anywhere, no crops were growing and the fields were full of brambles, nettles, weeds and thistles.

But the worst was still to come. He approached the centre of the estate. There was the Castle Tower that he had seen so beautifully drawn in the 1950 report but it was a ruin. The blackened walls were still intact but it was a burned-out shell and no longer resembled Orford Castle. The barmkin wall to secure cattle and protect the castle was reduced to a pile of stones covered in earth; the pretty manor house which had been attached to the tower had been burned to the ground and over three-quarters of the roof of the magnificent stable block opposite, was in a state of collapse. Jim felt a crushing weight on his shoulders, one which he did not think he could carry and he stood in the middle of all this mess, incredibly depressed. Downham had been right about the clouds; where was the silver lining? The excitement and exhilaration over the possibility of inheriting the title and the estate vanished like a burst balloon as he stood there and surveyed the scene of neglect and devastation all around him.

Not able to snap out of his depression, he wandered aimlessly towards the one-quarter of the stable block, still standing. He was surprised to find a smart, well-groomed horse inside with a tiny foal. Without thinking, he spoke gently to the horse to calm it and then nearly jumped out of his skin when a girl's head appeared upside down from the hay loft entrance above him with a great mop of curly red hair, and demanded "Who are you?"

James was about to reply 'Jim' when he remembered that he had already taken a decision to use his formal title, just in case he went ahead with this crazy scheme. "I'm James," he replied.

The girl held on to the sides of the loft entrance and performed a very neat summersault, landing directly in front of him with a cheeky grin. "I can see who you are. You're the next Mountjoy, come to make our lives even more difficult."

"May I have the pleasure of knowing your name, fair lady."

"I'm Rowan. Now, what do you want?"

Jim desperately needed to talk to someone and he took a snap decision to open up to the girl and see what he could learn to help him in his decision.

"OK, come outside and I'll tell you why I'm here and perhaps you can help me make a decision."

They walked into the light and Jim could see that she was a tall, slim and attractive young lady, probably in her early twenties and was clearly a bit of a tomboy. She had a lovely smiling face and, as she spoke, her face was animated and open.

"Yes, I'm supposed to inherit the management of this estate and I came here today in a positive mood, ready to start the task, but I'm appalled by what I see. The road is in a state of collapse, the fields have gone wild, the cottages are falling apart and the Castle, which I had assumed was intact, is a burned-out hulk. What should I do, Rowan? Should I just walk away and forget it?"

His speech and his sense of despair had obviously struck a chord with the girl and her attitude changed immediately. "No James, don't do that, I'm sure you can do something to help us."

"But, where would I start, what are the priorities?"

Quick as a flash, she came back with a response wiser than her years. "People. The estate isn't land or buildings, its people. Give the people hope and trust and everything else will follow."

"I like your answer and I'm willing to follow your advice but I should level with you from the beginning, the one thing I don't have is money. So, help me, give me some ideas on how to give the people hope and earn their trust, without the money to be able to mount grand recovery schemes."

They chatted for a long time and gradually, little ideas emerged on how to move things forward. Rowan was anxious to insist on openness and the need to take people into his confidence, to be honest with them and above all, to do what he said he would do.

"Would you be willing to help me?" Jim asked.

"Yes, so long as you're honest with me, as well. By the way, where's your chauffeur-driven car?

Jim pointed to the bicycle propped up against a pile of stones.

"Oh, you really aren't rich then," Rowan concluded. "What are you doing about lunch?" He looked at her blankly and she went on "I've got some sandwiches in the hayloft. Hang on a mo and I'll share them with you."

He watched her as she walked away, tall, slender, intelligent and rather lovely. "I think I'd like to get to know you better," he mumbled to himself.

She returned a few minutes later with a beautiful smile on her face. She shared the sandwiches and a couple of apples between them and they continued chatting as they ate. By now, the mood between them was much more open and relaxed.

"Would you be prepared to give me a conducted tour of the estate, tomorrow so that I can see the whole place and meet everyone?" he asked.

"Sure," she replied. "But it's pretty big. If I ride my pony, you could ride your bike, so long as we follow the pathways." The plan was agreed.

"And where are you planning to stay tonight?" Rowan asked.

"I was intending to sleep rough, but I would like somewhere dry. Would you allow me to sleep in your hayloft?"

"I'll check with the horses to see if they wouldn't object to your company. I suppose that means that you have no plans for dinner, either," she added. "I'll have a word with my parents and see if the dinner will stretch to four." And she disappeared after lunch to check with them.

Jim sat there in the sunshine, awaiting her return. She had given him tremendous encouragement but, as he gazed about him again at the devastation, doubts crept back into his mind. Everything was broken. He could do a certain amount to help but much of it was simply beyond him. He needed some practical help, someone from Blue Peter who could take two bits of ticky-tacky and a cardboard loo-roll and could make them into absolutely anything at all ....!

Susan's boyfriend!

That was almost exactly what she had said about him. He would give her a call later and mention it.

Rowan returned and told him that her parents would be delighted to have him to dinner that evening. Jim thanked her and then asked "Please can you tell me about the people on the estate. Who they are and what they do?"

"You've probably already gathered that everyone on the estate used to work for the estate but they are all retired now, apart from me. I believe that the estate manager introduced a few new people before he died but, even they have now reached retirement age. They're all skilled, experienced people in their own field. There's a blacksmith, joiners, farm hands, cowmen and all the others skills needed on an estate like this, but they've lost heart. They've watched the estate decline into its present state and they don't care anymore; they've lost their sense of pride, they've no leadership and they're just drifting, waiting to die."

"What's their greatest fear?" Jim asked.
"That they'll be thrown out of their tied cottages. You've probably already worked out that a lot of them don't pay their rent on a regular basis."
"And what's their greatest hope?"
"That's more difficult," Rowan told him. "It's partly that they can stay in their cottages until their dying day, but its more than that. Most of them have been on the estate for fifty years or more. They remember how things were under the 11th Duke. The estate was smart and active; they were proud of being part of a successful estate and they would love to relive those days and regain that sense of pride."
Jim was quiet for a while, absorbing what the girl had said; he had no doubt that she was right but how could he possibly put it into practice.

They talked for several hours, exploring possible tactics and approaches until Rowan jumped up quite suddenly and said "Come on, dinner will be ready. Dad was the gamekeeper and I think there could be game on the table."
She led him to a reasonable sized cottage which did not seem to be falling apart quite so much as some of the others he'd seen. Caleb and Elizabeth met them at the door and welcomed him warmly, invited him in and led him to the table.
Elizabeth opened the oven door in the kitchen range and produced a seemingly endless array of food dishes for the table and placed a large pheasant in front of Caleb for carving. First, however, he bowed his head, as did the rest of the family, and said grace. James was touched and joined in the 'Amen'.

"This is very kind of you to invite me to dinner," Jim ventured.

"On the contrary, your lordship. We are honoured by your presence," Caleb responded.

"Please, just call me James," Jim asked. "I haven't even decided whether to accept the title, or the burden of the estate, yet."

"Oh, but you must," Caleb interposed. "We need someone young to lead us and help us restore the estate to its former glory."

"Well, I've been talking with your daughter who has given me some excellent advice." He saw an odd exchange of looks between Caleb and Elizabeth. "But the task is enormous and, unlike earlier generations, I don't have the money to plough into the estate."

He changed the subject. "Elizabeth, that pheasant was excellent. Do you still breed birds, Caleb?"

"Yes, not the thousands I used to raise in the past, but I still raise a few hundred each year for us to eat on the estate."

That triggered a thought in Jim's mind. "Is there an opportunity for us there? Could we raise some income from shoots on the estate, or even from selling the birds?"

"I don't see why not," Caleb told him. "Years ago, there used to be shoots here every few weeks."

"Right" Here's a challenge for you, Caleb. Have a think about the possibility and how to progress it and we'll talk again when I've decided whether to take on the challenge of the estate."

Jim was taking his leave a little later and thanking them profusely for an excellent meal when he remembered to ask "Do you know what time the shop opens in the village? It was Elizabeth who replied. "Yes, it opens at eight o'clock."

He turned to Rowan. "I'm going to pop down there first thing and I'll meet you at the stables, when I get back."

It was getting dark as he made his way back to the stables and that reminded him to add a torch to his shopping list. He washed himself at the tap outside the stables and then hoisted himself up into the hayloft, rearranged some straw to make a bed, and was asleep in moments, quite oblivious of the nocturnal activities of the resident mice.

Chapter 6

Jim had spent so long sleeping rough in recent years that he slept peacefully and was not even stiff when he awoke. He let himself down to the ground, went behind the stable to relieve himself and then used the tap again to give himself a good wash.

Back in the loft, he emptied to contents of his rucksack and stacked them tidily in one corner, then jumped down again, slung his rucksack on his back, mounted his bike and set off down the road to the village. Going downhill was decidedly easier.

The shop was empty when he arrived and he was able to quickly assemble the items he needed, packed them in his rucksack and set off back to Dunkield.

Rowan was already at the stables when he got there and he received a bright and cheery 'Good Morning'. She had already taken care of the foal and fed the horse, Beauty, which was standing saddled and ready. He dumped his rucksack in the hayloft.

"If it's convenient, I'd like to try to visit every cottage on the estate today, including the ones which are unoccupied. If I decide to go ahead, I will need somewhere to sleep, beside the hayloft."

"Yes," Rowan replied. "We can do that. Ready when you are."

She set the pony into a gentle trot and Jim had no difficulty keeping up with her on his bike. From the 1950 Estate report, he had a clear picture of the estate in his mind but he enjoyed the journey, saddened by the state of the fields and the cottages but happy to see some of the other attractive features. At the far end of the estate they visited one of the widows, Martha. She was in her late eighties but was still sprightly and fit. She had a small vegetable garden which appeared well stocked and she had a chicken coop with half a dozen or more chickens wandering around contentedly. Jim chatted with her for several minutes, trying to gauge her feelings on the run-down condition of the estate and then asked if she would be willing to show him her cottage. She was clearly house-proud and everything inside the place sparkled like a new pin although the walls had not seen a coat of paint in decades and were badly cracked in places. He also noticed that some roof tiles were missing and asked if the roof leaked. "Oh, only when it rains, and I keep a bucket handy for that ", she replied cheerily. He made some notes on his mobile.

Next, they called on one of the retired joiners, Keith. Jim asked if he still did any joinery work. "Oh, yes. I like to keep my hand in," and he showed them his workshop where he was working on some furniture; it looked good. They talked at length about the state of the estate and Keith said it was a crying shame how things had deteriorated. The cottage was not bad, but seriously needed some paint and patching up.

The next place they called at was Ted's cottage. It was probably not one of the most salubrious cottages, but Ted was proud of it. He led them out the back where a huge sow was lying in a pen, clearly close to farrowing. "How many are you expecting," Jim asked.
"I'll be disappointed if there's less than eight," he replied.
"Then what do you do with them?"
"I sells them at the market," Ted replied proudly.

They went on to the blacksmith's cottage and Jim enquired if he still used his forge.
"Yes, I fire it up every few weeks, there's always something that needs fixing." But his cottage was the worst they had visited so far.

The next two cottages were vacant and Jim asked where the keys were.
"Oh, we don't lock things round here," Rowan replied and opened the door to the first one.

Rose Cottage was in pretty poor shape and desperately in need of some attention. Bramble Cottage was not bad, however. It had a serviceable kitchen and bathroom, there was a bed in each of the two bedrooms and, with a couple of days cleaning, the place could be habitable.

"This one will be fine for me," he told Rowan.

They covered a further half-dozen dwellings and, increasingly, Jim chatted with the occupants, trying to understand their lives. Before continuing on, they stopped in a pretty little dell and Jim produced some sandwiches he had had made up in the shop. When Rowan thanked him, he said that he would also like to invite her to join him for dinner, this evening but could she please bring two plates, two mugs and some eating irons. She smiled at him and accepted graciously.

They set off again, straight after lunch and rattled through the remainder of the cottages although it was nearly six o'clock by the time they got back to the stable. Rowan immediately set to, feeding, watering and tending to her pony and ensuring the foal was happy. When she emerged, Jim was standing outside gazing up at the ruins of the castle and Rowan came and stood beside him.

"When I was little," Rowan began. "I used to dream that the castle had been rebuilt; and stood tall and strong and beautiful. In my dream I would be standing here beside the stable in my best dress, gazing up at the battlements. Just then, a fine, tall gentleman would come striding along the driveway. He would stop beside me and smile at me, then he would pick me up in his strong arms and carry me into the castle."

Jim could not think of an appropriate response to this revelation of her secret dreams; fortunately, Rowan solved the moment by asking what time she was required for dinner and she left for her cottage.

It was a mild, moonlit evening and Jim spent a few minutes finding an appropriate, sheltered spot for his dinner party. He found a good log for them to sit on, well away from the stables and unpacked the camping stove and saucepan he had purchased this morning. He had all the ingredients for a prawn risotto and, without starting the cooking, got everything organised. When Rowan reappeared three-quarters-of an hour later she had changed and clearly made an effort to make herself look good.

"You look lovely," Jim told her. "But what happened to the tiara?"

"I couldn't open the safe," she joked as she handed him the plates and mugs.

He opened the prosecco and poured a generous slug into each mug, handed one to her, saying, "This is my thank you to you for all your help and encouragement over the past two days." Then he lit the camping stove and started to prepare the dish.

"So, James. What have you decided? Are you going to accept the challenge?"

"Could I possibly have another couple of hundred years to reach a decision on that question?" he responded.

"No! I demand to know, here and now."

The contents in the pan were starting to bubble nicely and Jim paused for a moment to reduce the flame before continuing.

"Rowan, you have been a tremendous help and encouragement to me on this since we met yesterday morning, but the prospect still scares me silly. If I go ahead, will you help me every step of the way?"

She put her hand gently on his arm and simply said "Yes, I'd love to, James."

He put the finishing touches to the prawn risotto, ladled some onto each plate and refilled the mugs with prosecco. He sat back on the log and looked at the girl, she was smiling at him happily.

"You're a nutcase James, but this is fun; thank you for inviting me out to dinner. Now I come to think of it, it's the first time I have ever been out to dinner, sitting on a log in the open air with a strange man."

"It's a pleasure, my lady. I've enjoyed your company and I hope I'm not that strange."

"What do you plan to do now?" she asked.

"First thing tomorrow, I shall ride back down into Carlisle. I need to meet with the estate's lawyers and deal with a host of bits and pieces. Then, unless I change my mind and chicken out, I'll probably be back in a week or so.

"Is there anything I can do in the meantime?"

"Yes, you can kiss me," he replied.

"Don't be so presumptuous. I hardly know you," she responded and she finished her meal, rose quickly, gave her thanks and departed leaving a slightly puzzled Jim.

He swigged the remains of the prosecco, washed the plates, cutlery and mugs under the tap and left them in one corner of the stables. He tidied up the remaining items and heaved himself into the hayloft, still puzzling what had gone wrong. OK, he may have been a little bold but why had she turned down his request for a kiss so firmly?

Unable to fathom it, he pulled out his mobile and called Susan.

"So," she asked. "Have you reached a decision?"

"I think so, but tell me, that boyfriend of yours......."

"Adam Davies?"

"Yes. Is he currently employed?"

"Sadly, no."

"Do you think I would like him?"

"Yes, Jim, I'm sure you would; he's a man's man. But why are you asking?"

"Well, the size of the task here is enormous and I'm not really great at practical things. How do you think he'd fancy a holiday in Cumbria, all expenses paid, working his butt off for nothing?"

"I think he'd jump at it, Jim," Susan said.

"OK, ask him and text me if he's interested. I've got a whole list of things I'd want him to bring with him if he does come."

"Will do, your lordship. By the way, your credit card and some letters from the bank have arrived."

"Good! Please could you send them on to me at Downham and Sparrow's offices."

"Will do. Bye!"

With that, he packed his rucksack by the light of his newly acquired torch, turned over and was asleep in moments.

Chapter 7

The ride back downhill into Carlisle the following morning was exhilarating; until he hit the traffic, that is. He arrived at Downham and Sparrow offices just as they were opening and went to find Jonathan.

"Ah! Good morning young man; or should I say 'Your Lordship'?"

"Not yet," Jim replied. "A few more questions first. The place is in an appalling state. Did you know that the Castle is a burned-out shell, a ruin?"

"Now you come to mention it, I had forgotten but I think I did know. There was a rumour that it was Frederick himself who set fire to it, as he was losing his marbles. What about the rest of the place?"

"Total neglect and decay. Plenty of those dark clouds you mentioned but I've yet to find the silver lining. The whole place is a mess and I'm still trying to work out where one would start. Anyway, any answers on those fraudulent invoices?"

"Yes. Our accountant has been through several back years. She has stopped the standing orders and has written to request repayment of over one-hundred thousand pounds. We've given them twenty-one days, after which we'll get litigious."

"Great! We are certainly going to need some money. Did you prepare that note about agricultural tenancies, rent increases and recovery of unpaid rent?"

Jonathan handed him a few sheets of paper.

"In simple terms, a farm worker has no automatic right to stay in a tied cottage, once he ceases to work although, as you will appreciate, no estate would continue to find workers if they made a habit of making them homeless as soon as they reached retirement age.

"There is a formal process for increasing rents and I have set it out in detail in that paper.

"The process for recovering unpaid rent generally relies on the tenancy agreement or, in the absence of one, on custom and practice. Your namesake, the 11ᵗʰ Duke, was pretty strong on administration and I've been back over some of the old tenancy agreements. I think it's safe to say that if any instalment is more than twenty-eight days overdue, you would be entitled to give notice to evict the tenant."

"Right, Jonathan. I'm fairly certain that I shall live to regret this, but the answer is 'yes'. I'm ready to proceed on both the title and the estate. Can I leave it to you to deal with whatever paperwork is required and could you also arrange for me to meet the bank manager?"

"With pleasure, your Lordship," said Jonathan as he bowed towards him in his wheelchair, with genuine deference.

"Now, I need to do a bit more research in the library and then there are more things I need to do around town." Just as he walked into the library, his mobile buzzed. It was a message from Susan to say that Adam had jumped at the idea. He sat down and sent her a long email of all the things he needed. It included his own bicycle from the shed; Adam would need transport. He asked her to go through his drawers and cupboards and pack any of his clothes which were in reasonable condition which she thought would still fit him, and also to send a sleeping bag and a second one for Adam, if there was more than one.

He spent half an hour looking up some additional information and then called the Agricultural Advisory Service Carlisle branch. When they answered he said that he needed some advice and the girl asked who was calling. Almost without thinking he said 'Lord Mountjoy of Dunkield', and had his first taste of the power of the title as he was put through to the chief advisor, Peter Longfellow, who asked "How can I help?"

"I've just taken over the Dunkield estate and I'd like to come and have a chat about the place. Could you spare me some time?"

"Certainly, your Lordship. Would one o'clock this afternoon be convenient?" Jim said that would be excellent and checked the location of their offices. He asked Melanie if she would organise some sandwiches as usual and then popped to the shops to buy some more items of clothing and underclothes as he felt the existing ones were getting past their 'best before' date.

Back in the office, there was a note on his desk saying "John Briggs, Bank Manager, here Monday at midday". Jim ate his sandwiches and set off for the Agricultural Advisory Service offices.

He was warmly welcomed by Peter Longfellow, a personable fellow in his late thirties. He showed Jim into a pleasant meeting room where coffee and tea had already been prepared.

"Now, what can I do to help?" he enquired.

"I mentioned that I have just taken over the Dunkield estate. I know absolutely nothing about land or farming but, even my inexperienced eye can see that the farm is in a dreadful state of neglect. So far as I can understand, the stock was wiped out in the Foot and Mouth epidemic in 2001 and the farm was never restocked. So, at a guess, it has probably not been farmed for nearly twenty years; the fields have gone wild, the walls collapsed, the hedges overgrown: there's no livestock, there are no active farm workers and the whole place is a mess."

"So, what would you like me to do?" Longfellow enquired.

"Two things; I'd welcome a visit there for you to have a proper look at the place and help prepare an action plan to take us forward. The second is that I'd like you to give me some quick-fix ideas now on little things we could do to make a big difference. I'm due to talk to all the estate tenants in a few days' time and I need some ideas to help to inspire them. Oh! And by the way, the estate is pretty well bankrupt."

"So, no problems, really!" Longfellow joked.

He poured coffee for each of them and then sat back in his chair to contemplate the situation.

"We really need some livestock; are there none?"

"There's a girl who has a pony and a foal, and one of the retired farm workers has a sow about to farrow, but not much more."

"Well, that's a good start. I suggest that you get the girl to leave the pony and foal out in the field for most of the time. Just having animals around, cheers everyone up. I also suggest that you agree to buy-in all the piglets when they arrive. Put them and the sow in one of the fields. They'll root around and grub-up the ground and it'll be fit to plant in a year or so."

Jim was busily making notes on his mobile. "Anything else?"

"How about letting your fields for grazing on an annual basis for other farmers to fatten up their weaned lambs and cattle. Round here, the rental income is calculated by the acre. It's not enormous, particularly if your fields are as bad as you say, but it would be a useful contribution and would certainly improve the quality of the land over a couple of seasons. The only thing you would be responsible for is ensuring that the walls and hedges are adequate to keep the beggars in.

"If you can fork out a few thousand quid, you could even buy in a few beef cattle to fatten-up on your own account."

"How easy is it to get rentals?"

"Fairly easy. I can certainly give you some contacts."

"Peter, I came in here not knowing what questions to ask and, despite that, you have given me answers. Thank you. I'd like to arrange for you to come up to the estate in the next few days and have a more detailed look. Do you think you might be able to make it next Thursday?"

Peter checked his diary. "Certainly, would ten o'clock suit you?"

Jim had liked Longfellow instantly and felt a huge sense of relief that there was someone knowledgeable that he could count on, on his side. After their discussion, he felt that he could weave a positive and believable story to share with the estate workers and that, with Longfellow's help they could start to do positive things.

Leaving the Agricultural Advisory Service, he made his way to a computer shop he had spotted. He had recognised that he was going to need a pc, not least so that he could have access to internet banking for the estate. He found a reasonably priced laptop which looked as though it would fit his needs and headed back to the hotel he had used previously and booked in for four nights.

He checked that they had a laundry service and then immersed himself in a hot bath, feeling that he had not washed properly for days.

He popped his dirty clothes in a laundry bag and deposited them at reception on his way out to dinner, choosing a different restaurant on this occasion.

Back in his hotel room he unpacked his new laptop and spent the next few hours setting it up. In between, he telephoned Susan.

"Hi Sue, are you sure Adam is up for this and have you told him I'm going to work him hard and he doesn't get paid?"

"Yes, that's fine but I don't know if I mentioned that he is dyslexic. Give him anything practical and he's your man but keep him well clear of numbers or any paperwork."

"Understood. Have you managed to find all the stuff I listed?"

"Yes! I've even managed to find two sleeping bags although I've warned Adam that, if I come up for a weekend, he'll have to share his with one of us."

"OK. Can you arrange for him to come up on the overnight coach on Monday evening and I'll meet him at the arrival point on Tuesday morning? If he has any hassle about the amount of luggage for the coach, give him some money and get him to bung the driver twenty quid."

"It sounds as though you are quite enjoying yourself, Jim."

"Truth is I'm absolutely terrified; but I've jumped now. It's just a question of where I'll land."

On Saturday morning he wandered around the shops looking for some things he needed. He bought a couple of lights for his bicycle and was just leaving the shop when he noticed an item for sale, second hand. It was a small carriage for towing a child behind a bike. It had two wheels, a box-like compartment and a long pole which connected just below the saddle of the towing bike. The child had clearly outgrown its transport but it would be ideal for carting shopping and so forth up to Dunkield. It was marked £20. He haggled with the store manager, settled on £10 and wheeled it back to his hotel to marry with his bicycle.

Jim knew that, if he was to occupy Bramble Cottage, he needed a complete set of kitchen equipment. He found a cheap kitchenware store and let fly. Plates, bowls, mugs, tumblers, cutlery, more pans, kitchen knives and cooking spoons, a cruet set and dozens of other items. Most items came in packs of four or six so there should be plenty of spares, even after breakages.

Fortunately, he had brought his rucksack with him, otherwise he would have struggled to get them all back to the hotel. He had not planned to return to the estate until the middle of the following week but it occurred to him that it would make sense to do a quick trip there and back on the Sunday to deposit as much of his stuff there as he could. In that case, it would also make sense to pile as much as he could into his 'baby buggy' so he went back to the shops and bought a couple of dozen tins of food and other things that would come in handy at any time.

He was up early on Sunday and packed for his journey. Lighter things were in the rucksack, heavier items in the buggy. The traffic was light and he made good progress for the first half of the journey but, as he started to approach the hills, he started to slow down considerably. He walked the last five miles or so and was almost in a state of collapse when he reached the stable. He called Rowan's name but there was no response and he could see as soon as he looked in that she was gone and so was the pony.

He rested for a couple of minutes until he felt that he was able to breathe again, more or less normally. He mounted his bike and set off in the direction of Bramble Cottage. The path was mostly downhill from there and he sat and free-wheeled for much of the distance. As he approached, he could see that the mattresses were out in the sunshine, airing against a wall. Beauty was tethered to a nearby tree and the foal was sleeping quietly beside her.

He dismounted and went into the cottage. Rowan was hard at work with a brush cleaning for all she was worth and didn't hear him enter. He came up behind her and she jumped a mile when he put his arms around her saying, "you little angel". This time, she did not resist but dissolved into his arms and responded fully when he kissed her full on the mouth.

"Oh James! You're back. I did so hope you would come back. But I wanted to get this cottage tidy before you arrived. Does this mean that you are going to accept the challenge?

"Yes, but I'm only here for the day to bring some things I've bought for the house. I hope to return full-time on Tuesday."

"But tell me, why was it alright for me to kiss you just now but it wasn't the other night?"

"You are a dangerous man, Lord Mountjoy. I feel strongly attracted to you but the other night you hadn't fully committed yourself and I didn't know if you would ever come back again. You have, so I've thrown caution to the wind. But don't you play me false."

She showed him around the cottage. There was still some cleaning to be done but she had made an excellent start and the place would soon be quite habitable.

"I'm glad you're here. I had a real struggle to get those mattresses outside. Can you give me a hand to bring them back inside before you leave? You can bring your things in, if you wish. The kitchen cupboards and drawers are clean."

She walked outside with him, admired the 'baby buggy' and helped him carry some of his purchases inside and unpack them.

"How many are you catering for? There's enough stuff here to provide for an army."

"I've got a friend of my sister's coming to give me a hand. I've never met him but she tells me that he is very practical and what I'm going to need is practical help like his and yours. Now, what can I do to help the cleaning process?"

"The cooker's pretty filthy. You could try chipping some of the dirt off that."

It was a lousy job but he had asked, and it was to be his cooker. Rowan had brought some cleaning materials and he had also included some in his own shopping. He worked away at it with enthusiasm, inside and out, for a couple of hours. At the end, it did look as though there was a marginal improvement. Unfortunately, most of the dirt appeared to have transferred to him and he looked filthy. He spent another half hour trying to clean himself up.

"And I suppose that you've not brought any lunch with you again," Rowan piped up, accusingly. "Come on, I think I've enough to share with you again. The wine is in the kitchen tap there and you could use one of your new cut-glass crystal, earthenware coffee mugs to drink it from." They sat and ate together at the table and it suddenly occurred to Jim that this was his first meal in his new home. He looked across the table at Rowan, his dining companion, and felt a huge rush of affection and gratitude towards her.

"So, you think you'll be back on Tuesday?"

"That's my plan at the moment. I've got a guy from the Agricultural Advisory Service coming up to see me on Thursday. Then, I wondered what you might think about getting everyone from the estate together on either Saturday or Sunday to introduce myself and share some thoughts?"

"It's a good idea, although we'll have to hope that it's not raining."

"Should it just be a straightforward lecture from me or could we do something like organising a 'Jacob's Join' where everyone brings some food and we all share it?"

"That's a brilliant plan, James. It will help to emphasise 'sharing' in the new estate."

"OK, I'll organise a barrel of cider. Don't start to spread the word until I get back on Tuesday. Now, let me help you get those mattresses back inside and then I'm off back to Carlisle and, once again Rowan, thank you for this wonderful gesture of help."

On the way home he stopped off in the village at the pub, tried the cask cider and asked the landlord to order a barrel and have it delivered to the Dunkield estate. While he was there, he visited the gents' toilet and noticed the vending machine on the wall. On impulse, he decided to make an investment in a packet of three and put them inside his wallet. One never knew when such items might come in useful.

Chapter 8

He needed a hot bath again when he got back to the hotel to remove the grime from the cooker which had transferred itself to him. His laundry had been returned to the room and they had done a good job. He bundled his latest washing, covered in grease from the cooker, into a laundry bag and deposited it at reception, telling the girl that he was leaving early on Tuesday morning.

He ate at a Chinese restaurant that evening and then returned to his room to start work on the things he wanted to say to the estate tenants. He made some progress but recognised that it was going to require a lot of thought so he turned his attention to making out some menus and shopping lists to see him and Adam through the coming week. Satisfied, he turned the light off and slept.

Even James knew that the days of wearing a tie and ones best three-piece suit to meet the bank manager were gone; in fact, even the chance to meet one's bank Manager was rare, these days. None the less, he dressed carefully and as smartly as he could and made his way to Downham's offices where he spent the morning in the library developing his knowledge of the estate. In the library files he found a picture of the Mountjoy coat of arms, took a photograph of it with his mobile and also asked Melanie to take a photocopy for him. The letters Susan had forwarded with the credit card and bank letters had arrived, much to his relief.

Jonathan had organised for the bank manager, John Briggs, to visit their offices because it was not easy for him to be too mobile in his wheelchair. However, he had asked Melanie to buy-up half of the Marks and Spencer food hall to lay on a magnificent buffet lunch. Briggs arrived promptly and Jim was introduced to him under his newly acquired title after which they sat around and munched their way through the buffet, drank copious quantities of wine and chatted generally. Jim's first-class honours degree from Cambridge went down well but he did find himself struggling a little and using poetic licence to create a believable story about his career and business experience since graduating.

They drifted into talking about the estate and here Jim was already able to bring forward some of his ideas to put the estate back on a sound financial footing. They went through the various accounts and their purpose and Jim particularly wanted to know if Briggs had any information about the unused bank account.

"Well, said Briggs, there is a balance of one-hundred thousand on that account, plus accumulated interest, but it has never moved, ever since the account was set up. I looked back through our files this morning and the only thing I was able to find was a pencil note at the very beginning, it seems to be the name 'Selina'." Jim looked at Jonathan who simply shrugged his shoulders.

"Are there any covenants or restrictions on that account?" Jim asked and Briggs confirmed that there were not.

"OK," Jim continued. "Then I think we should assume that there is no reason why those funds should not be brought into play. I was going to ask you to provide us with an unsecured temporary overdraft facility of a quarter of a million but, in the light of that, I think we can manage on one-hundred-and-fifty-thousand."

"I'm not sure I can help with the unsecured bit," Briggs interposed.

"Oh, come on," Jim quickly put in. "Your bank has had this account since before Adam and Eve were thrown out of the garden. We're looking at one of the largest estates in the whole of the north-west. That has to be worth getting on for a quarter of a billion at today's values. Besides, my plan is to hugely increase the throughput on the account, all of which will generate additional income for your bank."

Briggs did not give in easily but Jim gradually wore him down and, by the end, he agreed to pencil in the overdraft, subject to receiving a believable business plan from Jim. He produced various papers and mandates for Jim to sign, had a last glass of wine and staggered away.

"Well done, Laddie," said Jonathan. "That's the first time I've seen him bettered."

"I've decided to go ahead with rent review notices on all the cottages, with the exception of the four widows. I want them left for another year." Jim told him. "Apart from Caleb, the gamekeeper, every other tenant is in arrears, so I suggest we ignore notice periods and just plough ahead. Here is a list of my suggested revised rents which I've indexed against the change in the cost of living index over the intervening period."

"I want the notices to be accompanied by a standing order mandate which every tenant will be required to sign. Please could you organise for them to go out at the beginning of next week?" Jonathan was not happy at short-circuiting the system and recommended that they should go through the formal procedure. That would be protracted and time-consuming; Jim stuck to his guns and Jonathan eventually reluctantly agreed to organise it. Before leaving, Jim collected the various bank papers and cheque books together, feeling rather pleased with the day's work; he had funds to start some serious work.

From there, he made his way to the local planning office and asked to speak to a planner. Again, the posh title worked wonders and he was shown into a meeting room by the planning officer, Michael Duffy.

"How can I help?" Duffy asked.

Jim explained that he had taken over the Dunkield estate and wanted to know if any of it featured in the regional plans for the county.

"Hmmm!" said Duffy, thoughtfully. "It's not an area I've had much to do with. Are you alright for a few minutes while I go and check a few files?" Jim said he was fine and

Duffy disappeared. It was nearly quarter of an hour before he returned, waving some papers.

"So far as I can see, our office has never included Dunkield in any planning exercise in the past. What I can say is that there is a wish to try to increase the housing stock in that general area."

"When you say, 'increase', how many houses would you envisage and what land area would they require?"

"It would probably need to be at least two or three hundred dwellings to justify installing the necessary infrastructure. Depending on the quality of the development and the housing density, that might occupy, say, forty or fifty acres." Duffy told him.

Jim thanked him, saying that he was looking at all the options for the future of the estate and that had been most helpful. In his mind he was thinking that the estate was vast and totally underused. Selling a chunk for housing would hardly dent the size of the estate but could generate some useful capital to work with.

On the way back to his hotel, Jim called in at the supermarket and purchased most of the items he had listed that he and Adam would need for meals for the next few days. He omitted butter, eggs and milk as he planned to get those in the village on the way up to Dunkield in the morning. He paid the bill with his new credit card and then used it to get some cash out of the machine as he was down to his last few pounds.

Back in his hotel, he telephoned Susan to check everything was going to plan. She was leaving shortly to accompany Adam to the bus station and to help carry his luggage and she told him the time the coach was due in Carlisle adding "Jim, be kind to him, won't you."

"You really do like this guy, don't you?" Jim fired back. She did not argue.

He opened his laptop. He was anxious to check his own bank account and also gain access to the Dunkield accounts. The hotel wi-fi may have been poor, but he knew there was none at Dunkield, and he would have to rely on tethering the mobile to the laptop, to enable communications with the outside world.

He entered the codes and passwords he had received and had no difficulty accessing his own bank account. He was pleased to see that he still had a useful balance. It occurred to him that he should probably keep a note of money expended on behalf of the estate. He could hardly charge food but thought that the kitchen hardware and his hotel bills were legitimate items and started to make a list.
Moving on, he had more difficulty accessing the estate bank accounts but did eventually get through and was pleased to see that John Briggs had already made a note of the overdraft facility on the accounts. Excellent!

He closed the laptop and went out to find somewhere to have dinner. On his return to the hotel he retrieved his laundry from reception and then asked to settle his account as he would be leaving very early in the morning.

Chapter 9

Jim set the alarm on his mobile and was up early the next morning. He packed all his shopping on to the buggy and his clothes into the rucksack on his back and was at the bus stop before the coach arrived. Only three people alighted from the coach and it was quickly obvious which was Adam. Jim strode up to him and greeted him warmly. "Hi Adam!"

"Hi Jim," he responded. "Susan said you would be hard to miss."

They watched while the coach driver unloaded the bike and luggage and then Jim helped him carry the various items across to where his bike stood.

Jim had brought some strong twine and Adam expertly helped him to tie the suitcase across the top of the buggy. Most of the rest of the stuff was in the rucksack on Adam's back and the only remaining problems were the sleeping bags which they helped each other to tie on top of their rucksacks.

"There's a breakfast bar on the edge of town," Jim told him. "I suggest that we ride to there and have breakfast and some coffee before we tackle the main part of the journey." And he led the way.

They locked the bikes together outside the 'All-day Breakfast Bar' and sat in the window where they could keep an eye on them. Jim checked what Adam would like to eat and they each settled for a full breakfast – with everything. While they were waiting, Jim said.

"I hope Susan has been honest with you. I can give you food and lodgings, but I can't afford to pay you."

"Yes, she has. But I'm on unemployment benefit and I probably don't need more than that, Jim. Anyway, tell me about this estate, you've inherited."

"Sure. But, before I start, can I ask a favour; please could you call me James. It's not to seem posh or to give myself airs and graces, it's because everyone else will know me as that, and I don't want to confuse them.

"The estate is a heap of brown stuff. Everything is worn out, broken or in a sad state of repair. I nearly decided not to go ahead. I'm not practical; that's why I needed someone like you who is, who can look at things, know they're wrong and click their fingers and make them better.

The breakfast arrived and there was silence whilst they both tucked in. They downed two cups of coffee each and Adam used the restroom while Jim settled the bill after which, they recovered their bikes and set off for Dunkield. The bikes were heavy and they made fairly slow progress; Jim was struggling, in particular. Suddenly, Adam said, "Look, I'm on your bike which you'd probably be more comfortable on and besides, you're pulling most of the weight in that buggy. Let's swap for a while and see if that works any better."

Well, it certainly worked better for Jim. The bike was lighter, it fitted him better, had lots of gears to make the uphill ride easier and he did not have the extra burden of the buggy. They did a further five or six miles like that and then Jim insisted that they swapped back for a spell.

They called in at the shop in the village and further burdened their machines with butter, eggs and milk. They swapped back and forth a couple more times until they eventually came to the steep bit at the end and Jim had to dismount and was walking. Adam was ahead, still manfully trying to cycle uphill when a van came around the corner, far too fast and he was forced to ride into the ditch to avoid being hit. Thankfully the van stopped before it reached Jim who was in the middle of the road. The driver got out and, as he and Jim went to rescue Adam from the ditch Jim saw that the van was from Richard's Mobile Shop. Adam was scratched but otherwise unhurt and the driver was apologising profusely.

"That will cost you two bottles of water," Jim announced and the driver fetched them from the van without a murmur.

As they drank to quench their thirst, Jim asked the driver "Do you go up to the Dunkield estate?"

The driver told him that he didn't and Jim asked if he would.

"Yes, I've got a spare slot on Tuesday mornings, I could call in at around ten o'clock."

Jim thanked him and asked if he would make that a regular fixture as from next week but suggested that he should drive more slowly on the estate roads. He agreed, then drove off again at top speed.

The two of them finally reached the start of the estate and Adam commented on the sad state of the gates as they passed. He was scathing as they swerved around the dead oak tree on the drive and was even more vocal when they reached the castle and he saw its burnt-out state. They stopped briefly at the stables and Adam said what a pity it was that the roof had caved in. Jim called Rowan's name but there was no reply and he saw that beauty and her foal were out so they mounted their bikes again and carried on down to Bramble Cottage.

Rowan was just coming out of the cottage as they arrived and Jim introduced her to Adam.

"Hi! Adam. I've just finished the last of the cleaning; hope you like the cottage."

"Thanks Rowan," said Jim. "You're an angel. We're going to unpack and we'll possibly see you back at the stables later," and they watched as she mounted Beauty and coaxed the foal to follow them.

The cottage shone inside. Rowan had obviously spent a great deal of time and effort making it spotless and there were even small vases of wild flowers in each room. Jim made a mental note that he must find some really nice way to thank her. He had already decided which room he was going to use and he showed Adam to the other one which he thought would be 'just fine'. They spent an hour or more unpacking and storing items in drawers and cupboards. Although he had forgotten to ask Susan for towels, she had thoughtfully included a large one for each of them and he hung them in the bathroom.

It was lunchtime by the time they had finished and Jim warmed up some soup and cut some chunks of bread for them both. As they were eating, Adam enquired where Jim thought they should start.

"I've not been inside the fallen-down part of the stables. Let's have a look and see what's in there and if its capable of being fixed."

They removed the buggy from the back of the bicycle and rode back up to the stables. Progress was decidedly easier without all the weight of the luggage they had carted.

Rowan was brushing down Beauty in the end stable which was still in good condition. Adam looked in briefly, acknowledged her and then went off to try to find a way into the rest of the structure. Jim remained there and went up to her and put his arms around her.

"Rowan, I don't know how to thank you for all you have done. You have made the cottage look lovely and I'm truly grateful. May I kiss you?"

She nodded nervously and he drew her into his embrace. The kiss was gentle at first but seemed to ignite a fire within each of them until they were almost frantic to kiss and hold each other for ever.

The beautiful mood was rudely shattered by Adam calling from the other side of the timber partition. "Jim, I mean James. James, come and see what I've found."

Reluctantly, he gave Rowan one last, long, lingering kiss and went outside. He called to Adam to ask where he had got in and was told it was beside the water barrel. Jim squeezed through the hole.

It was surprisingly spacious inside and he was able to stand up. As his eyes adjusted to the gloom, he realised that he was actually in a barn, not stables. And that he was looking at a cornucopia of farming equipment. That was exciting but perhaps the most exciting thing was a big, grey Massey-Ferguson tractor, standing in the middle.

"It's probably fifty or sixty year's old," Adam told him. "But we'll have a look and see if it moves. But that's not what I brought you in to show you. Come and look at these timbers. See this beam, this is the cause of the problem. Its broken here and has brought down the whole of the rest of the roof with it. I think that, if we were able to raise it back into position and brace it with some decent timbers, we'd be able to secure the ends, fix it back in place and the roof would be as good as new."

"How would you raise it?" Jim Asked. "And where would you get the timbers to brace it?"

"Well, we might be able to raise it by brute force, otherwise, there's a jack on the bench and we'd have to do it a little at a time. As for the timbers, there's lots around. But I'm going to need some tools and I could do with some experienced help."

"Adam, if you can get the roof back up by Sunday, it would be the best possible example of renewal and regeneration for the estate and hopefully help to inspire people. There are three retired joiners or general handymen on the estate, Keith, Mark and Dave. You go and put some spuds on for our dinner and I'll go and see if they'll help.

Rowan was still working in the stable next door when they emerged and Jim asked her if she thought the chippies would be prepared to lend a hand; she was decidedly unsure.

"Anyway, I'm going to visit them now and ask them." And he double checked which cottages they were in. "A couple of things for you Rowan. Firstly, please would you ride round to all the tenants tomorrow and tell them we're going to have a Jacob's Join at three o'clock on Sunday. Bring some food to share and bring a beaker to drink some cider. Secondly, if we're going to mess about in the other side of the stables, I think we need Beauty and the foal out of here tomorrow while we're working; just in case. And, by-the-way, the agricultural advisor suggested that having beauty and her foal gambolling about in one of the fields could be an added 'feel-good' factor for everyone. What do you think?"

Rowan said that she was already thinking it was time for them to be spending time outside and she would fix it.

Jim went around to visit the three joiners in turn but gave the same message to each.

"I need some help and wondered if you'd be prepared to assist me tomorrow morning. I want to see if it's possible to repair the roof of the barn. Do you think you could lend a hand for a couple of hours at nine o'clock, with your tools?"

He didn't get any rejections so simply thanked them and said, "See you in the morning."

Back in Bramble Cottage, he told Adam that none of the joiners had said no, so, let's hope.

The potatoes were nearly ready and Adam apologised that he had no idea what Jim planned to eat with them. They went through the fridge together and cobbled together a reasonable meal which they sat and ate together. They chatted about the run-down condition of the estate and how and in what order they should tackle it. At one point, Jim asked Adam if he had a driving licence and he confirmed he had, asking why he had enquired.

"Well, this keep-fit cycling lark is great for the soul and wonderful for the environment, but it's pretty inefficient if we're going to tackle this place seriously. I think I'll look for an old van next week that we can use to fetch and carry things in and get down to Carlisle and back. Adam thought that was a sound plan.

Towards the end of the evening, Adam called Susan to say that he had arrived safely and he liked the look of the place. Jim emailed Melanie at Downham and Sparrow to ask for the contact details of the estate's insurance agents.

He figured that a review of insurances was probably overdue.

Chapter 10

They were both up, breakfasted and in the barn by eight the following morning. Rowan had moved Beauty and her foal to an adjacent field and was already out on her rounds. Adam busied himself purposefully, clearing the maximum possible space for them to work in and searching out the timbers he needed. Jim bumbled around aimlessly but did try to memorise the hoard of equipment in the building. The three joiners all arrived together promptly at nine o'clock and Jim made the introductions, all round. Adam carefully explained his plan and then went through it a second time. There were some questions for clarification but they seemed reasonably relaxed that it made sense. Jim fervently hoped that it did.

Under Adam's direction, they worked well together and all started to push, shove and lift in unison and, to Jim's utter amazement, the offending timber moved in the right direction. By ten o'clock, it was in its proper position and suddenly, the roof was an awful lot higher than it had been. At this stage, they moved into the bracing and fixing stage and Jim knew that he was entirely out of his depth so he cycled back to the cottage to collect some beers for them all.

By the time he returned, two new stanchions were in place and a couple of the guys were up ladders, hammering for all they were worth. When they were satisfied that all was secure, they came down and stood about, drinking their beers.

"Will it hold," Jim asked.

"You could land an elephant on that roof," one of them suggested.

"The twisting has warped some of the roofing and Its going to need re-felting at some stage," Adam put in. "But there's an old tarpaulin over there. Give me a hand to get it up on the roof, I'll nail it down to keep the place dry."

Between them, they got the tarpaulin up on the roof and then Jim and Adam took their time to thank the guys and make certain they knew how their efforts were appreciated, before they drifted off together. The whole exercise had taken less than a couple of hours.

When Rowan returned at lunchtime, she was astounded. "So far as I can remember, that roof collapsed before I was born," she told Jim. "You've fixed it in a morning; that is really going to give a message to the tenants."

"How have your invitations been received?" Jim asked her.

"Well, the usual mumblings from the usual malcontents. But everyone is up for it."

Just at that moment, there was a terrifying roaring sound from inside the barn. Until the roof had been raised, the big barn doors at the end had been jammed. Now they rushed to open them before Adam asphyxiated himself. He backed the tractor out of the barn, coughing and spluttering and then did a lap of honour round the entire building, before bringing the machine to a halt and jumping down.

"Not bad Eh? It has got to be fifty years old at least and probably hasn't moved for twenty.

Rowan left to go home for lunch and Jim and Adam made their way to Bramble Cottage.

"I've heard that farm workers usually take their lunch, their 'baggins' out with them so that they don't have to keep going home at lunch time," Adam commented. "Makes sense, perhaps we should do the same."

They were back at the barn after lunch. Adam got up on the roof and finished nailing the tarpaulin down and also nailed plastic sacks over some of the remaining holes. Jim was inside the barn. He had decided that, if the weather was bad on Sunday, this would make an ideal venue, provided he could clear sufficient space for everyone. He was working away when Caleb entered the barn.

"Rowan tells me you have a magic wand and it certainly looks like it; that's a good piece of work," he said, looking round the barn. "You asked me the other night about breeding pheasants and possible shoots. It's a little bit late in the season to start breeding many more chicks this year, but I'll have a go and we can make a real effort to breed lots for next year."

"Thanks Caleb, the estate is going to need every penny it can earn. Now, whilst you're here, you've been on the estate for most of your life. Tell me, have you ever heard the name 'Selina'?"

Caleb jumped visibly and turned white. "Your Lordship, I've made a habit of never telling lies but I'm going to tell you now that I've never heard that name and I'll thank you never to ask me again." And he left the barn quickly without another word. Hmm! Now, there's a mystery, thought Jim.

He continued tidying the barn and, by the end of the afternoon, there was plenty of space to fit everyone in there easily and he spent half an hour with a broom, sweeping the floor. When Adam came down from the roof, he said that there were a couple of bits of machinery in the nettles behind the building and they wandered round to have look. There was something which was clearly a roller and neither of them could think of a use for that currently. They didn't know the name of the other main item but it was a rotary flail of some sort which Adam thought was used to turn hay while it was drying.

"Now that we have the tractor," Adam said. "There are two items we will need. One is a trailer and the other is a mower, so that we can start to clean the fields up."

"We've got an Agricultural Advisor coming tomorrow and we could ask him about those. I found him very helpful at our last meeting so why don't you sit in on the session tomorrow and see what we can learn? Come on for now, I think you've earned some dinner."

Peter Longfellow arrived very promptly at ten o'clock the following morning in a respectable Land Rover saying

"You need to get rid of that dead oak tree on the drive, it's enough to discourage anyone."

Jim introduced him to Adam and Longfellow suggested they start the day with a tour of the estate. "I'll drive, you direct," he said to Jim.

They climbed in and Jim directed him to the very furthest part of the estate, which was the lowest point, down towards the village. They climbed out and Peter examined the fields and pronounced that the soil was thin and very stony and that it was going to need a lot of fertilizer and other treatment before it would be productive.

He turned the vehicle around and they progressed slowly back up hill, stopping at almost every field and climbing out to examine it carefully. Longfellow was good. He was able to comment on the quality of the soil or any deficiencies, just by examining the vegetation and Jim, who had brought a notebook with him, spent a lot of time scribbling notes. After the disappointment of the lower fields, they found that the soil in the higher fields was of a much better quality and should be much more productive.

They moved slowly back towards the barn and then Jim directed him to drive to the other extreme of the estate, skirting the forest, at which point they turned around again and drove slowly back, examining the fields as they progressed. As they reached Ted's cottage, Jim said that he was the one with the sow about to farrow. Jim knocked on his door, introduced Longfellow and asked if they could see the sow. He led them to the sty round the back of the cottage where the sow was wallowing in the trough.

"Mr Longfellow thinks I should buy all your piglets and put them and the sow into one of the fields to fatten, Ted. What price should I pay Mr Longfellow?"

Peter said one figure and Ted shook his head and said another, Peter said a slightly higher figure than his first and Ted dropped his first slightly to a point where the difference was fairly small. Jim put his hand up to call a halt. "I'm going to accept Ted's last figure. Ted, I'll buy all the healthy ones at that figure, but the runt comes free. When they're big enough, I want you to move them and the sow into bottom meadow and look after them for me. Make sure that the walls and hedges are tight and that they have plenty of water."

Ted was as happy as a pig in ..... well, he was happy and the party moved on.

Jim had cycled down to the village shop earlier that morning for some fresh bread and things to make sandwiches. When they arrived back at the barn, he invited Longfellow to join them for lunch and a chat at Bramble Cottage. Adam made the sandwiches while Jim prepared drinks for them all and then they sat round the table and ate and chatted.

Peter opened the batting. "I can see that you weren't exaggerating the other day when you said that things were in a dreadful state; fields wild, walls down, hedges overgrown and an awful lot of neglect. So, let's talk about what we can do."

"There's no point in thinking about trying to make hay this year. The fields all need to have a mower over them to cut down the weeds and the grass, preferably before the weeds go to seed again this year and start spreading their seeds. Do you have a mower? No? OK, we'll come back to that."

"I mentioned the idea of letting fields for other farmers to fatten their stock. As I said, it doesn't earn a fortune, but it gets your fields under control for free. If you're interested, I have a list of half a dozen local farmers who would rent a field or two and I've made a note of the suggested rates. Don't forget that you need to make the fields stock-proof."

Jim interrupted. "Yes, letting the fields is something I definitely want to do and as early as next week, if that's possible. Incidentally, I managed to persuade the bank to lend us some money, so I'd also like to go ahead with your idea of buying some beef cattle for fattening."

"Fine James. I suggest that a dozen would be a good number to start with, just to get the feel of things." And he mentioned a likely sum. "Would you like me to go ahead and arrange that?"

"Yes please," Jim replied. "But would it be possible to involve my two cowmen in the process so that I can get them to take ownership?" Peter thought that was an excellent idea.

"I notice that you have a fine-looking Massey-Ferguson. It may look as though it's out of the Ark, but they're great machines and they go on for ever. You can attach a huge range of equipment to it. What other machinery have you got?"

"We've found a heavy roller and a hay turner. We know we need a trailer and you've mentioned a mower. How do we go about getting those?" Jim enquired.

"Looking at the state of the fields, I think you could also do with getting your hands on a topper to get rid of the coarse long grass and thistles before you start. The sheep won't eat that. There are sales of farm equipment nearly every week, somewhere in the area," Peter told them. "There's one at Full Fold Farm which is just a few miles away, next Tuesday afternoon. But beware of local bidding rings trying to push the prices up. It's illegal, but regarded as a local sport."

"Can we attach hedge cutting equipment to the tractor?" Adam asked.

"Definitely not," said Peter. "There's no protection on your machine and you'd kill yourself. I suggest that if you need hedging done, you subcontract a local farmer with the proper equipment and rent him by the day." He mentioned a range of farmer-to-farmer hire rates.

"As we discussed, I'm going to prepare a detailed development plan for regenerating your estate'" and he told them the cost involved before continuing "But I've one other thing to mention while I'm here. I know a young farmer; he's twenty-one. He's been farming since he was three years old and he's in his final year of a day-release course at the Agricultural College in Carlisle. He knows every bit as much about farming as his father does, possibly more. But his father keeps him on a tight leash, won't allow him his head and doesn't pay him more than pocket money. I'm not trying to thrust him on you, but I'd like you to meet him; he'll make a good farm manager in a year or two."

"How would he get here? Jim enquired and was told that the lad rode a motor bike.

"Yes, I'd certainly like to meet him. Can you arrange it? What should I expect to pay if he has the use of a tied cottage?"

Peter suggested that he start him on just a little more than the minimum wage and told him that the lad's name was Doug Midgley.

Jim thanked him warmly for his help and they both went out to see him off.

"Well, what do you think?" Jim asked idly.

"A good bloke and lots of great ideas," was Adam's response.

"And, are you happy to hang around here for a while, Adam?"

"Definitely! I'm enjoying myself. I've spotted a whole stack of little things that need doing or mending so, if you've nothing else planned for this afternoon, I'm going to take myself off and start tackling them." Adam concluded.

Jim spent a few minutes tidying up the results of the lunch and then cycled to the third vacant cottage to check what condition it was in if he employed Doug Midgely. There was plenty of dust and lots of spiders and it needed a good clean but he wasn't going to let Rowan do that. The place was in reasonable condition and the lad could tidy it for himself, if he came.

Next, he rode back to the barn. He called Rowan's name at the stables and she answered from the hay loft above.

"Hang on, I'll come and join you," he called as he swung himself up into the loft.

"I'm not certain that I finished thanking you for all the work you did on the cottage," he said and he pulled her down into the hay with him and kissed her. She responded warmly and they fooled around for a few minutes, again getting more and more heated until she suddenly sat up.

"That's enough," she said. "I know too many stories of Lords who have their wicked way with young women and then disappear, leaving some poor girl in the family way."

"Pity, I was enjoying myself," Jim told her as he pulled a length of straw out of her hair.

"So was I," Rowan replied. "Far too much!" And she let herself down into the stable.

Jim followed and then went into the barn. It was looking good and he was pleased. He'd cleared a big area for folks to stand and tried to put anything that was not needed out of the way, against the walls. It occurred to him that if tenants did bring food, they would need somewhere to put it. His eyes fell on the long work bench. It was piled high with rubbish and he spent the next few hours clearing it and stacking the contents tidily away under the bench. Afterwards he gave it a good brush-down with a stiff brush. A white crochet tablecloth would have finished the job nicely but might have been slightly over the top.

He was just finishing when the drover arrived with the barrel of cider. Jim helped him to lift it on to one end of the workbench, and left it to settle.

Adam was just going out to start work on Friday morning when Jim called.

"I'm going down to the shop in the village today. Anything you want?"

"More beers and some peanut butter," Adam called back.

"It doesn't take much to make some people happy," Jim thought.

"He made out a shopping list and then telephoned the estate's insurance agent on the number Melanie had emailed him. He introduced himself and told the agent that he would like to arrange for him to visit the estate to review the insurance policies and cover and they agreed a date and time. Before ending the call, he added a request to put the Massey-Ferguson tractor on cover, noting he was expecting that it would be used on roads, occasionally.

He decided to use his own bike to run down to the village, rather than the bone-shaker, he felt more comfortable with it and besides, it had dozens of gears to help him on the ride back up hill. He was halfway down the hill when his mobile rang in his pocket. He braked and brought the bike to a halt and answered the call. It was Doug Midgley.
"Mr Longfellow tells me that you may have a post available that could be of interest. When could I come and see you?" Jim asked when would be best for him and Doug told him that his day release course was on Mondays. They agreed that he would come over at the end, about five o'clock.

At the shop he went around and picked up the various things he needed making sure that they had sufficient for their meals for the next few days. He included beers and some peanut butter and some very nice chocolate biscuits and Battenberg cake for the meeting on Sunday as his contribution to the 'Jacob's Join'. He added a copy of the local newspaper and the Farming Weekly. Lastly, he queued at the post office counter to get a form to licence the tractor. He piled his purchases into his rucksack and set off up the hill. Yes, it was definitely easier with the gears.

While Adam came and went over the next couple of days, Jim concentrated on preparing his speech for the tenants on Sunday afternoon. He knew that it was a make or break point. If he could get it right, he could take them with him. If not ....

Chapter 11

On Sunday, Jim timed himself to arrive at the barn at exactly three o'clock. The place was packed. He found a place to stand and stood still looking at them until there was absolute silence, then he took a deep breath and launched into the speech he had memorised.

"Thank you all for coming here to meet me today. As you know, I am Lord James Mountjoy, the 13th Duke of Dunkield. I've already met most of you briefly as I have toured the estate but I wanted to share with you my thoughts for the future.

"I've got some good news, but I've also got some bad news and I want to get the bad news out of the way first as I think that's more honest. *(He saw a few heads nod.)* So, I've arrived here and what have I found? Cottages, roads, hedges, walls, fields in a state of total decay and no one doing anything about it. It's a mess.

"So, who is responsible for this mess? Why, I hear you respond, Duke Frederick, of course!
Rubbish, I say. Absolute rubbish. Frederick may have been a lunatic whilst he was around, but he has had absolutely nothing to do with the estate for nearly twenty years whilst you have sat here and watched the decay, day by day, you've watched the place fall apart and done absolutely nothing about it. You can't continue to blame Frederick. It is you, every one of you who are responsible for this mess.

"So, let's throw lots of money at the problem and make everything better.
There's a problem. The estate is nearly bankrupt, and I shall tell you why?
It is nearly bankrupt because almost every one of you has failed to pay your rent for donkeys' years. In most cases, rents are a pittance and have not been reviewed for nearly

forty years. They are pennies and yet you still haven't bothered to pay them and the estate has had almost no rental income.

So, who is responsible for the estate finances being in a state of collapse? You are, not Frederick, and some of you have told me that you're not particularly proud of the state things have got into. The entire place looks like a pig-sty and you've eaten the pigs. We're in a mess.

"What are we going to do?

Well, the estate lawyers have advised me that no worker has an automatic right to remain in his tied cottage, after he ceases work. So, the answer is easy, I evict every one of you from your cottages, sell the entire estate and go back down south with a lot of money in my pocket.

Hands up everyone who thinks that's a good idea. *(There were no hands raised, but several shouts of 'shame'.)*

"Yes, I agree. That would be a shame. So, let's try another idea. Some of you are thirty years or more behind with your rent so let's be generous; let's say that everyone who can bring their rent up to date by the end of this month can stay but the rest will be evicted. Hands up all those who will still be here at the end of the month. *(Five hands were raised, the four widows and Caleb and there was silence.)*

"That doesn't seem to strike you as a good idea, either. So, how are we going to solve this problem? Any ideas? No? Right, I'll tell you what we are going to do.

Firstly, instead of eviction notices, you are going to receive rent review notices in the next few days to bring your rents in line with current values. That will be a huge apparent increase for some of you but only because it is so long since they were last reviewed. The rents will still be reasonable by today's standards, not extortionate.

Secondly, you all have bank accounts for your pensions or benefits so, you are going to be asked to sign monthly standing order forms so that, in future, the rent will be paid, on the dot, every month. I have decided to omit the widows from this review but we will have to look at them sometime in the future. Also, if the review causes anyone genuine hardship, come and see me and we will talk the matter through and we'll come to some agreement.

"Thirdly, if you can't bring your unpaid back rent up to date by the end of the month, how are you going to repay it? Well, for the moment, I'm not going to ask for cash, instead, I'm going to ask for your help to put things right.
Between you, as I have said, you have caused the problems of this estate and brought it to the brink of ruin and between you, I want you to help me lift it back up by its shoelaces.
All of you are retired but most of you are still able-bodied and I have checked who is as I've been going around. I am going to ask you to come back and work for the estate, to repay your debt with light work, instead of money. And I don't expect you to work a fourteen-hour day,

"Look at the fantastic example Keith, Mark and Dave have set in repairing this barn which has been unserviceable for twenty years or more. They've put it right. They didn't take ten weeks working a fourteen-hour day. They did it in two hours, earlier this week and it's a fantastic bit of work. They've shown how, working together, we can make this estate work again and I'd like to thank them from the bottom of my heart. *(Here Jim started an applause which was picked up by quite a lot of his audience.)*

"I want all of you, if you will, to follow their example and give a couple of hours a day to help get things running again, just as they did. Will you do it? *(There were positive nods all round and Jim knew he was winning.)*

"By the way, what I'm asking is probably illegal and if you want to take me to court, you may well win. But, before you go to court, please vacate your cottage because I'm going to have to sell it to pay the fine. *(a bit of laughter.)*

"Now let me tell you some of the good news; the things we're going to do.

We are going to review our entire stock of cottages, the cottages you live in. They've been neglected for thirty or forty years and we're going to bring them up to an acceptable standard. I'm going to ask our three joiners, Keith, Mark and Dave to lead that work and to prepare a priority list for the order of refurbishment. If there's any disagreement, I will arbitrate. The only suggestion I would make is that you put Rose Cottage at the top of your list so that we can use that to house anyone temporarily displaced while their cottage is worked on.

I'd like the widows and wives to help, particularly with things like cleaning and curtains and anyone else to help who has an hour free. Obviously, all materials required will be paid for by the estate.

What I'd really like to do, if we can, is to get through all the cottages and smarten every one of them up within the next twelve months. I want you to be proud of where you live. If I can find some additional labour to help, I will, although I've no idea how at the moment.

"Let's move on to talk about the fields; they are in a right old state of decay. They've not been occupied since the Foot and Mouth outbreak and we're going to tackle them in a number of different ways. Firstly, we're going to buy a topper and a mower and get them under control. Secondly, we're going to stock them, progressively. I've agreed to buy all Ted's piglets when they arrive. He's going to put them with the sow in bottom meadow so that they can snout about and turn the soil over. You're responsible Ted to see that the walls and hedges are secure, and that the pigs have plenty of food and water but I doubt that's going to tie you down for more than a couple of hours a day.

"Next, we're going to sublet some of the fields for grazing. I'm expecting several flocks of sheep to arrive next week and our farm workers, Mike, Corny, Big Des and Charlie, I'd like you to take charge of them. Again, make sure they have access to water when needed but also, make sure every wall and hedge of the fields you put them in is lamb-proof, I don't want us to lose a single head. Again, I don't expect it to take more than a couple of hours a day. If you have any problem with foxes, I gather that Caleb has a pop-gun.

"Talking of Caleb, he has volunteered to try to increase the level of game on the estate so that we can start to think about organising shoots to bring in some income for the estate. He tells me it could take a year or two but we've got to start somewhere. Thank you, Caleb.

"Banks are incredibly mean but I've managed to persuade ours to lend us a bit of money and we're going to buy in some beef cattle to fatten up on our own account. I've told our Agricultural Advisor that I want to go ahead with that but I've asked him to involve you, Jake and Matthew, because they'll be your babies and I know you'll love them, dearly.

"Don and Paddy. You're the experts on walls and hedges and I want you to work with all the other chaps to make sure the animals are secure. You know the old rule, 'walk the boundaries at least once, every day'. There is quite a lot for you to do but I hope you can make a real difference in a couple of hours a day.

"Now, who haven't I mentioned. *(He looked towards the giant figure of the blacksmith, John Strong)* Ah! Little John. *(that caused a ripple of laughter).*
John, I've got three tasks for you. Firstly, I expect that there will be a number of little requirements for bits and pieces of hardware coming from the refurbishment of the cottages. Secondly, I'd like to commission you to walk the entire estate and check on every gate, hinge and catch and any other ironwork you come across such as the

perimeter railings, and mend or replace anything that needs it.

Thirdly, and this is the biggie, I want you to refurbish the main gates to the estate to show that we are proud of our estate and of who we are. Can you do it? *(John nodded.)* Thank you.

"Now, we're going to have a little party and share our Jacob's Join and a glass or three of cider but just before we do, I want to invite you to another party. On Christmas Eve this year, I want us to close our smart gates that John has repaired to our smart estate with smart fields, smart hedges a smart road and everything else we're proud of; and there'll be the biggest and best party this estate has had in decades.

Who wants to come to my party? *(There was a lively cheer.)*

I can't hear you. Who wants to come to my party? *(this time there was a massive cheer and Jim knew he'd won them.)*"

He stayed around in the barn for a period to see if anyone wanted to ask him questions and to drink a couple of glasses of cider and then retreated to Bramble Cottage where he lay on the bed, shattered. The speech had taken it out of him. He was just drifting off to sleep half an hour later when there was a light tap at the door and Rowan came in and through to the bedroom.

"James, that was absolutely brilliant. You hit exactly the right note, told them all the bad news and still got them to commit to working for you for nothing. They're still all up in the barn chatting away happily and they think you've given them pride in themselves again, already.

"Do you think I could work the same magic to charm you into bed with me? Jim asked.

"No way! But I do like you. Let's take it slowly. Anyway, I just came to congratulate you."

"Are you going back to the barn," he asked. "If so, would you spread the word that Richard's Mobile Shop will be coming to the barn at 10am on Tuesday, every week, starting next Tuesday. I forgot to mention it."

"Will do." And with that, she was gone.

Chapter 12

Jim started Monday by telephoning the six farmers on Longfellow's list who had expressed an interest in using his fields for fattening lambs. One had found alternative arrangements and one tried to beat him down on price, well below Longfellow's suggested price. The other four each had sizeable flocks and he arranged for them to be delivered over the next few days, assigning one of the farm workers to each flock but insisting that two be present to count each flock in and agree the number as they arrived. He noticed that they appeared to be counting in a foreign language.

Yan, Tyan, Tethera, Mether, Pimp and so on up to *Giggot* or twenty at which point the teller transferred a pebble from one pocket to another and started again from the beginning; *Yan, Tyan, Tethera.* He was told that it was an ancient Cumbrian counting system inherited from the Celtic and still used for counting animals: Jim was utterly amazed when the two tellers counted the stones in their pockets at the end and came up with the same total number.

By Thursday, all the flocks had arrived, the air was full of sheep noises and he felt that the tenants already had a bit of a spring in their step.

Although the farm did not really rank as an upland farm, the sheep which arrived were predominantly upland sheep with flocks of Herdwicks and some of Swaledales. He found the Herdwicks difficult to understand. Apparently, they had partially died out at the end of the nineteenth century and no less a personage than Beatrix Potter had been responsible for their revival. What was puzzling was why they had survived at all; their wool was apparently wiry and unpopular and their meat was little better.

Swaledales on the other hand, he was told, were crossbred with Blues to produce excellent lambs which were then sent south for breeding. Whatever, he was pleased to see the fields full of livestock.

Doug Midgley arrived on his motorcycle, shortly after five o'clock on Monday, complaining about the huge oak tree blocking the driveway; it was becoming a standing joke. He was short and stocky, looked like a farmer and his weather-beaten face and thinning hair made him look older than his twenty-one years. He shook hands firmly and, when Jim waved his arms expansively in the air and asked "What do you see?", replied without a moment's hesitation, "Neglect".

"Come on," Jim encouraged. "Tell me more." That opened the floodgates and Doug held forth for nearly ten minutes on all the problems he could see around him; some of it he might have picked up from Longfellow, but most of it was certainly his own.

When he eventually slowed down, Jim asked "What would you do about it, and where would you start?" That generated another long and lucid response and, even though Jim found the broad Cumberland accent a little difficult to follow at times, he was left in no doubt that the lad had his head screwed on properly.

"Tell me about the problem with your father," Jim asked.

"Age! He's too young," Doug replied. "Mum and dad had me when they were quite young. He's only forty-five now and has decades of work in him still. I've been helping on the farm ever since I could walk but, in his eyes, I'm still the little kid, running around the farmyard, getting in the way. I've a load of ideas on how we could do things better but we can't even have a sensible conversation about things anymore."

"Here you'd have at least half a dozen fathers, all of whom will believe they've forgotten more than you'll ever know." Jim told him. "It would be up to you to get their trust and respect and to get them to work with you, not for you in the early stages."

Jim led the lad up to Bramble Cottage and made a cup of tea for them both. Then he sat him down and told him all the initiatives that he had put in place, all of which were about to start; Doug nodded appreciatively as he went through the list.

"What hours do you expect to work in this job?" Jim asked.

"Farming's not a job," Doug replied. "It's a calling and a career, even when you're in bed you're on duty, 24/7. I have that calling and I expect to work every hour that is necessary."

Jim couldn't fault his answers.

"I'm not sure what Peter Longfellow will have told you about the job, so let me give you my version. At some stage I shall be looking for a farm manager, but not yet. I don't know enough to tell you what to do. What I need for the moment is someone who knows instinctively what has to be done, gets on and does it, and brings the rest of the men along with him willingly. Do you think you could do that?"

Doug never hesitated for a moment. "Certainly."

"OK," Jim replied. "We'll give it a month's trial to make certain its working for both of us and then extend it to three months. You will have the use of one of the cottages on the estate and here's a note of what your monthly salary will be. If you need some cash to get bits and pieces in the meantime, that can be arranged. Is that satisfactory?"

Doug was over the moon and thanked Jim again and again. The following Sunday was the first of the month and they agreed that he would bring his things over and occupy the cottage on Saturday and officially start on the Sunday. He had three months of his day-release college course still to run and would continue to attend that on Mondays and see it through to the end.

Before he left, Doug said, "You do know that we need to move the sheep regularly, don't you? Otherwise they catch worms and if the whole flock gets worms, you've got real problems. Ideally, you should move them after three weeks and not bring them back to the same field for six weeks after that."

"Right," Jim told him. "Put that at the top of your 'to do' list, for when you arrive.

On Tuesday morning, Jim was at the barn with several other tenants, awaiting his turn in Richard's Mobile Shop. There was some friendly banter amongst those queuing and Martha, one of the widows, turned to him and said she thought he was quite right, they had sat around and watched while the estate decayed. She was going to find which cottage the joiners were working on and go and offer her help. Several others in the queue were nodding their heads.

The van was well stocked and Jim was happy to purchase a good basket of shopping, rather than having to cart it up from the village. As he was being served, the driver turned to him and said "You need to do something about that dead oak tree on the drive. I had to swerve right onto the grass to get past."

Adam had checked the oil and the brakes on the tractor while Jim was shopping; they had a very early lunch and set off together. Adam was driving and Jim was perched precariously on the huge mudguard with a number of oil cans strapped to the back of the tractor. They deliberately went via the petrol station so that they could top-up the tractor and the cans with diesel and check the tyre pressures but they were still among the first to arrive at Full Fold Farm.

The first person Jim saw when they arrived, was Doug Midgley. They greeted each other and Jim introduced him to Adam.

"What are you doing here, Doug, "Jim asked,

"Wasting time," Doug replied. "I told dad last night that I was leaving and he threw me out, on the spot. I knew there was a sale on here today, so I'm just here for somewhere to go."

"Right, stick with us and you can come up to the estate at the end of the sale and move into your cottage right away." Doug thanked him. "What are you hoping to buy here?" he added.

"We're looking for a trailer, a topper and a mower," Jim told him and the three of them sauntered round all the lots for sale. There were two trailers; one was in excellent condition and very smart, the other was old and worn, but in perfectly serviceable condition with reasonable tyres.

"The good one will go for a high price, and is up for sale first" Doug told them.

"I don't think the tatty one will attract many bids. I think that's the one to go for."

"No!" said Jim. "I understand why you say that, but I want to raise our standards. Let's bid for the smart one, if we don't get it, we can always go for the other."

They found a topper and a mower and examined them carefully. Both of them were quite ancient but looked in a serviceable condition. Jim had been studying the classified advertisements for second hand machinery prices in the copy of the Farmers Weekly he had bought and he asked Doug what he thought the two items and the trailer would go for. If they sold for the figures Doug suggested, he would be perfectly happy.

Adam saw a petrol driven chain saw for sale and asked if he could buy it to start chopping up some of the dozens of dead trees around the estate. Jim said absolutely not, it was a liability. If he wanted a petrol driven chain saw he would buy him a brand new one, under warranty with protective goggles, gloves and helmet. They saw a couple of fence-post augers and a few other bits and pieces which they might go for if the price was right.

Finally, the auction started. The farm had been dairy farm so most of the lots were of no interest to them and it was over two and a half hours before the auctioneer announced the lot of the first trailer. "What am I bid?" Jim was just about to raise his hand when Doug snatched it down hissing, "Not yet!"

The bidding was desultory and the auctioneer was about to sell when Doug told Jim to raise his hand. There were a couple more bids and then the auctioneer knocked it down to Jim at a price very close to the guess Doug had given. Jim was elated.

They went through the same procedure for the mower and the topper and got both of them at even lower prices than Doug's guess and they rounded the afternoon off with fence post augers and a soil tamper for practically nothing.

At the end of the auction he went and settled up while Adam and Doug connected the trailer to the tractor and got a few guys to help them lift the mower and the other items on to the trailer and secure them.

"You better follow behind us and sound your horn if you think anything is about to fall off." Jim told Doug, as the procession moved off.

They made it back to the estate without any mishap and parked the tractor and their acquisitions. Jim told Doug to follow him and led him to the vacant cottage.

"We can help you with crockery and cutlery but you're on your own for most of the other stuff you'll need. Anyway, unpack your things and then pop down to Bramble Cottage and we'll see what we can help you with and provide you with a bit of supper for this first evening. He told Doug as he left.

Jim was looking through last week's local paper later that evening.

"Adam, there are several vans in here that sound as though they would meet our needs. Let's get down to Carlisle early on Thursday, buy this week's paper and see if we can find something suitable. This lack of transport is loony."

Jim was up early next morning but found that Doug had beaten him. He could see the lad, several fields away, walking the boundaries of the estate. He was clearly trying to get his mind around the size of the problem and was out all day.

Jim concentrated his attention on an area much closer to the centre and was pleased with what he saw. There was activity everywhere.

There were sheep in several fields. He could see Mike and Corny keeping an eye on them and went over to chat with them and check they were happy. They were, and reckoned it was 'gradley' to see some livestock about the place again. The hedgers and dry-stone wallers, Don and Paddy, were working in another field and he asked them how big the problem was that they were working on. Apparently, it was a 'bit of a bugger', but they'd have it sorted in a couple of hours. Jim watched them for a couple of minutes, fascinated by what they were doing. They had taken all the dead wood out of the hedge and were hacking three-quarters of the way through the remaining stems in the hedge, close to the ground. He asked if that killed the wood.

Don chuckled. "No, what we're doing is called layering. We're cutting or pleaching part-way through the wood so that we can bend the stalk without breaking it but the sap can still flow and keep it alive. Then we weave the stems together horizontally to make a tightly knit hedge that a lamb can't get through. It encourages new growth in the hedge and within a couple of years, even a mouse will have difficulty getting through it. Years ago, me and Paddy used to win all the local competitions for our hedge layering."

The work looked neat and tidy and Jim told them so and congratulated them.

Jake and Matthew were checking out various fields to see where they wanted to put their charges when the beef cattle arrived. Jim had just had a call from Peter

Longfellow and went across to tell them that he would be picking them up at the barn at eight-thirty on Friday morning to go and view some cattle. He saw John Strong, the blacksmith, several fields away, examining all the gates and fittings, as requested. Finally, he saw that Adam had attached the new topper to the tractor and was making short work of one overgrown field. Over the course of the next few weeks he used it in no end of fields, and later followed it with the mower. There was activity everywhere, and it felt good.

Jim retraced his steps and made for Rose Cottage, the one remaining unoccupied cottage which was the one he had asked should be prioritised for refurbishment so that it could be used to accommodate tenants while their own cottage was being refurbished.

Keith, Mark and Dave were all hard at work there and Jim asked them to give him some idea of the size of the task he had set them. They were very cheerful and said that they were quite enjoying doing a bit of practical work again but their main problem was plastering.

"Most of the cottage walls on the estate are wattle and daub and many of them are crumbling. We can all do joinery and splash a paint brush about but none of us is a plasterer and that's our greatest need."

Jim had no idea how to solve that one but promised to keep his eyes open.

He was uncomfortably aware that an overdraft facility from the bank depended on him producing a convincing business plan for the estate and that he needed to get down to work to prepare this. He also knew that he was starting from an incredibly thin knowledge base. He spent several evenings drafting and redrafting various sections of the plan covering income, expenditure and capital requirements and then called in Doug to help with costs, sales prices and a general reality check. That led to a further iteration with a raft of new assumptions and values. Before submitting it to the bank, he asked Peter

Longfellow to cast his eyes over it and that resulted in yet more amendments. One thing that became obvious during the exercise was that scale would be a significant issue. Although he was now starting to generate activity across the board, he would need to hugely ramp-up the level of activity to generate a self-sustaining level of profitability for the estate. However, at least he was starting to understand the rules of the game. He sent a copy to John Briggs at the bank and arranged to meet him a couple of weeks later to discuss it. Briggs asked for clarification on various issues but was basically prepared to accept the plan against the promised overdraft facility.

Chapter 13

On Thursday morning, Jim and Adam were seated in the 'All day Breakfast Bar' outside Carlisle whilst the Massey-Ferguson sat outside. It was just after eight o'clock and they were reading the latest edition of the local newspaper, between mouthfuls of breakfast.

They circled half a dozen advertisements for vans which looked like the type and price range of vehicle they were looking for and Jim telephoned the numbers in the advertisement and arranged to call to inspect them. Two were not available to see that day but they toured the remaining owners,

The first two vehicles they saw were in a pretty poor state with bashes and scratches all over them. The third one was perfect. It was in a good, clean condition and had relatively low mileage. Adam spent some time with his head under the bonnet checking it over, he kicked the wheels and got underneath the vehicle to prod and poke. He was satisfied. Jim haggled on the price and agreed a deal and the payment process with the owner who then, kindly, offered to drive it up to Dunkield at the weekend, with a friend who could give him a lift back.

As they left there, Jim said "Come on, let's find an agricultural merchant. I want to open an account for supplies and, while we're there, I'll buy you a chain saw to celebrate." They found an appropriate place on the edge of town, completed the paperwork to open an account and purchased the much-needed chain saw.

They stopped in the village on the way back to pick up a form from the post office to tax the van and, as he entered the shop, Jim saw an advertisement in the window '*Skilled decorator, looking for local work*' and he made a note of the number.

Back in his cottage, Jim first went on line for quotes to insure the van. As neither he nor Adam had any no-claims bonus entitlement, the price was frightening, but there was no option and he accepted one of the prices quoted.

Next, he called the number on the advertisement he had seen. When the fellow answered, Jim asked what particular skills he had.

"Oh! I'm an all-rounder; painting, decorating, plastering, the lot."

"And why the emphasis on 'local work'," Jim asked.

"The guy went a bit quiet and said, I've just lost my licence and I can't drive to go all over the place as I used to. I need local work to earn some money to keep the family together while I'm banned from driving."

"Come up and see me at Dunkield in the morning, "Jim told him, and they agreed a time.

He wandered across to the barn feeling that lots of things were starting to come together. He was pleased to see Rowan there as he'd not seen her for a few days. He was about to put his arms around her when she stopped him.

"Don't do that, you naughty man; you know what happens when we get too close together."

"Yes! We both enjoy ourselves," he replied. "OK, I'll behave for now. But I wanted to ask you if you know anyone on the estate who might be able to help with bookkeeping and a bit of administrative work?"

"Do you mean, besides me?" Rowan asked.

"Why, have you got experience of that type of thing?"

"For your information, your lordship, I'm not actually just a Bimbo. "I've just finished an MA(Hons) degree in Business Studies and Accounting. That's how I got Beauty, she was a present from Caleb and Elizabeth for my graduation. We didn't know she was in foal at the time. That was a bonus."

"And there was me thinking that you were just a very, very pretty face. Will you help me?"

"Flatterer! There's not a whole lot of work available up here so, I may be prepared to consider a decent offer. And now, I may kiss you, briefly." It wasn't particularly brief; but it was very pleasant.

He was just about to head back to his cottage when a huge cattle truck arrived with Jake, Matthew and Peter Longfellow in the cab. They had purchased twelve head of cattle for fattening. Jim watched while the vehicle was backed up to one of the fields and the animals unloaded. They went ballistic as they were freed into the field and ran round and around in sheer joy. It was great to watch. Jim could see that Jake and Matthew were already deeply in love with their charges and gazing at them admiringly. It was another step forward in the regeneration of the estate and he thanked Peter for his help and support. Peter was looking round admiringly; he could already see that things were changing.

At dinner that evening Adam told him that Susan had asked if she could come up for a weekend. Jim said that the answer was 'certainly' but suggested that she left it for a few weeks until they were more settled in, and then stayed for a week's holiday. Adam was happy with that.
"I'm planning to take my new toy down the drive tomorrow and show it to the famous dead oak tree and see if they can come to some arrangement," he told Jim.
Sure enough, early on Saturday morning, the sound of a chain saw could be heard half a mile away down the drive as it was introduced to the dead tree.

The decorator arrived mid-morning and Jim had a long chat with him. His name was Mike Burgess and he seemed a pleasant enough fellow and was clearly ashamed of having lost his licence. He had a wife and small child to support, and another baby on the way. Jim made it clear from the beginning that he was not prepared to pay contractor's rates and would only be interested on a day-rate basis, paid monthly but, if it worked out, he might be in a position to offer him the continuity of work for several months, possibly until his driving ban ended.
He took Mike across to Rose Cottage where the team had made really good progress already. He showed him the

cracking problem in the ancient wattle and daub walling. Mike was not phased and said that he had plastered many such surfaces.

Jim told him the rate he was prepared to pay and said "You'll be working with the team from the estate. Let's start with a fortnight's trial to see if its working from both sides. If it is, I think there should be plenty of work ahead of you."

Mike thanked him and told him the quality and quantity of plaster he would require. That was a shipping order, in itself.

Burgess had just left when the fellow turned up with the van they had agreed to buy. Jim spent a little time checking the ownership documents and the condition of the van before the vendor left in his mate's car.

Jim drove the van to where Adam was working on the drive and, as soon as he got close enough, he could see that, in the battle with the ancient oak, the chain-saw was definitely ahead on points. There was plenty of tree still left to go at but the driveway was already passable.

"I'll go and get the tractor and trailer so that I can help shift some of these logs you've cut, out of your way," Jim told Adam. He was back ten minutes later and they put a decent load of logs on the trailer.

"If you're ordering anything from down town," Adam said. "Please could you order twenty bags of cold-lay asphalt so that I can start filling some of these pot holes in the drive."

"OK, I have to get a ship-load of plaster for the new decorator and Caleb has asked for a couple of sacks of grain for his pheasants and Rowan needs some hay for her pony." Jim told him.

"So, you've taken the decorator on" Adam commented.

"Yes, I've got to do everything I can to encourage the tenants to keep up the level of activity. We've started strongly and I want to keep the pressure up."

He met Doug as he was driving back to the barn and offered him a lift. He'd seen him working with the others over the past couple of days but hadn't had chance to catch up with him since he'd arrived and it was a good opportunity to chat.

"Can you give me a hand to unload these logs?" He asked, and Doug was happy to oblige.

Jim had already discovered that north Cumbria could get quite damp when the sky was in a bad mood, although locals had assured him that they got nowhere near as much rain as south of the hills in the central Lake District. "Its how they makes the lakes," they would proudly inform him; "down near Borrowdale, they reckon that the only time it doesn't rain in the entire year, is when it pours". However, it started to rain as they finished stacking the logs and lashed down as though the weather was determined to set a new record. They dashed into the barn together but were soaked in the few seconds it took them to cover the distance.

"How have you explained your presence to the others," Jim asked when they had recovered their breath.

"I've told them the truth," Doug replied. "I'm a poor farmer's boy who's fallen out with his dad and has been chucked off the farm. You've taken pity on me and sent me to see if I can be of any help to them. They've accepted that and we seem to be getting on all right." Jim was relieved.

"But I'm glad to have the chance to chat with you," Doug continued. "I've spotted a whole heap of things that need doing and I've got lots of ideas for developing the farm." And he spent the next half hour pouring out a range of thoughts and ideas, all of which made total sense to Jim.

"Those all sound like sensible ideas to me." Jim told him. "If any of them simply need small amounts of money to take them forward then the answer is 'yes, go ahead'. If you need labour, that's more difficult. I don't want any of the guys taken off the tasks I've given them just yet. But I suspect that some of the tasks, like looking after the sheep, are not going to keep them particularly busy, so it's up to you to coax them into spending a bit of time on your projects, providing mine don't suffer."

"Thank you, your lordship. That's just the sort of support I wasn't getting at home. I'll plough on."

"And thank you Doug," thought Jim as the lad left. "Someone who sees what needs to be done and gets on with it. Brilliant!"

Jim could hear Rowan moving about in the stable, next door and went to talk to her.

"I seem to have employed two people already, I've never had to handle PAYE and there's an absolute stack of administrative stuff starting to build up. Have you decided if you're prepared to help me?"

"Do you think that's wise? We seem to have a disturbing effect on each other, whenever we're together." Rowan replied.

"I could try tying your hands behind your back so that you can't molest me," Jim suggested.

"Well, that sounds like a fun game to try some time, but I don't think I'd get much done." Rowan parried.

"No, I'm serious," Jim continued. "I really need some help. There's not enough to keep you busy full time but I'm happy to pay you on an hourly basis to start with; plus all the hay you can eat."

She took a gentle swipe at him, and missed. "I'll take that as a 'yes'." He said,

"I'll have to think about finding somewhere to make an estate office at some stage; but for the moment, you can come and use the pc in my cottage, while I'm out."

Just then, Adam came past looking very tired and very wet.

Jim called out "Get yourself bathed and changed, Adam. We'll go down to the pub and you can have your first decent meal of the week."

He turned to Rowan and asked if she would care to join them. She declined, saying that Elizabeth would have prepared dinner for her and It would be impolite to change the arrangement at the last moment.

As they were driving down to the pub, they passed the former obstruction of the oak tree. Adam had retained a number of long, straight branches for future use. Otherwise the tree had been reduced to firewood. "You've done a great job there," Jim told him.

"And you've done a great job, too." Adam responded. "It's difficult to believe that it's just a week tomorrow since you did your speech; and the whole estate is starting to look better, already."

Chapter 14

By eight o'clock on Monday morning, Jim was down at a builders' merchants in Carlisle with his tractor and trailer, asking to open an account. Normally, that would have required a month or two of paperwork and references; the name The Lord James Mountjoy of Dunkield cleared it in minutes. In his student, socialist days, he would have abhorred such deferential, bourgeoisie capitalist nonsense. Now it came in rather handy.

He had the trailer loaded with twenty bags of cold-lay asphalt and twenty bags of plaster and was on his way within the hour. At the agricultural suppliers he added a couple of bags of corn for Caleb and half a dozen of the old-type smaller hay bales for Rowan and was back at Dunkield before eleven o'clock.

He dropped half a dozen bags of plaster off at Rose Cottage for Mike Burgess, who he was pleased to see was already hard at work. The rest of his load he unloaded and stacked neatly in the barn.
Adam came by just then, put five bags of asphalt back on the trailer, together with a wheelbarrow, a shovel and the soil tamper and drove the tractor off for the main gates to start the mammoth task of filling potholes along the main driveway.

Jim took the van and headed down to the village for some bits that he needed. He was just about to head back home when, on impulse, he drove into the static caravan park and up to the office. He asked the chap in the office what they did with static caravans which had outlived their usefulness. He was told that they either broke them up for scrap or sold them off, depending on their condition. Jim asked if they currently had any for sale and was shown two. One had a lot of mildew in the rooms and smelt decidedly musty; the other was in quite good condition. It had two bedrooms, one of which would make an excellent estate office, a lounge-dining room with a kitchen area and a separate bathroom.

Jim asked if they had their own equipment to move the vans and was told that they had a trailer with a winch to load the vans, but no tractor. They hired that in, as required.

He could see from the way the van had been pushed out of the way that it had probably not been used for several years. He asked the chap the price of the decent van and immediately offered half that price. He saw that the guy was about to haggle and held up his hand.

"Look, let me take the dimensions of the van to see if it would fit where I have in mind. If it does and you're prepared to take my offer, I'll buy it." And he left the chap looking stunned and open-mouthed.

He stopped off at the gates to the estate to see how Adam was getting on, filling potholes. He had already covered forty or fifty yards and the drive already looked better.

"I should probably have asked for some tar to pour into the holes before filling them but this is just intended to be a quick and cheerful solution and we can go back and refill any holes that reappear." Adam commented.

"It looks a tonne better already," Jim commented.

Before leaving, he paced the width between the two gateposts and concluded that the caravan would fit through. He got back in the van and drove back to the barn, checking all the way that there would be no obstruction to halt the passage of the caravan, now that the dead oak tree was gone.

At the Castle, he paced the site of the old manor house which had burned down and decided that the static caravan would fit there perfectly. Over dinner that evening he shared his idea with Adam who agreed to go with him to check the van out and see if their tractor would pull the trailer.

They decided to leave a second visit for a couple of days to let the guy stew and Jim spent those days in a thorough review of progress on the estate. All the lambs were happily gambolling around their fields and Don and Paddy confirmed that the boundaries were now lamb-proof and they were moving on to other hedges and walls. Jim made a mental note to speak to Peter Longfellow and see if he could bring in more sheep for fattening. Jake and Matthew were tending their cattle lovingly and Jim found that they had already given names to several of them.

The joiners, Keith, Mark and Dave, with help from the plasterer had nearly finished renovating Rose Cottage. It looked splendid and they were about to move on to their next cottage which was for one of the widows and was in a pretty deplorable state. The lads were clearly working well together and seemed to have a real sense of purpose but he made a special point of checking that the arrangement was working for Mike Burgess and that he was happy.

John Strong was at his forge and was repairing a couple of gates which were defective and was fabricating several bits and pieces of ironmongery he had found were broken. Ted's sow had farrowed and he had moved it and its offspring to bottom meadow and the entire pig family were looking very happy.

Finally, Jim sought out Doug Midgley to see what he was up to. He showed Jim some of the projects and ideas he was working on. Everything looked sensible and Jim was pleased to see that he had some of the farm workers working with him in perfect harmony. Doug looked as happy as Ted's pigs.

Having left the caravan park to fester for a few days, Jim took Adam down to see the static caravan, later in the week. They had discussed strategy before they got there and Adam was quick off the mark.

"Look Jim, I really don't think this van is worth what you've offered for it. See this, its bent and that bit is broken and as for this, that'll cost a mint to fix. "

And the caravan park owner stood there perplexed, watching his commission disappear.

"I might be prepared to compromise a bit on the price," he ventured and the sum effectively halved again. Adam asked to have a look at the trailer and confirmed that the Massey-Ferguson could join to the tow-bar. He just hoped that it could take the weight.

Jim checked the inside of the van again and noted all the items which had been left inside it.

"OK, I'll take the van and all the contents at the lower price." Jim told him. "We'll come and load it on Saturday and we'll move it first thing on Sunday, when there's not too much traffic about."

"You're going to need some bricks to mount it on," Adam told him as they drove away. Jim ordered them for delivery the following day and then spent time clearing the site of the old manor house to provide a base for the static caravan.

Winching the structure on to the trailer was a relatively easy job. It was slow because the hand operated winch was highly geared, deliberately, to take the weight and the exercise took about three hours on Saturday afternoon.

On Sunday morning Adam drove the tractor down to the caravan while Jim drove the van with Doug Midgley and a couple of the men. By the time they arrived, Adam already had the tractor hitched up to the trailer. Adam engaged a very low gear and edged the leviathan forward. When they reached the entrance to the park, Jim sent two of the men ahead to warn any oncoming traffic and get them into gateways or otherwise off the road and the entourage moved slowly forward at walking pace.

It took them over an hour to reach the entrance to the estate at which point Adam asked Jim to put some stones behind the wheels of the trailer. He turned the tractor engine off and left it for half an hour to cool. Eventually, he restarted the engine and inched the trailer carefully between the gateposts. Jim was shocked to see that the spare space between the posts was rather less than he had estimated but the vehicle got through safely and continued on up the drive. Adam had completed repairs on more than two hundred yards of the drive and that made the passage easy. It was rather bumpier when they got to the section he had not yet tackled.

At the site of the old manor house. Adam manoeuvred the trailer into the correct position for unloading and the static van was winched slowly back to earth. At this point, Jim fetched beers from Bramble Cottage for everyone who had helped, then thanked them all and told them that was enough for today. He sat on the tractor wheel-arch while Adam drove the trailer back to the caravan park where they picked up the van and returned.

Jim was dying to play with his new acquisition and move in although he did feel a little guilty at abandoning Bramble Cottage, after all the work Rowan had done to make if habitable. At dinner that evening Adam told him that there was quite a lot of work required before he could use it fully. Jim should continue with his proper job of organising the estate and he would work on the van in the meantime.
However, Jim found it difficult to keep away and each time he just 'happened' to be passing, there was more progress; the van was standing on bricks, the electricity was connected, there was a water supply, and so forth.

However, when Jim returned from town on Wednesday, he was met by a very serious-looking Adam who simply said "Jim, we have a problem. There's something you need to come and see." Without explaining further, he led him across to where he had been digging a hole for a sceptic tank and lifted a piece of sacking. There in the hole was a human skeleton.

"I'll call the police." Jim said and he took out his mobile and made the call.

Glancing round, he saw Caleb standing staring at the scene from some distance away. He went over to him and on some intuition asked, "Selina?"

Caleb nodded.

"You better come up to the barn and tell me the story." In the barn they sat on bales of hay and the story poured out.

"It was Lord Frederick. Despite the fact that he was no spring chicken, he managed to lure a girl from the village into an affair and the lass got pregnant. I often saw her come and go and it became obvious that she was in the family way. When the bairn finally arrived, she brought it up here and presented it to him. He was already going mental at that stage and he lashed out at her with a stout stick and killed her right here. I was passing and went to try to stop him and saw her fall. The master told me to bury her and that if I ever told anyone I would be thrown off the estate with my wife and would never get work again. I did as he told me and I've lived with the dread of that day, every day since." He paused for breath and Jim seemed to feel some of his pain.

"There's something else you should know. I found the baby over there under that mountain ash, the rowan tree. She'd been born with a great mop of red hair and the moment I picked her up, I christened her Rowan. I took her home to Elizabeth and we kept her and brought her up as our own daughter. Rowan doesn't know it but Selina was her mother and Lord Frederick was her father."

Just then, the sound of a police siren could be heard in the distance.

"Thank you for telling me," Jim said. "I think my pheasant chicks are going to need a lot of extra care and attention over the next few days. Please could you go and see to it."

The police arrived and quickly established a 'Scene of Crime' area with a 'Do Not Cross' tape barrier. Jim and Adam were questioned at length but, given that they had only been around for a few weeks, were soon eliminated from the inquiry. Forensic established that it was the body of a young woman and that she had probably been dead about twenty years. The local police found that they had an unsolved disappearance on their records of a young girl from the village called Selina Brown just over twenty years ago. Dental records for Selina Brown corresponded with those of the skeleton.

At this point, Jim told the police that Lord Frederick Mountjoy had gone completely mad about twenty years ago and had burned the Castle and the manor house to the ground. He had no reason to believe that he was implicated in the death, but left the question hanging in the air. He added that Frederick had died five years ago in an advanced state of dementia. The police were not particularly efficient and the late Frederick's mental illness seemed to provide an easy explanation and possible motive for the crime. The previously unexplained disappearance of a local girl and Frederick's subsequent death seemed to rule a neat line under the whole affair. At the Coroner's Court the inquest found those conclusions logical and acceptable and the matter was closed, leaving Adam free to complete work on the sceptic tank.

Jim moved into what became known as the 'Estate Office' and transferred his belongings from Bramble Cottage, leaving it free for Adam to occupy it on his own. He suggested that Adam should tell Susan she could come and holiday there when it suited her.
He still felt slightly guilty at abandoning Bramble cottage after all the work that Rowan had put in to make it habitable but he was very happy about his new home and settled in immediately. It was great to have the freedom

and space and to be able to sit in the lounge in the evenings, read a book and relax.

In the estate office the furniture was removed from the second bedroom and a long bench installed as a desk under the window which had a commanding view over a wide area of the estate. He installed some power points, moved two chairs from the dining room table to the bench and set up his laptop. He would need to get a second pc for Rowan to use but, Hey Presto! – he had an office.

Doug popped into the office a couple of mornings later while he was working there.

"I've found a farmer in the village who has a tractor with the proper equipment for hedge-cutting and I'd like to use him. Normally, we wouldn't cut the hedges until September but everything here is in such a state that I'm sure we'll get a derogation." And he told Jim the farmer-to-farmer day rate for hedging.

"Where do you want him to tackle?" Jim asked.

"I'd like him to do both sides of the drive, right up to the tower to make the place look neat and presentable. Then I'd like him to do round half a dozen fields down by the stream. They're a bit boggy and it would give them a chance to dry out if we open them up a bit. I reckon it should take him thirty to forty hours in total."

Jim did some quick mental arithmetic and told him to go ahead.

"By the way, I've received Peter Longfellow's suggested plan for the estate. I've read it; you have a read through and then we'll get together with him and discuss it."

When Doug left, Jim went off to see the widow's cottage that the team were currently working on. It was already nearly finished and they had transformed the place. It was going to be really lovely and he congratulated them wholeheartedly, on their work. They told him that the widow was due to move back in next week and went on to tell him the next cottage they planned to work on. He turned to the plasterer, Mike and asked how the arrangement was working for him. He was perfectly happy but said that he was going to need some more plaster in the next week or two. Jim told him that he would organise it and invited him to carry on working with the team.

Having finished his work on Jim's estate office, Adam had moved back to filling holes in the drive. He needed some more asphalt and Jim ordered that and more plaster for delivery together. By the beginning of the following week Adam had completed the drive and filled every pothole from the gateway, right up to the Tower. From there, he set himself the task of cutting up every dead tree on the estate and logging them for winter. There were at least a couple of dozen trees which qualified, so it was no mean task.

In between that work, John Strong asked his help to lift the gates off the gate posts at the entrance to the estate. Adam constructed a strong 'A' frame and they removed one gate at a time and transported them on the trailer to John's forge for him to work on them.

Rowan finally condescended to visit the estate office and they sat down together and talked about how it should work.

"In about a week's time, we need to pay the wages for Doug and Mike. Your first task is to find out all about PAYE and make sure we pay them properly and on time by bank transfer. Then, I'd like you to check that we've received all the completed standing order forms for the revised rents and submitted those to the banks so that we start receiving the new rents promptly at the beginning of the month. I've started a cashbook on the pc. I'll show you how that works and I'd like you to keep it up to date. I'd also be grateful if you'd handle day to day things and ordering stuff such as more plaster and checking and paying the bills. You can work on my laptop for now but I plan to get a desktop pc which we can leave here in the office and I'll network it with my laptop. Do you have a mobile 'phone? "Rowan shook her head. "I'll get you one. The only way we can get on the internet up here is to tether the pc to a mobile. I'll leave you to play with the system for a while but give me a shout if you get stuck." He gave her a quick kiss and left her to get on with things.

Jim hadn't seen Caleb since the day the body was discovered, and he wanted to have a quiet word with him. While Rowan was working, he popped out and found him working near his cottage.

"How are the pheasant chicks, Caleb?"

"They're doing fine, your lordship and they asked me to thank you for your concern. And that goes for me, too, Sir. I didn't want to have to live through all that affair again."

"Are you going to tell Rowan about her parents?"

"I'm not sure. Elizabeth and I have discussed it and not come to any decision."

"Caleb, you've got a guilty secret and I've got one too. I don't know how Rowan feels about me but I like her a lot. If I find that she feels the same way about me, I may be coming to you someday soon to ask her hand in marriage. This is not a proposal at this stage but, if that happens, I think she should know about her parents before she makes a decision. Can I leave it with you?" Caleb nodded.

With that, Jim left to go back to the office to check if Rowan needed any help. She didn't; she was perfectly capable of sorting herself out. He asked her to call Peter Longfellow and invite him up for a chat any day next week, to suit him. He left his mobile with her and told her he was going down into Carlisle to get a new pc and a phone for her.

He took the van and drove slowly along the drive, looking at the increasing activity all around him. He stopped at the field where Jake and Matthew were standing, gazing adoringly at the beef cattle.

"How are they getting on?" He asked.

"Gradley!" He was told and he asked them if they could handle more. He was told that there was enough grass in the field for twice as many and there were vacant fields all round if he wanted to fatten up more cattle. He thanked them and went on his way to town.

The pc he wanted was not going to be used for calculating the trajectory of moon rockets or for playing high-powered computer games so he purchased a fairly basic desk-top with a good size screen and, in the same store, bought a mobile 'phone, similar to his own. The chap in the shop set the phone up for him and he tried to guess how high Rowan jumped when he rang his own number and it rang on her desk. When she answered he told her he was just checking up that she was still working. He asked her if there was anything she needed from town; there wasn't.

He went on to do some shopping at the supermarket and added a very pretty bowl of flowers to his basket.

Back at Dunkield he marched into the office and placed the bowl of flowers in front of her.

"For my favourite administrator," he said. She gave him a lovely smile and thanked him.

He sat on the chair next to her and started to unpack the new pc and set it up. As that was whirring way doing its own thing, he handed her the new mobile. That's for you. Put my number on it and we can keep in touch and relay messages to each other.

The chemistry and the magnetism of the attraction between the two of them was intense. At one point they each found that they had stopped what they were doing and were gazing silently at each other. It was a spooky moment and they both leant forward at the same time and kissed each other.

"Wow!" said Jim. "We're going to have to sort ourselves out or we'll never get any work done. I'll go and make some coffee to sober us up."

Chapter 15

Susan was due to arrive on Friday afternoon for a week's holiday. Peter Longfellow was due earlier in the afternoon and Jim deputised Adam to go and collect Susan in the van while he was in his meeting. He had asked Doug to join him for the session and they had both read Longfellow's plan for the estate, in advance. They did a tour of the estate again in Peter's Land Rover before the discussion and he was full of admiration for the huge amount of progress that had been made since his last visit. The place was starting to buzz.

Back at the estate office they sat in the lounge and Jim made tea for them all before starting the discussions.

"Peter," he ventured. "I'm really grateful for the work you've done on this plan for the estate as well as everything else you've done to help us since I started. Doug and I have discussed your report and we are in complete agreement; indeed, you'll see that Doug has already started a number of the initiatives of his own accord and we plan to do the others as soon as we can.

"I think that the thing which has helped particularly has been having livestock around. It has helped the estate to live, literally. I'm wondering if we could handle more livestock. We've no end of fields still empty. Should we buy in some more beef cattle to fatten? Could we let more fields for sheep grazing or, indeed, should we be thinking of buying sheep on our own account for breeding? What are your thoughts?"

"Well, I'm absolutely amazed at the progress you've made already." Peter began. "And yes, I don't see any reason you shouldn't expand the livestock although at some point you are probably going to need full-time stockmen or shepherds. Doug is perfectly capable of organising and choosing your next investment in livestock and I'll keep an eye open for farmers still wanting grazing to fatten up their stock."

They discussed some of the other recommendations in detail and between them agreed the way forward for the next few months.

As Peter rose to leave, he added "I'll keep on popping in every few weeks to keep an eye on progress if that's OK with you." They both accepted his offer and went out to see him off.

Doug was just about to leave when Jim held him back for a few moments.

"Doug, is the arrangement working OK for you?" He asked. Doug said it was and that he was enjoying himself enormously and was grateful for the opportunity James had given him.

Jim added. "Good, in that case I think we can say that you've passed your probation period with flying colours: congratulations, and keep up the good work."

Just then, Adam drew up in his van and Susan emerged from the passenger seat.

"Oh Sue! How lovely to see you! Welcome to Castle Ruins." And he kissed her cheek.

"It doesn't look all that bad to me and Adam tells me you walk round with a magic wand, making everyone work hard and making everything beautiful," Susan replied.

"No, Adam's the magic bit. Thank you for lending him to me. Now, you two better go off to Bramble Cottage and get acquainted but I'd like you to join me here for dinner tomorrow evening if you can tear yourselves away. No doubt we'll see each other around in the meantime. Bye!"

They drove off towards Bramble Cottage and Jim wandered up to the stables. Rowan was there and offered no resistance when he put his arms around her and kissed her.

"I've invited Adam and my sister, Susan to dinner tomorrow evening and I've come to ask if you would join us. They're deeply in love and I'd hate to sit there all evening by myself playing gooseberry while they make eyes at each other." And he kissed her again."

"Well, that's not the most flattering invitation I've ever received for dinner but I'll check my diary and, if I'm free, I may just possibly come and join you." This time, it was she who kissed him and she held onto him for ages.

Jim was amused to see that Adam had Susan up early the following morning. They were in one of the lower fields where Adam and his chain saw were making short work of a dead tree. Susan was there in her posh green wellies, chucking logs onto the trailer as Adam cut them. He liked the fact that Adam had coaxed her out there and he liked the fact that she was prepared to muck in and help.

Rowan came to him that morning with red rings around her eyes and she had obviously been crying.

"James. Dad told me last night about my real parents and I feel a little bit numb. So far as I'm concerned, Caleb and Elizabeth are my parents and always will be but, for some reason, I feel a little bit cheated that I didn't know the truth before. Dad said you knew. How does it affect our relationship?"

"Lord Frederick is buried over there beside the Tower. When Selina's remains are released, we'll bury them beside Frederick and you can go and pay your respects whenever you want to. As for us, I think that you are a very special young woman and it's obvious that we increasingly feel drawn to one another. I've been in touch with the Genetics Department at Cambridge University. They say that, with effectively six unrelated mothers between us and our common ancestor, there is absolutely no reason why we should not get up close and personal, if we want to."

Tears were flooding down Rowan's cheeks. She kissed him again and thanked him and then ran off to talk to Beauty and her foal. She needed to be alone and Jim knew not to follow. She saddled-up Beauty and the two of them galloped from one end of the estate to the other and back again until Rowan felt she had worked her way through the problem and come to terms with the new version of her parentage.

In his university days, Jim had been a bit of a legend in halls for his fabulous dinner parties. Tonight, was to be the real test and he spent the entire afternoon preparing for it. The starter was to be a cold fish platter. He had prawns, smoked salmon, smoked mackerel, crab and crayfish tails, with an appropriate garnish and accompanied by a delicious sauce. The main course was venison which he had marinated in lime juice and it was accompanied by new potatoes, broccoli, broad beans and asparagus. The sweet was ginger biscuits soaked in sherry and interleaved with whipped cream. There were some rather delicious chocolates and coffee to follow. He had chosen appropriate wines to accompany each course.

Adam and Susan were the first to arrive and he sat them in the lounge area and served them aperitifs. Rowan was late, very late and he was starting to wonder if she would turn up at all. When she did, it was spectacular. Her usual jeans and sweater had been abandoned for a most beautiful gown and a pretty necklace. Her hair was stunning and set off her face to perfection; Jim went quite weak at the knees, just looking at her. Adam rose from his seat to greet her and Jim stuttered quite self-consciously as he introduced her to Susan. She was the belle of the ball and she looked absolutely beautiful.

Jim offered her an aperitif, which she declined and a few minutes later, he invited them all to the table and poured the wine. The starter was a great success and the wine flowed, as did the conversation.
He waited a respectable time then cleared the plates and served the main course apologising for the lack of dishes and silver service. He had an appropriate wine to accompany the course. They lingered over the meal and Jim saw that Susan was watching Rowan quite intensely as they chattered on.

At one point, Susan asked Jim how he had managed to make such a difference in such a short space of time and Rowan interrupted to answer for him. "He's done it by giving people some self-respect; giving them a reason to get up in the morning and giving them something to care about. He's transformed their lives." Jim was a little embarrassed but thanked her.

At the end of that course, Rowan sprang to her feet and cleared the dishes away while Jim produced his masterpiece dessert from the fridge with, of course, a pudding wine to accompany it.

There was something magical about the evening and the conversation never flagged for a single moment and it was relatively late when Adam and Susan finally rose to leave. Just as they were going out, Susan pulled Jim away from the others and whispered in his ear, "Jim, Rowan's absolutely gorgeous and she adores you. Marry her, quick!"

It was a warm evening and they all stood outside talking for a while. Susan turned to Jim and asked, "What do you want from all this?"

He paused for a brief moment and then said, "Sue, you know better than anyone that I have done absolutely nothing to deserve this good fortune. It came completely out of the blue. As a result, I don't really feel that it's mine in the normal sense of the word; I don't own it. I'm more here as a caretaker to help restore the estate for the benefit of posterity. It may sound a bit corny but it's that sense of stewardship which has driven me thus far and I've felt a wonderful sense of satisfaction in the progress we've made, to date.

He looked up at the ruined remains of the burnt-out Castle Tower, bathed in moonlight and added "And someday, I'd like to restore that tower; that would be the ultimate achievement." Adam was standing nearby and added "I'm with you on that, James."

Jim and Rowan remained outside for a short while after the others had left.

"You know that has always been my secret wish too," she said. "What I didn't tell you before was that the fine gentleman who came striding along the driveway, lifted me into his arms and carried me into the castle with him, always had red hair and a beard."

Jim was standing behind her and he put his arms around her and held her in a loving embrace. She did not resist and the chemistry flowed between them, stronger than ever.

"Oh James!" she sighed. "Every time I'm near you, I feel that I want to tear my clothes off and drag you into bed."

He gently cupped his hands over her small, firm breasts and fondled them through the thin material of her gown, and said "I feel exactly the same way, so don't let me stop you."

She sighed and placed her own hands over his to hold them there firmly, then turned her head to kiss him lovingly. After a few moments he felt her shiver in the cold evening air and led her back inside and through to the bedroom. He undressed her slowly, hanging her gown carefully over the back of a chair and playing with her body as he progressed. They slid beneath the sheets together, entwined in each other's arms, exploring each other frantically.

He reached out his arm to find his wallet and the contents he had purchased at the pub but she guessed what he was doing.

"Don't worry," she said. "It's been obvious since we met that it would end like this. I went to the doctor a few weeks ago and she put me on the pill. Take me, please James, make love to me, now!"

In the early hours of the morning she stole away to her own bed. Jim heard her go and kissed her as she left.

He suspected that Caleb would hear her too, when she arrived.

But it had been beautiful, magical. And he knew that he was in love.

Chapter 16

Rowan's entire life had been thrown into turmoil by the revelation that she was not Caleb and Elizabeth's daughter. Her existence since her earliest days had been warm, comfortable and secure, safe as part of their little family unit. There had never been the slightest hint in all her years of childhood or adolescence that things were not as they seemed.

As a child, she had always had the entire estate as her playground and she grew up in the outdoor world of fields and trees and streams. Caleb had often called her a 'little tomboy' but, at the same time, she was enfolded in their unstinting love and care. At five years old she had gone to the local primary school in the village and either Caleb or Elizabeth had walked there with her every morning and returned to walk back home with her at the end of the day. She remembered now that one of the children at primary school had once asked why her hair was so red. When she had asked Elizabeth, she had simply said that God chose the colour of one's hair and she should be happy about it.

At eleven, she had passed an examination which had taken her to the high school in Carlisle as a weekly boarder. She had not really liked that and longed for the weekends so that she could roam free again on the estate. However, she was bright and had no problems with the school work and strong 'A' level grades had gained her a place at Carlisle University on a business studies and accounting course. She had lived in halls there, returning home only for holidays and the occasional weekend visit. She had obtained a good degree, despite enjoying her time at Uni and her good looks and vibrant personality had quickly attracted a bevy of boyfriends. In her spare time, she had worked in the bar at the student's union and had saved up all her earnings and tips.

After graduating the summer before James had arrived on the estate, Caleb and Elizabeth had presented her with Beauty and she had spent the summer riding and enjoying the freedom to roam the estate again. She had used her savings to take driving lessons and had passed the driving test on her first attempt. She knew that, if she found a job and wanted to continue to live on the estate, she would need to be able to drive to get between the two. But Caleb and Elizabeth recognised that, after years of studying, she was entitled to a few months of idle enjoyment and had made no attempt to pressurise her into finding a job, although they could probably have done with the extra income.

And then, James had arrived. She had seen old photographs of Lord Frederick in his younger days and immediately recognised that James was a Mountjoy as she peered down at him through the hatch in the hay loft. She had summersaulted down in front of him and been quite cheeky. He had explained why he was there and she felt an immediate empathy with him over the size of the problems he perceived on the estate. As they talked together, she recognised his genuine desire to set things right and she felt drawn to him.

She had shared with him her thoughts on the problems of the estate and how to tackle them. She had shared her lunch and, with Caleb and Elizabeth's agreement, invited him to dinner. She had sat beside him at dinner, mesmerised by his conversation and his presence; there seemed to be an invisible chemistry between them. The following day she had really enjoyed escorting him around the estate and introducing him to the various tenants and again, she had felt the genuine interest he had shown in each visit.

That evening, he had invited her to dinner; perhaps the craziest dinner invitation she had ever received in her life. They had sat, side by side on a log in the open air while he cooked risotto over a camping stove. Again, she had felt powerfully drawn to him as she sat beside him, smelling his scent and listening to his words as he tried to reach a decision on his future. But he had not yet fully committed himself to taking on the challenge of the estate and when he asked for a kiss, she refused, not really knowing if he would return. Despite that, she had set about cleaning Bramble Cottage in the hope that he would come back and take control. When he did and embraced her in the cottage, she knew it was for real and fully responded to his kisses. She went weak at the knees to be in his arms and feel his embrace.

She had been so proud of him that Sunday when he had spoken to all the tenants in the barn. He had made them face up to the truth but, in the process, had taken them with him and gained their respect and their help.

James's effect on her was strong and immediate whenever they were together, and she was slightly frightened by the intensity of her feelings, there was an almost animal-like attraction between them. For a little while she tried to avoid being alone with him but, when he came up to the hay loft and started to kiss her and caress her, she would gladly have let him take her there and then. It had taken enormous will power for her to sit up and call a halt to proceedings.

When he had suggested that she should work for him she had again resisted, scared that she would be unable to handle the closeness and intimacy. When she finally agreed, she found on several occasions that they had both ceased working and were simply gazing into each other's eyes. It was then that she had known that eventually they were going to end up as lovers and she had taken an early opportunity to visit the doctor and ask to go on the pill.

Caleb's revelation that she was not their daughter but the child of the late Lord Frederick and some unknown girl from the village was a bombshell, changing everything she had known about herself and her life. She had spent the day with Beauty and her foal, thinking it through.

She tried to envisage Lord Frederick and Selina but could find no warmth of feeling or emotion towards them.

She thought long and hard about Elizabeth and Caleb. They had loved and cared for her from her first day and had treated her as their own child in every way. Their silence over her real parentage had been to protect her and she could not fault their motives. Also, she knew that she loved them dearly and would always think of them as her parents.

Her real concern was for James or, rather, for James and herself. She knew now that he was her future and that she wanted to marry him. If they were related, would that be some form of incest or could it cause a problem with their genes which might affect any potential offspring? He had assured her that he had checked out the genetic facts and was comfortable that the family relationship between them was sufficiently distant for it not to be a problem. Of even greater importance was the fact that he had cared enough and taken the trouble to check it out; it meant that it was important to him too.

That evening when James had invited her to dinner with Susan and Adam had been special. She had liked Susan immediately and felt comfortable in her and Adam's company. The conversation flowed warmly that evening but, when Susan had asked James how he had managed to make such a difference on the estate in such a short time, she responded spontaneously on his behalf. Afterwards, she felt a little embarrassed at her interjection and sprang up from the table at the end of the course to help to clear away the dishes.

They stood outside seeing the others off and then Jim had put his arms about her and fondled her breasts. She had held his hands there tightly so that he would not stop and she had known that tonight was the night. Involuntarily, she had shivered as a thrill coursed through her body. He had led her through to the bedroom and slowly undressed her and taken her to heaven. She had no regrets.

Jim had arranged for the two of them to spend time with Susan and Adam that week. Susan said she had always wanted to see Hadrian's Wall and, as they were relatively near, could they visit it? Neither Jim nor Adam had ever seen it, so they agreed to make a trip there in the van. Both Jim and Adam were big chaps and sat in the front of the van, while the poor girls were scrunched up in the back on cushions. They drove along the old Roman military road, through Once Brewed and Twice Brewed, and found a spot to park and get access to the wall.

The area they had chosen was good. Here, after two millennia, much of the wall in this part was still largely intact. It blocked valleys and ravines and scaled almost unclimbable heights. It was impressive and they spent a couple of hours following its path. They found a café a little way from the wall where they were able to get soup and a sandwich for lunch, and thoroughly enjoyed their day out and all their other outings that week. Rowan knew that, day by day, she and James were growing ever closer together.

Unbeknown to her, Jim had felt the same way. He loved her happy and bubbly personality and the way in which she responded so positively to every situation. She was fun to be with and Jim treasured every moment in her company that week.

Towards the end of the week Jim invited Susan and Adam over for coffee and asked if they had discussed what they wanted to do for the future. He had been amused to see that, each time they returned to base, Adam was quickly out in the fields again and had Susan out there in her wellies, working away. She seemed to be enjoying herself and he wanted to know if they had any plans.

Adam was the first to respond. "James, I'm having the time of my life here; I've not had so much fun since I was at play school. I'm still receiving unemployment pay and I'm hardly spending any of it. I'd like to stay and continue working with you, if you'll have me."

"That's fine with me," Jim replied, "although at some stage we need to check if its legal for you to remain on unemployment pay. If not, we'll have to put you on the payroll. What about you, Sue?"

"We've had a lovely week together and Adam has been trying to persuade me to sell-up down south and come and live here. I've fallen in love with the place and I must admit, it's very tempting. I'm sure I could get a job in Carlisle although the salary would probably be a fraction of what I can earn in London. What I've decided to do is go home on Saturday as planned and see how I feel when I've settled back in. I'm genuinely undecided, so I may be back. In the meantime, you look after Rowan. The two of you are made for each other."

"Well, you'd be very welcome if you do return and you and Adam could share Bramble Cottage. There's two bedrooms, after all, if you need to get away from each other." He joked.

On Saturday, Jim kissed Sue 'goodbye' and waved her off as Adam drove her towards Carlisle to meet the London-bound coach. Adam was quite subdued when he returned and Jim took a few beers up to Bramble Cottage later that evening for them to share. He asked what Adam was planning to work on over the next few weeks.

"I'm going to continue getting all those dead trees logged, ready for winter and then, before the bad weather sets in, I want to get that tarpaulin off the barn roof and get it properly covered in roofing felt."

"And do you think Susan will be back?" Jim asked. All Adam would say was "Hope so."

A few weeks later, Jim was in his office going through the estate finances. Rowan was doing an excellent job of keeping the cash book and other records in order. He had spent a surprising amount on the cattle, machinery, wages and other items but he was keeping a careful eye on the balance on the account and had not yet started to use the overdraft facility. Thankfully, money was starting to come into the account for the first time in years. All the rents were being paid into the account by standing order and there had been some useful contributions from letting the fields for grazing. It was time to start thinking forward. He found Doug and invited him over for a chat.

"Doug! I want to do a bit of a review of where we've got to and what we should be doing next. We've got half a dozen fields of sheep happily grazing and we've got the beef cattle starting to fatten up nicely and, so far as I can see, the men are coping perfectly adequately with the work. What do we do next?"

"Well, the fields that the sheep and the cattle are in are all looking substantially improved from when we started and we're moving them from field to field to keep the flocks and herds healthy. There's quite a lot of woody stuff that's grown in the fields, such as gorse and broom and brambles that the animals won't eat and I've got the men going round each field in turn, chopping that back and burning it. It'll make the fields even better for next year. The sheep are all yearlings and the farmers won't be planning to put them to the ram, this year.
I suggest that we continue to move them all to new overgrown fields from time to time and continue to take the rentals. Next spring, we can either offer to buy some of these yearlings or buy some at market, put them to the ram next autumn and start our own flock."

"As for the beef cattle, we could certainly cope with more if we can afford them; the one thing we have is lots of land. I think that buying in calves to fatten up for market is probably the way forward for us here. We need to be careful to observe all the regulations about the registration and movement of cattle, but I'm on top of all that. And, as for the men, they're happy at their work at the moment but I think some of them are starting to slow down a little and we may need to take on younger farm hands at some stage."

"Thanks Doug, that all makes sense. Can I leave it to you to organise moving the sheep to new fields and getting the hedge and wall team to work with them to ensure that those fields are lamb-proof, as well? As for the beef cattle, I'm happy for you to double the numbers when you find the right stock. I understand your comments about the men and I'm still thinking about that one. I'll get back to you when I've worked out the way forward."

Peter Longfellow came by a few weeks later. He'd been a regular visitor ever since Jim first arrived but it was a little while since his last visit. As always, he was amazed at the progress since then. Jim told him Doug's suggestion that they should see fattening beef cattle as their main way forward for the future.
"I've done some calculations since that discussion and I estimate that we would need to have between two and three hundred cattle to make the project viable." Peter thought that was probably about right but added that, at some stage they would need to erect a large cattle-shed to house them for their last few weeks before sale so that they put on the maximum amount of weight. That sounded expensive.

"Ted's piglets are growing very fast; they seem happy in that field." Jim mentioned. "At what stage should we look to sell them, always assuming we can prize them away from Ted; and should we be thinking about further pigs?"
"They should have gone to market weeks ago. I know Ted loves them but you should be planning to sell them on at four to six weeks and the sow should have been back to

visit the boar again by now. That field they're in could easily hold half a dozen sows so I suggest that you get Doug and Ted to look for some new sows and get them breeding. You need to be looking for between two and two and a half lots of piglets a year from each sow.

Peter also reminded Jim about the increased record-keeping for cattle which was now required by law. Jim said that he understood that Doug was handling that but asked Peter to call on him to check that he was happy that was being maintained properly. Peter called back a few days later to say that he had seen the records and they were fully compliant.

Adam finally finished his mammoth tree-cutting exercise. He had used his initiative and had delivered huge loads of logs to all the widows and the invalids on the estate. There was still a pile behind the barn which looked as though it could have fed a power station for a year.

Having finished off the dead trees, Adam then moved on to re-roofing the barn. He removed the temporary tarpaulin covering and used that to cover the log pile to enable them to dry. Then he asked Jim to order eighty rolls of roofing felt. Remembering that Adam was dyslectic, Jim suggested that they had a quick remeasure, just to check. The remeasured calculation came to less than half that amount.

He was using some sort of bitumastic compound to fix the felt down, rather than nails and he worked really hard at the job, up and down ladders for several days. On the final day, he was fixing the last length of felting along the ridge of the building when he managed to fall off. At the eaves, the roof was only really about head height so the damage was limited to a badly sprained ankle. However, it slowed him down for a week or so and the final piece of felt flapped around in the wind until he was well enough to get up on the roof again and fix it. Afterwards, he spent nearly a week coating the walls with wood preservative, inside and out. When he had finished, the barn looked substantial and smart.

The intimate liaisons between Rowan and Jim had become a fairly regular fixture and they usually found time to relate to each other, several times each week and they were growing ever closer to each other.

She was working in the office one afternoon when Jim came in and told her that he wanted to talk.

"It will be Christmas in less than a couple of months. I think that everyone on the estate has performed magnificently since I arrived, I promised them a party and I'd like to try to make it special. Can you help me to plan it, please?" Rowan said that she would love to; did he have any initial thoughts?

"Well, it sounds ambitious, but I'd like to try to offer a hot meal. There's a guy who advertises in the local paper for 'Hog Roast, brought to your door'. Apparently, he part-cooks it at his place, then brings it to your party in his van and finishes off the cooking in a gazebo, outside. I thought we could offer slices of hog in a bun and, if we can think of some way of cooking that volume, we could cook some potatoes and vegetables and some gravy to serve with it. I thought we'd use paper plates and disposable bamboo cutlery so that there would be minimum tidying up afterwards."

"That sounds great," Rowan responded. "I'm sure I could get half a dozen or so of the wives or widows to prepare some sweets for dessert to finish the meal off."

"Yes, that would go down well. We'll organise loads of cider and beer and wine and even the odd bottle of spirits and we'll go for disposable plastic glasses for that, as well."

"Hey! There's a guy down in the village who plays the accordion and calls for square dances. How about lining him up to play while we eat and have a proper barn dance afterwards?" Rowan added.

So, the plan was born. They spent their spare time over the next few weeks getting everything lined up. The Hog Roast man was booked, the accordionist was booked, the plates, glasses and cutlery were purchased; it was going well. The one thing they had not really resolved was how to cook the vegetables and keep them warm.

"Right," said Jim. "This is a case for a real expert. Where's Adam?"

Adam's solution was simple and practical. I've got some bricks left over from the base to the static caravan and I'll build a long barbeque. I need you to get a couple of large chafing dishes, James. We'll use new potatoes that don't need peeling and we'll ask half a dozen of the wives to cook a pan-full of them each and bring them to the barbeque where we'll put them into the chafing dish to keep warm. For the vegetables, I suggest tins of mixed carrots and peas from the supermarket. We'll open the tins and empty them into the other chafing dish and leave them to warm gently on the barbeque. Anything else?

"Adam, you are just totally wasted on this planet," Jim quipped.

It was a few mornings later when Rowan and Jim had their first little tiff. Rowan marched into the office and announced "I've decided; I'm going to move in with you."

Jim was concentrating on some figures and responded, perhaps a little too brusquely, "Oh not you're not."

"Why not?"

"It wouldn't be fair on Elizabeth and Caleb and their values."

Rowan was having a bad hair day. "You don't love me; you're just using me," and stormed out of the office before Jim could utter another word. He was quite upset and should probably have chased after her but he was trying to complete the figures he was working on and in any case, he knew beyond any shadow of doubt that he did love her and he loved her dearly. Also, he had been totally genuine in his concern for betraying Elizabeth and Caleb's values and respect. It was one thing for him and Rowan to grab stolen moments together to misbehave in secret; to live together openly would have been something entirely different.

He watched from the office window as she went up to the stables and collected Beauty's saddle and harness, then carried them into the field and saddled up the horse.

She rode off at quite a pace, obviously still in a mood and he saw her cantering along in various directions over the next couple of hours. Eventually, he saw her riding back towards the field where she kept the horses. She cantered the horse towards the low wall at one side of the field; he had seen her jump that wall dozens of times and he watched as the horse sailed effortlessly into the air.

At that very moment, two RAF fighter jets on a training mission screamed out of the sky with an ear-shattering noise. Jim jumped but the noise totally spooked Beauty and she twisted in mid-air and he watched as Rowan went sailing through the air and landed somewhere out of sight beyond the wall.

He leapt up from the desk and tore outside. He jumped over the wall and ran to where Rowan was lying. She was very still. He checked that she was breathing and checked for a pulse. Fortunately, she had had the sense to wear her riding helmet but she was out, cold, and he had no way of knowing if she was injured. He was frantic, aching for her to open her eyes and had no idea what to do.

When she had still not moved after several minutes, in desperation, he did the only thing he could think of, he shook her gently and shouted "Rowan, Rowan, wake up! I love you. Will you marry me?" and he bent down and kissed her on the lips.

He saw her eyes flicker open and gaze at him intently in silence for a few moments before she said,

"I thought you'd never ask. But yes, I'd love to. "

"Good, because I've decided that you're really rather nice and I'd like to spend the rest of my life with you.

"Are you hurt?" he added, almost as an afterthought as he saw her start to move.

She tentatively moved her arms and legs and wiggled around a bit. "Yes, pretty well everything seems to hurt, but I don't think that anything's broken." He helped her slowly to her feet, allowed her to stand for a few moments to check that everything was alright and then half carried her towards the office where he gently sat her in a chair and went to make her a cup of coffee.

"Were you serious about us marrying?" she asked when he returned.

"Yes! But don't tell anyone yet. I'd like to announce it to everyone on Christmas Eve. I'll take you down to Carlisle in the morning. We'll buy an engagement ring and I'll give it to you at the party."

Later that evening they found time to celebrate their engagement together although he had to be very gentle, she was quite badly bruised. But they did keep their engagement a secret from everyone else until the Christmas Eve party.

On the night, the barn was full to bursting. Everyone was in a festive mood and there was a great deal of hilarity and fun as they all arrived. Once again, Jim timed his arrival to be there after everyone was assembled. He stood at one end of the barn, towering over everyone else, and waited until there was complete silence before starting.

"I promised you a party to remember, and we're going to have one tonight but first, a few words.

When I arrived, I asked for your help to bring this estate back to life and restore our pride in it. You have responded magnificently. Just look at us now."

Here is John Strong, He's just returned from the entrance to the estate where he has closed our gates, as I promised. Smart gates on the entrance to a smart estate, a smart drive with smart hedges. Smart fields full of animals, all a world away from where we were in the spring. I'm proud, very proud of what you have achieved and I know that you are proud, too. Thank you."

"We've got fields full of sheep and fields full of our own cattle, fattening for market. We've got some healthy pigs although Enid tells me that she hasn't been to bed for weeks because Ted still insists on taking the piglets to bed with him. It's all looking good and here we are in our smart barn. How has it happened? Well, you know the answer. It has happened because of you. I asked for your help and you have responded magnificently."

"I asked you for a couple of hours a day to help to put the estate back together again and you have given that time unstintingly. Indeed, I know that many of you have given even more freely of your time, thank you. We're still not profitable yet, but we're going in the right direction. So, here's my first message and I think it's a good one for Christmas. You have paid your debt. There are no more back-rents outstanding. All your debts are cancelled and forgiven. *(There was a warm round of applause and cheering at this.)*
I'm going to need continuing help from a lot of you for the future but, from here on in, I'll pay you for the time I ask."

"The other really exciting thing that has happened is that we have nearly finished the refurbishment of the cottages and I know that a lot of you have benefitted from that. Your homes are smart and presentable and much nicer to live in. There are still half a dozen to complete. Mike Burgess will be with us for a few months still and I hope that, by the time he leaves, all cottages will be up to standard. Thanks to Keith, Mark and Dave who have headed-up that work, it's been really good news, hasn't it?" *(There were a lot of very appreciative noises.)*

"Now, in order that some of you can settle back in your rocking chairs and start to enjoy your retirement, we're going to have to bring some young people in to take your place. We brought one young upstart in earlier in the year, Doug Midgley. I know that a lot of you feel that he has made a huge contribution to our work over the past few months and I'd like to tell you now that I am promoting him to be our farm manager. Give him your support." *(A very surprised Doug waved his hand in acknowledgement of this unexpected, but welcome news and there was wide applause.)*

"It's time to feast but, just one more thing before we do. Where's Caleb?" *(Caleb waved his hand in the air.)*
"Caleb, in front of all these people, I have a favour to ask you. Please may I have the hand of your daughter Rowan, in marriage?" *(The noise, the cheering and the applause were tumultuous. When Caleb could finally be heard he simply said. "Yes, your lordship; with all my heart.")* Jim took Rowan by the hand, put the engagement ring on her finger and kissed her in front of the assembled crowd.
The music and the feasting started and, as he had promised, it was the biggest and the best party the estate had seen in decades. Some of them were still celebrating as the clock struck midnight and it was Christmas Day.

Chapter 17

Jim spent time over Christmas to work on some budgets for the coming year. He now had a far greater understanding of costs and knew that it was a make-or-break year. He had to get the farm generating a profit before the end of the coming year and before he got through all the available funds and he revised and updated the estate business plan he had prepared earlier, to reflect the current situation.

He called Doug in for a chat a few days after Christmas and told him his new salary as farm manager. He was delighted at that.

"However," Doug commented. "If you really plan to run the number of bullocks you've suggested, we need to get serious about a few things. In particular, we need to get self-sufficient in feeding the cattle. We've been lucky last year; because we had so many fields going wild, they could gorge themselves in the fields right through the winter. This year we need to grow some additional winter feed for them. I want to plant lots of fodder beet for them and grow a good crop of hay and also make whole crop silage. To do that, I need some more farm machinery. There's a massive sale of farm equipment in the middle of January and I'd like to see if I can get a plough, a harrow, a seed drill and a baler for the hay and some other bits and pieces. Is that OK with you?"

Jim gave him a budget to work to and told him to go ahead, adding "As soon as the grass starts growing again, I'd like you to keep your eyes open for any beef calves and buy them in whenever you're happy with the price and their condition. We've got to get the farm into profit, this year, if we're to continue to grow and the sooner we start, the better."

"You heard what I told the men the other night about their debts. In fairness, I didn't feel I could continue to use them as slave labour any longer and, in reality, those back-rents were never really going to get paid in cash. So, can you also have a think about how we need to man the farm for the future. Wages are a major cost on the estate so I need to plan carefully and keep the cost to the minimum necessary."

Doug said he'd get his mind round it and come back with a plan and he went off very happy.

"So, your wedding. How, when and where do you want it to be?" Jim asked Rowan when they were together a few days later.

"I'd like it to be on the first of May." Rowan replied. "I'd like to invite everyone from the estate and half a dozen friends from school and university and, I'd like it to be here on this estate, preferably in the open air inside the old Castle Tower."

"May Day is fine with me," Jim told her. "I agree that we should invite the whole estate and the only other person I'll want to invite is Susan. Inside the old tower sounds like a bit of a challenge but I'll get Adam to have a look at it and make certain its safe."

They went on to discuss some of the details and the catering arrangements. After the success of the Christmas Eve party, they felt they were ready to tackle anything.

"You've been working on the budgets with me," Jim continued. "You know that we can't afford to fork out for a honeymoon in some exotic place. Would you settle for a couple of nights in an hotel?" Rowan was quite happy with that.

Adam called in for coffee later that week. Susan had stayed with him again over the Christmas holiday and Jim enquired if they had come to any understanding over her future.

"She adored the party on Christmas Eve and you know that she is absolutely thrilled about your engagement to Rowan. She thinks you've made a great catch; but no, she is still totally undecided about her own life."

Jim asked Adam what he was planning to work on now he'd re-roofed the barn and demolished all the dead trees.

"That's what I wanted to talk about," Adam told him. "I'd like to start on the restoration of the Castle Tower but I think it's going to be a very expensive project. What do you reckon?"

"In that case, no!" Jim replied. "I'm going to have to be very careful with money over the next twelve months although Rowan has suggested that she'd like to get married inside the ruins of the tower so I was going to ask you if you could spend a little time just levelling the ground out and making certain the structure is safe. Could you do that?" Adam agreed, readily.

"Then, there are two other things I'd like you to work on. The main driveway crosses streams at two points. I've had a look at the bridges recently and I'm not happy about the condition of the far one. Please could you have a look at it and see what needs doing. The second thing is that I'm planning to increase the number of pigs in bottom meadow. Please could you talk to Ted and find out what sort of pig hut the sows like and knock me up half a dozen of them."

Always happy to have something to work on, Adam got up, ready to start his tasks.

Doug came over just as Adam was leaving and Jim added "Just one more thing Adam; Doug's going to a major farm equipment auction next week. I know you like auctions; would you mind going with him to give a hand?" Adam was fine with that and sauntered off.

"You asked about manning for the coming year," Doug started. "The guys did so much work on walls and hedges last year that the task has changed. With the fields secure, we don't need anything like as many men to keep an eye on the stock. Popping by, two or three times a day is probably sufficient unless there's a break-out. That goes for both the sheep and the cattle.

What I'm going to need this year is men who can plough and sow and till. The other farm workers reckon that Mike and Corny used to be the best men on the tractor. It's an intermittent job, they're both prepared to work flexible hours and, frankly, they can keep an eye on the stock whilst they go about their work."

"Matthew is a bit past it now and wants to put his feet up but Jake has turned out to be a good stock man and I'd like to keep him on more or less full time. With the number of bullocks you're planning, it'll be pretty well a full time job for him. I've talked to Ted about the pigs. He's happy to do a few hours a day to keep an eye on the pigs and make sure they're fed and watered so I think we're OK there. I'm going to suggest that we keep Don and Paddy on a string. We've no walling or hedging requirements just now but there will be and I plan to bring them in as we need them. I've talked to them both and they're happy to work that way. Finally, a young lad from the village came up the other day to see if he could work on the farm. His name's Ginger, he's just sixteen and he's left school with no qualifications. He'll be more trouble than he's worth initially but he'll be cheap and I'll see if I can train him up. So, let's see how we go from there and we can always bring some of the others in if need be."

As always, Doug's ideas made sense. They discussed and agreed hourly wage rates and Jim told him to go ahead, as outlined.

Doug and Adam went off to the auction on a freezing cold day when snow was forecast. The auction was poorly attended because of the weather and they managed to get everything on Doug's 'wish list' at knock down prices, the total sum being only about half the budget Jim had given him. They brought their trophies home on the trailer and unloaded them behind the barn. By the morning, their acquisitions and everything for many miles around were covered in snow. It snowed on and off for several days and drifted heavily; as much as eight to ten-foot-high in places.

The world was white and silent and beautiful – and deadly for the stock.

It may have been many years since the estate held animals but the old-hands knew the dangers and every able-bodied person turned out to help. They dug the tractor and trailer out of the snow and loaded bales of hay on the trailer and set off to search the fields for stock. Sheep had a tendency to crowd along a protective hedge or wall, to shelter from the snow. That was fine until the snow drifted and covered them completely and the only solution was to dig them out, one by one. Then they carried bales of hay across the fields to where the rescued sheep were standing and left them to look after themselves while the rescuers went on to the next field to repeat the exercise. It went on for days; they quickly ran out of hay and had to telephone the owners of the flocks to bring their tractors up to the estate with more hay and winter feed.

The bullocks were slightly less hard work, they tended to crowd together for warmth and to stamp the snow down as it fell. As a result, they did not get buried and were easier to feed.

The snow lay on the ground for over a fortnight. In the cottages, everyone sat and shivered, pipes froze. The snow brought the powerlines down and they were without electricity for over a week and there was general hardship and misery. Everyone looked out for their neighbours and did what they could to help each other. Despite this, one of the invalids succumbed to the cold. In fairness, he was over ninety but it was still sad. It was even sadder when the widow, Martha, died a few days later. Jim had the bodies moved to the barn and ran them down to the undertakers a few days later when the roads became passable. The following week he attended the village church for their funeral services and to pay his respects.

The thaw, when it came, was equally dramatic. The fields flooded but the fall of the land was towards the streams and rivers in the valleys and the drainage was good; as a result, none of the cottages suffered. Some of the villagers lower down the valley were less fortunate and there were reports of serious flooding.

When the snow finally melted, they found that they had not lost a single animal but the event brought home to Jim the importance of winter feed and Doug's insistence on becoming self-sufficient.

Through February and March, Mike, Corny and Doug himself could be seen out in the fields ploughing, harrowing and sowing. Animals were moved from field to field as they exhausted the grass in each field and it was a huge relief when the grass finally started growing again at the beginning of April.

Doug and Jake attended the market each week and usually came home with another cattle truck full of beef calves for fattening and the numbers were building up nicely in the fields. They had also bought-in a sizeable flock of sheep on their own account which they planned to put to the ram in the autumn.

Rowan was proving very capable in maintaining the estate records and finances. Jim was in the office with her one day when she turned to him and said "Just thought I should mention it; we've just got through the last of the hundred thousand we started with. I'm about to start drawing down on the overdraft facility."

In the post the next morning there was a letter from the bank.

> *Dear Lord Mountjoy*
> *In line with other financial institutions, the bank has been reviewing its lending policy in the light of the current economic situation. I am writing to inform*

you that I have been instructed to withdraw your overdraft facility, with immediate effect.

As you have not yet started drawing down on the facility, I hope this will not cause any inconvenience.

Yours sincerely

John Briggs

Chapter 18

"Inconvenience!" Jim roared as he stomped round the office. "Inconvenience!" He was incandescent with rage.
He had been relying on the overdraft as part of the year's funding he had budgeted; he had commitments all over the place and he was not going to be able to meet them without the bank funding. It was more than inconvenience; it was a disaster. The whole pack of cards was about to collapse about his ears.

What costs could he cut? Mike Burgess had finished refurbishing the last of the cottages and had left a few weeks ago when his driving ban ended. The men were currently working minimum hours so there was little to be saved there. Doug's wages were a real cost but Jim desperately needed him; he could let Ginger go but his wages were half of two-thirds of sweet bugger-all and wouldn't save much. He needed to think.

He grabbed his bicycle from outside the office and mounted it with no plan and no idea where he was going, he just needed air. Without thinking, he started to ride uphill towards the top end of the estate. It was hard work and got the blood pumping. The problem was going round and round in his head and he noticed nothing around him as he rode.
He was panting heavily when he finally arrived at the very top point of the estate and he paused to rest and look about him.

Since he had arrived at Dunkield, he had fallen in love with the area. It was a beautiful part of the countryside and the Dunkield estate in particular had become very dear to him.
Around him were the gentle rolling fells of north Cumbria but, from here, he could see the massive outline of Skiddaw and the other imposing and more severe hills of the central Lake District to the south. To the north, he

could just glimpse in the distance the silver threads of the River Eden and the River Esk, glinting in the sunlight. And, in front of him, set out before him like a patchwork quilt, he could see perhaps three quarters of the Dunkield estate, and it looked good. There were neat fields filled with sheep and cattle, all a world away from the run-down estate he had inherited twelve months before. He was proud of what he'd achieved and he did not want some stupid bank manager screwing the whole thing up through ignorance. No!

He got back on his bike and started to free-wheel slowly down the hill, trying to take in everything as he passed. He rode straight past the barn and kept on going, past Bramble Cottage and Rose Cottage and all the way down to the lowest point of the estate. It was where Peter Longfellow had pronounced the soil stony and poor quality on his first visit and he had made no attempt to try to address that problem yet, that was something for the future. That was the moment when he remembered his visit to the planning office in Carlisle a year ago; and the light suddenly dawned.

What had the planning officer, Michael Duffy said? 'They wished to try to increase the housing stock in that general area'. If he could sell some land for housing development, he could almost certainly raise sufficient funds to solve his financial problems. Jim was back on his bike in moments, pedalling for all he was worth, back towards his office.

He found his copy of the 1950 Estate Report and sat down at the desk to study it. It was a very comprehensive report and had detailed plans of every field on the estate, each field carefully marked with its acreage. There were three fields at the bottom of the estate with a total size of forty-two acres; they were the stony fields that Longfellow had labelled as poor quality soil and there was an added advantage that they were clearly separated from the rest of the estate by an ancient bridleway and were not visible from most of the rest of the estate. Perfect!

Jim telephoned Peter Longfellow.
"Peter, you've been a huge help to me over the past year. I've got an issue I'd like to talk over with you. When can you spare me some time?" They arranged to meet the following morning.
He outlined his plan to Rowan and asked her to hide the cheque book. He needed to put an absolute hold on all expenditure until the issue was resolved. Although it was probably not traditional to involve estate employees in such matters, he went to talk to Doug about the situation and asked him to skip auctions until the matter was resolved. There was little point in lying or trying to hide the truth, it would quickly become obvious.

He was in Longfellow's office, first thing the following morning. He started by telling Peter of the crass treatment meted out by the bank and how it now placed him in an almost impossible situation.
"Typical!" Peter commented. "I know of several farmers round here who have received the same appalling treatment from that bank. You would think that a bank in a rural area like this would be more in tune with the needs of their customers."

Jim went on to outline his thoughts on the possible sale of land for housing development. It was only a relatively small area in relation to the total size of the estate, it comprised a fairly infertile piece of land and it could provide the funds to enable Dunkield to continue and to implement all the plans for its development. He showed him the proposed area on the Estate Report and told him of his conversation with the planning officer, twelve months earlier. That was clearly not a green light, but was a useful indication of their possible reaction to an approach for planning permission.

"As a general principle, I hate seeing agricultural land going to housing and, given the appropriate treatment, the quality of the soil in those fields could be improved, over time. However," Peter continued, "It's not as if you are short of land on the estate and if this is what it takes to keep the estate afloat then I can hardly oppose it.

"How much is a chunk of land that size likely to raise?" Jim asked.

"It depends on the agreed housing density and other factors but you would almost certainly be talking well into seven figures."

"That would definitely make it worthwhile. How do we start and how do I get some cash in the meantime?"

Peter suggested that he should prepare a presentation pack, including copies of the estate plan for the area in question and also a location map. Before sending it out, he should go to see the planners again and see if they were willing to be quoted about wishing to increase the housing stock in the area. If so, he should include the comment in the presentation pack. Jim asked if he should apply for planning permission before going further but Peter told him that it was a slow and expensive process and any developer would almost certainly want to re-submit an alternative plan with their own ideas.

"When you've got that together, you need to send it to some major housing developers. There are two which specifically operate in North Cumbria and I would suggest also approaching two or three of the nationals."

Jim thanked him for his input but then asked "But how do I pay the wages next week?"

Peter told him that one of the major banks had an agricultural branch in Carlisle, and he named the bank. "They are much more switched on to the needs and problems of the farming community. I know the manager well and I think he'll give us a fair hearing. Get a copy of your accounts for last year and your budget for this year, together with your business plan, and I'll arrange for us to go and talk to him."

Jim said he would get those together within the next forty-eight hours, if Peter could organise a meeting.

Leaving Longfellow's office, he called in briefly to see Jonathan at Downham and Sparrow aware of the fact that it was several months since his last visit. Jonathan was genuinely pleased to see him and wanted all the news from Dunkield estate. Jim told him of the way the bank had let him down and that he was planning to sell some land for housebuilding to raise some cash. They chatted for a few minutes but Jim was anxious to get back to his office to start preparing the papers he had promised Peter. "Just one thing before you go," Jonathan said as he was heading for the door. "I've prepared all the papers and submission for your hereditary peerage to be recognised, and to be listed in Debrett's Peerage. Please could you check the details and sign the various papers where I've marked them at some stage so that you can officially be recognised as the Duke of Dunkield." Jim promised to put it on his 'to do' list.

On his drive home, his mind was going through a list of all the things he had to do; it seemed interminable but then another thing added to the list when he remembered that he was due to get married in just over two weeks' time. Help!

"He had applied for and received the licence to hold the ceremony on the estate and the vicar from the village had been booked months ago. Adam had told him that the surface inside the Castle Tower was firm and flat and the structure was safe but Jim couldn't remember where they had got to on the catering and other arrangements. As soon as he got back, he needed to talk to Rowan.

Rowan was in the office working away when he arrived. She was anxious to know the outcome of his trip so he gave her chapter and verse of his meeting with Longfellow and the course of action they had agreed.

"Do you think it will work?" she wanted to know.

"I'm fairly hopeful that we can sell some land for building but I've no idea of the timescale or how much it will raise. As for getting short term cash from a bank, I really don't know."

"Anyway, can we talk about our wedding?" Jim asked. "I can't remember where we've got to on the arrangements.

"That's changed a bit," Rowan told him. "I've been round to invite everyone on the estate to the wedding and all the wives and widows, without exception, got together and insisted on doing the catering. I've no idea what they're planning but, particularly in view of this business with the bank, I'm very happy to accept their offer."

"I didn't want our wedding to be a cheap affair; Rowan. Do you think we should delay it until things are easier?" Jim asked.

"No James, not unless you're getting cold feet, that is." Rowan responded. "I want us to be married now but I'm happy to make it really basic and simple, without any glitz. I was going to spend a fortune on a wedding dress but Elizabeth told me that she still has the dress she wore when she married Caleb. I tried it on the other night and it fits beautifully so I'm going to wear that. It'll be a sort of mark of respect for all Elizabeth and Caleb have done for me over the years."

"Let's also skip the couple of nights honeymoon away until we know we can afford it. The only extravagance I'd like to ask is to have that accordionist from the village again to make the party swing; is that OK with you?"

"Could you come through to the bedroom for a little while and remind me why I'm marrying such a wonderful woman," Jim asked. And she did.

Chapter 19

Peter Longfellow telephoned the following morning. "Slight hitch!" He said. "The bank manager I wanted you to meet is away until next week. We could go to see one of his minions but I think we'd get a better hearing with him, so I suggest we wait."

"Pity," James replied. "But you know the guy so I'll leave that with you. In the meantime, I'm going to see the planners again to try to get their feedback."

He called Michael Duffy at the planning office and arranged to meet him that afternoon.

When he arrived, Duffy introduced him to a colleague, David O'Hara saying "I mentioned that I don't personally deal with the area near your estate. "David does, so I thought it would make sense to involve him in the conversation this time."

Jim had prepared a draft of the presentation for the area and explained the plan. There was an area of forty-two acres on the northern edge of the estate which was not currently being farmed and he would like to offer it for sale for housing development. He reminded Duffy of his comment last year about wanting to see an increase in the housing stock in that general area. Did that still apply?

O'Hara was adamant that he could make no official comment until his committee had considered a formal application for planning permission. However, he showed Jim some of the zoning plans. "What I am prepared to say is that it is on the edge of an area which is zoned for housing development. And, although you must not quote me, I personally believe that the planning committee would probably look favourably on an application in that area."

That was good enough for Jim and he left with a copy of the zoning plan under his arm.

He spent the next couple of days working on the presentation pack and trying to make it look as professional as possible. On the front he included a copy of the photograph of the Mountjoy coat of arms that he had taken with his mobile at Jonathan's office. He also included a specific clause that any purchaser would be required to build a wall closing off that end of the estate from the proposed housing, before any other building work commenced.

The pack looked good when it was finished and he mailed it to five building companies with a covering letter and kept a copy back, ready to show the bank manager.

Bills for services already rendered arrived by almost every post. There was no way they could pay them and simply had to allow them to build up in a drawer.

Adam came to ask Rowan to order some materials for a project he was working on. Until now, Jim had not seen him to tell him about the problem with the bank and he took the opportunity to bring him up to date. He was clearly shaken by this reversal to their plans.

The days until next week seemed to be the longest ones he had ever had to struggle through. He was bad-tempered and tetchy and could find no way to settle to any of the tasks in front of him. His mood was not helped when Longfellow telephoned on Monday to say that the bank manager could not see them until Wednesday and he had to fester on for two more days.

By the time the meeting actually took place, Jim was fully fired up. He outlined the reasons for the problem, listed the achievements since taking over the estate, produced a copy of last year's accounts, went to great lengths to present the business plan going forward and accompanied it with detailed budgets showing that he expected to be in profit by the end of the current year. As a coup-de-grace, he presented a copy of the proposal to sell part of the land for housing which he anticipated would completely wipe out any lending. The manager was intelligent and he followed all Jim's points and it was also clear that

Longfellow had bent his ear earlier and put in a good word for him.

The manager said that he understood the background, the plans and the proposals. He asked a number of supplementary questions and finished the discussions by saying that he was in favour of the proposed loan. However, the amount was above his own personal lending mandate and he would have to put it before his lending committee but he was reasonably confident that it would get through.

On Friday afternoon Longfellow telephoned Jim to tell him he had just heard that the bank's lending committee had turned down his application; he was clearly embarrassed. A formal letter of rejection arrived in Monday's post.
Jim did not know which way to turn and the news put a damper on the plans for the wedding. He called in Doug and asked him to work out which was the least damaging way to dispose of some of the animals they had purchased, in order to raise some cash to pay outstanding bills. Doug gave him a list of the order to proceed and added "I'm OK for cash at the moment. You could put my salary on hold for a month or two, if that would help." But he left looking like everyone else, as though the world was collapsing about his ears.

Final demands were starting to arrive by every post and there was nothing they could do about it. Rowan disappeared on Thursday to submit to Elizabeth's ministrations to prepare her for the wedding. Adam took the van down into Carlisle to collect Susan and Jim sat there at his desk trying to figure out which were the least damaging things to sell to raise some cash to pay current bills, fully aware that was a short-term expediency and did nothing to help the rest of the year. For the first time, he wondered if he should be talking to Jonathan Downham about possibly filing for bankruptcy. He could not see his way through and was starting to feel desperate.

He picked up his mobile and dialled Jonathan's number. Melanie answered and he asked to speak to Jonathan. "I'm sorry, he's with a client at the moment. Can I ask him to call back?"

"Yes please, Melanie. I mentioned to him the other day that the bank has withdrawn the overdraft facility they promised. Its left me in an impossible position and I need his advice on whether I should be filing for bankruptcy. Please would you ask him to call back as soon as he can." She promised to tell him as soon as he was free. The call ended and Jim sat there with a feeling of desolation, emptiness and fear creeping over him. He had reached the end of the road; there was nowhere else to go.

He saw Adam return with Susan and waved disconsolately as they drove past to Bramble Cottage. Quarter an hour later they arrived back at the office, on foot; Susan was carrying some papers in her hand and Jim greeted her warmly, despite his overwhelming feeling of depression. She plonked herself down in a chair and announced "Right, big brother. Adam tells me that you have a small problem, so I've got some news for you. First the bad news; I've come to stay, long term." Adam had a silly but happy grin on his face.

"Now the good news. I put our house in Bromley on the market earlier this week and it sold in days. The purchasers are anxious to exchange and complete as quickly as possible. You own half the house so, if you'd be kind enough to put your signature just here, I'll put the contract in the post and we can exchange as soon as possible. One half of the sale proceeds are yours and that should be more than sufficient to extricate you from this hole you seem to be in.

It's bound to take a while until we actually get the cash: in the meantime, I have twenty-five-thousand in savings and I'm going to lend it to you to see you through until the sale completes. I've already transferred the money into your personal account. Any questions?"

Jim just sat there stunned with his mouth open and tears running down his cheeks. What could one possibly say to that?

"I'm going to keep my half of the money and, if Adam and I find that we really can't bear to live together, I'll buy a little cottage somewhere else and go and hide from him. Now, if you'd tell me where Rowan is, I'd like to go and help her prepare for her wedding."

After she had left, Jim continued sitting there in stunned silence, unable to comprehend or accept that his problems might finally be over. It could take two or three months until the sale completed and he received his half of the proceeds. The twenty-five thousand was not enough to solve all the immediate problems in the meantime but he could probably pay something towards each of the outstanding creditors to keep them happy, whilst he waited for the main sum. He sat there calculating the best way to share the windfall around. The main plan of purchasing more cattle to bring him back on plan would have to wait until the house sale completed.

Adam, practical as ever, had the appropriate solution. "Fancy coming down to the pub for a pint?"

As they were going down the drive, they spotted Doug. Adam stopped and Jim insisted that Doug got in the van, muddy boots and all. Doug asked where they were going.

"It's my stag-night," Jim announced. "We're going there and back twice to see how far it is."

It was noisy in the pub and no sooner had they ordered their first drinks than Jim's mobile started ringing in his pocket.

"Yes? .. Hello…. Pardon?   Sorry, I can't hear you…. Hang on, I'll go outside."

"Right, this is James Mountjoy speaking, who's calling?" It was Jonathan Downham.

"James, you mentioned the other day that the bank has pulled the plug on the overdraft facility and Melanie has passed on your telephone message enquiring about filing for bankruptcy. I thought that you were made of sterner stuff, James. You do know that we're holding all the refunds from those fraudulent invoices on our Client Account, for you, don't you?"

"No, how much is there?"

"Well, money is still coming in, but we're up to about ninety-thousand, so far."

It was all Jim could do to avoid issuing a string of extremely rude swear words.

"No, I had no idea you were holding that. Please, Jonathan, could you do a bank transfer for the whole amount to the Estate's number one account, today?"

Jonathan said that he would do it immediately; Jim thanked him and rang off. He stood there for a few moments quite dazed, not sure whether to blame himself or Downham. If he had known about the balance, all the histrionics of the past few days would have been totally unnecessary. And now, within the space of an hour, two lifelines had been thrown to rescue the plans for the estate. He was torn between euphoria and hysteria and not at all certain which one to plumb for.

Head reeling, he stumbled back into the pub and told Doug and Adam that the finances were back on track and that Doug should go ahead with his plans for stocking the farm. He decided that a celebration was called for and ordered whisky chasers for the three of them, intending to get completely drunk so that his brain could try to catch up and get to grips with the change in fortunes.

As the driver, Adam paced himself but the other two were pretty merry at the end of the evening. As they left the pub Jim mumbled, "Adam, you're a good bloke. I believe I'm getting married tomorrow; will you be the Best Man at my wedding?" If Adam replied, Jim didn't remember.

May Day dawned bright and beautiful. Jim drank a totally unhealthy quantity of strong black coffee in an attempt to sober up, with limited success. Adam arrived and set him the task to run to Rose Cottage and back without stopping and then sent him to shower and change; that helped.

The wedding was set for midday and, as Jim entered the ruined Castle Tower through the ancient archway, he had to admit that it was an impressive setting with the blackened walls towering above them, almost cathedral-like. Everyone from the estate was already gathered there, plus the few friends Rowan had wanted to invite.

The accordionist suddenly started playing a lovely piece of music and Jim turned to see Rowan advancing through the arch towards him; she looked absolutely stunning and he knew he would love her for ever. She was dressed in a slim-fitting dress which showed her figure to perfection and she had a coronet of spring flowers woven into her hair; she looked lovely.

Rowan was on the arm of her father, Caleb, who looked very proud to be walking his daughter to her wedding. She was accompanied by Susan as her maid of honour. A table at the front had been covered with a white cloth to make an altar and the two of them stood before the vicar and made their vows as he performed the wedding ceremony. It was simple and it was beautiful. At the end, he pronounced them man and wife and invited Jim to kiss his bride. He accepted the offer to the cheers and acclaim of all assembled.

The accordionist played a passable version of the wedding march as they processed back out through the archway together and towards the barn.

The women of the estate had arranged for the reception to be in the barn and the newlyweds entered to find a magnificent cold buffet set out on tables covered in clean white tablecloths. There was food for everyone and lots left over and, despite all the problems of the past few weeks, Jim had remembered to order lots of beer and cider and sufficient champagne for everyone to toast the bride and groom.

As best man, Adam felt he had to make a little speech; it was short and sweet and surprisingly amusing and he got a good round of applause at the end.

With all the recent excitement, Jim had given no thought to making a speech and simply thanked the assembled crowd for their support and for providing such a delightful wedding feast. Then the accordion player struck up and there was wild dancing and fun for the next several hours. As soon as they reasonably could, Jim and Rowan slipped quietly away to start their married life together.

Chapter 20

It was still only half-light when Jim awoke next morning. He lay there silently, gazing at his sleeping bride; even in her slumber, she was beautiful and he savoured the moment, drinking in the loveliness of her face. After a few minutes he started to blow gently at her face to wake her. There was no response for a long time but eventually, one sleepy eye opened and then another.

"Good morning, Lady Mountjoy."

Again, there was no immediate response but then an arm curled out from under the bedclothes, hooked around his head and pulled it towards hers so that their lips were touching and she held him there for a long time while they kissed.

Another pause, and then her other arm was on his chest and the hand started to slowly snake its way down his body until it reached a part of his anatomy which appeared to respond actively to her caress. From there, things took their natural course but, by the end, Lady Mountjoy was most definitely fully awake and very actively participating in proceedings.

"Right, your ladyship. Are you ready to get up yet, or what?"

"What!" she replied playfully and grabbed hold of him again.

It was hunger that finally persuaded her to leave her bed in search of breakfast, and they sat at the breakfast bar in their dressing gowns, devouring bacon sandwiches.

Between mouthfuls, Rowan said "Susan told me about selling your house in Bromley. Does that mean that the financial problems are solved?"

"Well, it got better than that. I didn't have chance to tell you yesterday but the solicitors were holding all the refunds from the fraudulent invoices on their Client Account. I'm a bit miffed that they didn't mention it before. Anyway, I've asked them to transfer it all to the estate account and we can get down to paying all the outstanding bills tomorrow. It also means that we can get back on track with our business plan for this year and I've told Doug to start going to the auctions again to build-up the stock of beef cattle."

"Are you happy about leaving our account with that bank after they dumped you and withdrew the overdraft facility?"

"Not really but all the standing orders for the rents are for payment to there and It didn't make sense to ask all the tenants to sign new forms so soon after the last ones. But I plan to leave the minimum possible balance there and I'll open an account at another bank so that we have an extra string to our bow if this should ever happen again."

"Do you want me to get those cheques sorted today?"

"No way! Today's our honeymoon; come back to bed and remind me where we'd got to."

*   *   *   *   *

They were both in the office early on Monday morning and cheques in full payment of all outstanding accounts went out in the post, first thing. They both breathed a sigh of relief at no longer having to fend-off demanding letters and telephone calls.

Jim left Rowan to bring the cashbook up to date and went to find Adam and Susan to thank them for their support at the wedding. They were both up at Bramble Cottage working on building more huts for the pigs. Adam was working on constructing them but had Susan sawing away for all she was worth, cutting timbers to length. Jim was still surprised at how well she was adapting to life in the country, so different from suburbia.

"I've come to invite myself to morning coffee," he announced and went inside to put the kettle on to boil. He made three mugs of coffee and brought them outside and they sat on a bench which Adam had recently constructed.

"I wanted to thank you both for your help and support at our wedding, the whole day was brilliant."

"Oh Jim!" Susan responded. "It was beautiful, I was in tears watching my big brother finally get married. The setting and the day were like a fairy tale."

"You do know who caught Rowan's bouquet when she threw it in the air," Adam asked, pointing at Susan with a silly grin on his face.

"Well, that's a good sign. I shall look forward to celebrating your marriage, as soon as possible." Jim told them. "And 'thank you' Sue for organising the sale of our Bromley house. It certainly took the pressure off our financial problems but I hope you don't live to regret it. Now you're here, what are your plans?"

"I've been looking through the local paper over the weekend." Susan told him. "There are loads of adverts for jobs that I'm qualified for. As I suspected, the salaries are rather lower than I'm use to but Adam has offered to run me down to town for any interviews I'm offered and, if I land a job, I'll get myself a little car and drive into town each day."

"And Adam, are you still happy to stick around here?" Jim asked.

Adam said he was and reeled off a list of all the jobs he had lined up for himself.

Within a week, Susan had found a job which suited her, bought a small car and she drove to work each morning.

Jim's next call was to find Doug and he came across him at the top end of the estate, examining the fields.

"Morning Doug! I'm not certain that either of us was particularly sober the other night but I think you got the message; the finances are back on course and I want to stock up to the planned level as soon as you're happy with the calves on offer and the prices."

"Yes, I got the message although I was surprised that you were sober enough to be able to take your vows after the way we drank that evening." Doug replied. "There are a couple of major cattle auctions coming up over the next week or two so I'm hoping that we can get back on course. I'm just looking at some of those fields Adam mowed last year. I think they'll be ready for haymaking in two or three weeks. I also need to spray the beet we planted.

We've got quite a bit of work coming up in the next month or two to get the sheep sheared and dipped. Could you call the owners and ask whether they're going to organise that themselves, or if they want us to do it? And, by the way, if we are to do it, I'm going to need to bring in some of the retired tenants to help with all that work." Jim said he would contact the sheep farmers but that Doug should go ahead and organise teams to help with the rest of the work. He was starting to appreciate how much of a year-round activity farming was.

Each of the farmers who owned the sheep was happy to organise the shearing of their own flocks, which took a big workload off Doug. Most of the sheep went to market over the next few weeks and the young bullocks increasingly occupied the fields they vacated. However, the next couple of months were still frenetic. Cattle trucks of young beef calves arrived almost every week and they were castrated and released into the fields. Doug also bought half a dozen new sows which had already been to the boar. There were two weeks of sunshine at the end of the month and it was all hands on deck to cut, dry and bale the hay and build hay stacks, after which Doug had some fertilizer applied to the fields in the hope of getting a second crop of hay or whole crop silage.

Jim saw Doug at work each day from dawn to dusk, seven days a week and out in all weathers. As the man had said, it was a calling, not a job. He was hardly surprised when Doug approached him one day to say that he needed some extra hands on the farm. Ginger had worked out better than expected but the level of activity was pretty intense. Could he look for a couple more farm labourers. There was no way Jim could refuse and within a week, Doug had recruited two new men, Mitch and Sean. With the death of Martha and the long-term invalid last winter, there were two cottages available and the new workers moved in.

Rowan was proving highly efficient with administrative issues and saw to the formal tenancy agreements and organising the standing order mandates for the rents as well as putting them on the payroll.

As the year moved into September, two fields which had been ploughed were drilled for winter wheat and the ewes which all now belonged to the estate were dipped again and the wool clipped around the tail, ready for tupping to begin. The fodder beet was harvested and stored. Doug bought some fine rams at the tup sales. They were fitted with raddle harnesses and released to the ewes, over the next few weeks.

As the growth of the grass started to slow, the stocks of whole crop silage and beet came into their own and the animals were well-fed throughout the winter. Fattened bullocks were gradually sold at the auctions. The prices were good that year and it was a relief to have money coming back into the account again, at last. Jim spent time checking the accounts and was pleased to see that, despite interruptions at the beginning of the year, the estate had performed to plan and had generated a small profit.

"We haven't had a traditional harvest celebration," he mentioned to Rowan at dinner one evening. "How about having a party for the whole estate again on Christmas Eve, as we did last year?" Rowan thought that was a great idea and offered to organise it.

"We'll do most of the same things as last year, including the accordionist and a barn dance but I think we could probably handle the catering ourselves, this year. I'm sure Susan would give me a hand. Adam has developed the long barbeque he made and, with a bit of ingenuity, I'm sure we could cope. I'll get the wives and widows to provide desserts, as they did last year."

"Great! We'll buy a gazebo to cover the barbeque but we must make sure it's well away from the barn. I don't want to risk burning that down."

It was already dark outside but he suddenly heard a motorbike go past on its way towards the village and realised that he had heard it on several evenings, recently. He mentioned it to Doug the following day and received a sheepish grin, in response.

"I assume by that you must have found a young lady in the village?"

"Well," said Doug. "It's a bit quiet up here in my cottage in the evenings."

"We're just planning to have another Christmas Eve party this year, Doug. Feel free to invite her up for that, if you'd like to." Doug thanked him and said he would ask her.

Once again, the party was a huge success. Jim resolutely refused to make a speech this time but simply held his glass high and wished everyone a 'Merry Christmas'. However, he took Rowan's hand and the two of them started the dancing and danced on until after midnight.

Doug did bring his girlfriend, Lisa. She was a pretty little thing and it was great to see the happiness on Doug's face as they danced together.

Jim hoped it would work out for them both; it would provide some stability in Doug's life.

Chapter 21

The year turned. The winter was mild and the grass was already starting to grow by the end of February. The winter feed for the livestock had proved fully adequate, there was no snow to cause emergencies and life on the farm got off to an early start.

Doug was well on top of things. He had spread fertiliser where he thought it necessary to encourage growth; the winter wheat was well advanced; fields had been ploughed and sown with root crops for winter feed for the following winter and an increasing number of fields were filled with cattle, slowly fattening. Lambing was still a month or so away.

With so much going on in the estate, Jim had given little thought to the prospectus he had sent out offering the lower fields for sale for housing. Responses had come in slowly over the past year but he had now received positive letters of interest from all five companies he had written to, including at least two indicative price offers. It was time to move it forward.

He called on Jonathan Downham to discuss the options.

"Are you sure you want to sell land, James? They're not making any more of it, you know!" Was Jonathan's initial reaction.

"Yes. I know! But its poor-quality land and there are two capital projects I need the money for." Jim told him. "The first is a sensible one. If I'm to continue in beef cattle, I need a large cow barn to fatten them up in before they're sold. That's expensive. The second project is probably foolish; I want to try to restore the castle."

"Well, I can't fault the first project and, as a sentimentalist, I can empathise with your ambitions to restore the castle. Do you know that there's an architect in Carlisle who specialises in restoring ancient buildings? I can't recall his name immediately but he's been working on the castle here and also on the cathedral for some time. It might be worth talking to him."

"Anyway, on the subject of the sale, sealed bid offers are popular for this type of transaction and usually result in a good price. I'll be happy to handle it for you if you'll let me have all the details. We'll tell them all the highest bid you've had so far and that usually sets the base level for the bidding."

"Thanks," said Jim. "I'll get the details to you in the next couple of days. In the meantime, I'll see if I can catch up with that architect you mentioned.""

"I've just remembered his name; its Gregory Price." Jonathan told him.

Downham's offices were quite close to the cathedral so Jim decided he might as well see if he could meet the architect while he was in the area. Inside, the cathedral he approached one of the deacons and asked if Price was on site and was told that he was working up in the tower. He climbed the steps, found Price meticulously measuring and recording the detail of individual stones and introduced himself.

"I'm from the Dunkield estate. We've got a twelfth century castle which was doing well until twenty years ago when someone burnt it down. The walls are still pretty intact and I'd welcome some views on how realistic it would be to think about restoration. Would you be interested in having a look and letting me know if you think it would make sense?"

Price said he would be delighted to take a look at the place, when would be convenient?

"Pretty well any time," Jim answered. "Here's my mobile number; give me a call and come up whenever you've a couple of hours to spare."

Leaving the cathedral, Jim went across to the museum. He had been fascinated by Jonathan's description of the Bishop's Stone recording the curse and the threat of excommunication by of the Archbishop of Glasgow in

1525 in his efforts to halt raids across the border between England and Scotland. He found the stone easily; it was huge and a bit difficult to miss. It was in a draughty underpass between the museum and the castle.

Part of the curse was carved on the fourteen tonne polished granite stone and the curse was terrible. If the Cardinal of Rheims had managed to reduce a poor jackdaw to a shrivelled wreck through his curse, this from Glasgow and the threat of excommunication should have instantly vaporised any poor wretch who still harboured any thoughts of border raids in their heads. If the curse had any effect, it was short-lived and the raids continued which was, perhaps, surprising, at a time when the power of the church was very great,

The stone had been carved and installed as a project to celebrate the millennium. Sadly, however, it had subsequently been blamed for a series of mishaps in Carlisle since its creation, including floods and foot and mouth disease outbreak. Demands for its removal had been discussed by the council but, so far, it stood firm.

Back at Dunkield he put together all the details that Jonathan had asked for to enable him to prepare the papers for the sealed bid and sent them off to him.

He told Adam about the meeting with Gregory Price.

"I know you're interested in the possibility of restoration. If the guy does come, you should join me for the discussion. Apart from anything else, you'll probably ask more sensible questions than I would."

He had obviously piqued Price's interest and he received a call from Gregory the following Sunday to say that he was in the area, would it be convenient to call? When he arrived, Jim introduced him to Adam and to Lady Mountjoy and the three men went off to examine the castle.

Gregory was immediately captivated by the place.

"I didn't know about this place; it's not in any of the textbooks although it deserves to be. It's almost unique. You referred to Orford Castle and I know that well; this is like a smaller version of Orford, built along the same lines. Orford is sometimes described as Byzantine architecture, built to a design thought to have been brought back from the Holy Land by the early crusaders and this is similar."

"What you describe as the castle, is really the central keep. Its circular with three rectangular 'clasping' towers spaced equally around its perimeter. All the staircases and walkways are built into the three towers so that you have uninterrupted circular rooms on each floor of the central keep."

"The keep would originally have been surrounded by a curtain wall which is now buried under the earthworks you see all around us. It would have been these outer defences, rather than the keep, which probably represented the main defences of the castle." He paused for breath and then continued. "The keep has been extensively altered over the years, which is hardly surprising, and the windows have been enlarged at some time after the place was no longer needed for defence."

"So, what are your initial thoughts about trying to restore the place?" Jim asked.

"Challenging! But ultimately worthwhile. Although we're standing on a relatively flat surface, I suspect that it is probably made up of all the timbers, detritus and other rubbish that fell down in the fire. There will probably be dungeons and storerooms beneath where we are standing, so you would have to start by digging downwards to clear the site before you could start to think about going upwards and I've no doubt that Historic England would want to take an interest in the work, the materials and any modifications. Yes, quite a challenge."

"You asked if it was worth restoring the keep; the answer is 'definitely!' This is a unique gem you have here. How it has escaped attention over the years, I've no idea but, as soon as Historic England find out about it, I'm sure they will want to encourage restoration. As to the cost, you are almost certainly into seven figures."

"That sounds rather frightening," Adam chipped in. "Will there be lots of grants available?"

"Sadly, no! There is very little funding available these days to help with such work. Historic England has no funds for it and the National Lottery Heritage Fund will only assist community or cultural schemes where there is some public benefit. There's just the odd chance that English Heritage might be prepared to cough up for a laser study of the subterranean area and possibly advice on structural stability.

"Look, I think this is tremendously exciting and I'd really like to be associated with the work, if possible. If you're in agreement, I'd be happy to apply to Historic England without any commitment on your part, to see if they'd fund a preliminary grant to study structural stability and laser examination of the areas below ground. At the same time, I could see if any grants might be available for the work if you decide to go ahead. Would you be happy with that?"

"So long as there is absolutely no commitment to any cost or to proceed with the refurbishment from my side, I'd be happy for Historic England to fund an initial feasibility study." Jim replied. "What sort of timescale would we be looking at?"

"Well," Gregory responded. "They're not noted for their speed of action and I have other work commitments as well. I think it would take at least six months."

Jim told him to go ahead and apply for a grant for the initial structural study and Gregory spent the next hour or so photographing the keep from every possible angle to provide the basis for the application. Before he left, Jim provided him with some notes on the history he had learned from Jonathan and from the Dunkield library at Downham and Sparrow's offices.

After Price's departure, he put the entire issue out of his mind; there was too much else to do. However, he did notice that Adam started to spend an increasing amount of time in the centre of the keep. He was obviously trying to find if there was any way of accessing the old dungeons.

Jonathan emailed to say that he had sent out the packs inviting sealed bids for the housing land. He had set a return date of six weeks.

Jim thought it appropriate to mention to Doug that he was contemplating the possible sale of some of the lower fields. Doug was fully aware that the quality of those fields was poor and had no problem with the decision.

"If the sale goes through," Jim told him. "And it is still a big 'if', I plan that we should spend some of the money on a huge cattle-shed where we can feed the cattle up, before taking them to market. I gather that there are all sorts of issues on location and run-off. Please could you think about it as you go around and try to decide on the best location." Doug was excited by the prospect and promised to have a good think about the siting.

And then it was lambing time. All the sheep on the estate now belonged to the estate and this was the first experience for Jim of lambing time. He had not previously been aware that sheep have been carefully bred over thousands of years to drop their lambs in the middle of the most atrocious, freezing and stormy night of the year. It all started fairly slowly which was just as well because the whole process was entirely new to him and he had a lot to learn.

Doug had recruited a number of the old hands on the estate to help the process and Jim was out in the fields with them, night after night checking on the flock and helping ewes to lamb. Many of the births were easy and natural but on almost every night, at least one ewe had to be helped but they lost only two lambs in the entire process. Rowan set up a nursery in the barn and, every few hours throughout the day and night, bottle-fed any lambs rejected by their mother. The yield was good averaging 190% per ewe and even the normally taciturn Doug suggested that he was not entirely displeased at that result. At the end, Jim was in a state of collapse but did feel that he had earned his spurs as well as the respect of the rest of the team. He retired to the estate office to get back on top of estate administration and left Doug and his team to get on with the work on the farm.

In the meantime, Jonathan Downham had received the sealed bids for the housing land and he invited Jim down to open them. One of the local builders and one of the national companies had backed out and declined to bid. However, this still left three very acceptable bids but two had a range of caveats attached, including planning permission. The final one was unconditional and they agreed to accept that. The bid document had specified completion within twenty-eight days of acceptance and, to Jim's amazement, it completed on time leaving the Dunkield Estate with more wealth than Jim had ever dreamt possible.

The sale would probably attract capital gains tax at some point and Jim made a mental note to talk to an accountant about how to minimise that. The livestock building should qualify but he needed to establish if the accumulated losses of the last twenty years qualified and also whether expenditure on rebuilding the keep would be an eligible off-set. In the meantime, he took advice on investing the proceeds to ensure that funds were available to meet the cost of any capital projects or capital gains bills, when appropriate.

Gregory Price emailed Jim a copy of his proposed submission to Historic England for a grant to cover a feasibility study. Jim called him to discuss a couple of issues but was basically happy with the draft. Price submitted the proposal and they sat back to wait. Gregory had been correct in surmising that the 'discovery' of the

Dunkield keep would cause interest and, within a fortnight, the estate received several visitors keen to view the find for themselves. It clearly achieved high profile at Historic England headquarters and they responded just six weeks later. They were not prepared to fund the full proposed study but would make a contribution of fifty percent of the budgeted cost. Price told Jim the level of cost involved for his half of the funding. It was crunch-time for Jim; he had to make a decision. The money from the sale of the land was certainly more than sufficient to meet the total cost of rebuilding the keep and it seemed entirely the right use for the funds. He sanctioned his half of the first phase.

Price was back on site within days and brought in structural engineers to assess the safety of the keep and the structural work needed to restore it. They introduced a high cherry-picker machine to enable them to reach the top of the battlements to check the condition of the battlements and parapets and also brought in a laser device to probe beneath the ground for cavities and possible rooms and dungeons. At Jim's request, Gregory started work on an outline design for the interior and a detailed schedule of specifications and, as that work progressed, involved a quantity surveyor to prepare a list of quantities, measurements and costs. As Price had pointed out at the beginning, he had other ongoing work and was not on site the whole time but he kept Jim appraised of progress and everything he was doing. The laser probe had confirmed Price's speculation and revealed a labyrinth of rooms and passageways below the accumulated detritus of fallen rubbish, timber and plaster. The structural survey had confirmed that the building was structurally sound for the renovation work to proceed.

All the subsections of the study were combined into a report for submission to Historic England. He took Jim through the proposed submission and the plans in detail.

"Look," said Jim. "I'm happy that Historic England should advise on all the exterior appearances, materials and features, as well as things like the positioning of the floors and the specification of the roof. However, inside this will be a modern dwelling, when finished, not a twelfth century castle and I want to be able to decide on the internal layout and the finishes."

Price accepted the point and specified this in the final report and this was submitted within ten weeks of starting.

Chapter 22

The completion of the land sale and the receipt of the enormous proceeds marked a turning point in the fortunes of the Dunkield estate. They could now afford to do almost anything they wanted and Jim set aside funds for a number of specific projects.

He wanted to use part of the money to set up two charitable trusts; one was for general charitable donations to deserving causes, the other was intended as a hardship fund for the benefit of any estate tenants who might fall on hard times.

He also set aside money for the maintenance of the estate cottages. Although all the cottages had been smartened up when he first arrived at the estate, he wanted to prevent them from declining into a similar state of decay again in future. He was also painfully aware that, almost without exception, the kitchen and bathroom fittings in them were pre-war. Installing double-glazing would also improve comfort levels. Bringing the cottages up to date would be a major expenditure but it did need to be addressed at some stage and he set aside a significant sum for this purpose.

In the meantime, he was anxious to push forward with the livestock building as quickly as possible. Doug had identified a likely site for the shed, out of sight of most of the estate and Jim submitted a planning application and obtained quotations for a suitable building. His plans for the future of the estate now envisaged handling four hundred bullocks or more, annually and that started to dictate the size of the required building. It also made sense to make provision to store hay, winter feed and possibly farm machinery under cover. That meant a very large building. One of the concerns of the planners was run-off of slurry and its possible effects on the streams, water courses and the aquifer. This required the installation of a substantial slurry tank. However, the planners were as helpful as possible and the application was approved fairly quickly.

Jim had already chosen the design for the building and received quotations and promptly ordered the building on a turnkey contract with the suppliers handling all the logistics. It was to be a largely prefabricated design and the sides would be mainly open to the elements with walls just sufficiently high to contain the cattle. The exception was on the west side where there was full height Yorkshire board designed to break the prevailing winds whilst still providing adequate ventilation and air movement inside.

Work on the base started within ten days of the order, the steelwork was erected shortly after and the entire building was ready for occupation within ten weeks. It looked good and marked a new stage in the professionalism of the farming operation and Jim made a point of inviting Peter Longfellow up to watch the first cattle enter the barn when it was completed. After that, cattle were moved into the shed three or four weeks before sale and it undoubtedly helped them to pile on additional weight, before they went to auction.

There were a couple of other spending priorities on Jim's mind. The first was to obtain two quad bikes for use around the estate. He knew that Doug walked miles each day and a quad bike would make his life easier. The second bike was for Jim and Adam to share, as needed. Each bike was fitted with a carrier to enable it to carry a bale of hay, sacks of grain or whatever else was needed. The bikes were an immediate success and Doug was thrilled at his. Adam also was pretty happy and Jim quickly found that if he needed to use that machine, he had to make an advanced booking. He also felt that it was time to get a second motor vehicle. The van was proving reliable and was excellent for collecting feed and equipment for the farm but, with the new-found wealth, he felt that supplementing it with a decent Range Rover would not be an extravagance.

Jim's other spending priority was a honeymoon for himself and Rowan. That was a sound diplomatic move and he left her to plan the where and when. Rowan had never possessed a passport and Jim had long since lost his in his hippie days so he also asked Rowan to apply for passports for both of them.

Susan come across to the office one evening after she returned from work; did they know where Adam was? The answer was 'no', they hadn't seen him for several hours.

"I'll go and start on the dinner; he'll turn up when he's hungry," she said and headed back to Bramble Cottage.

She was back a couple of hours later. "Adam's still not turned up and I'm getting a bit anxious. Any idea where he went or what he was working on?"

The quad bike was missing and, on an intuition, Jim wondered if he had possibly gone to poke around inside the keep. The two of them walked up to the castle keep together. Sure enough, there inside was the quad bike which Adam had been using but there was no sign of him. They searched around the area, calling his name but there was no response.

"Maybe he's outside," Jim suggested, so they walked right around the outside of the keep, calling Adam's name. Still there was no response. By now, Jim was also getting quite concerned and led the way back inside the keep and started a careful examination of the perimeter walls. About half way round he found a place where the ground had obviously been disturbed and several large lengths of timber had been moved, as well as some soil and turf revealing a small hole against the wall. He stuck his head down the hole and shouted "Adam, are you down there?" There was no clear reply but he thought he could hear a moan coming from somewhere beyond the hole.

"Quick Sue; get back to the estate office and ask Rowan for a couple of torches. Bring my mobile as well, I've left it on the desk and we may need help." And Susan ran off to the office.

Meanwhile, Jim started to try to widen the entrance to the hole; it was difficult to clear the entrance without causing soil and other rubbish to fall back into the hole but he made some progress. By now, it was starting to get dark and he was glad when Susan arrived back with some torches, accompanied by Rowan.

Jim shone one of the torches down into the hole. There was a drop of seven or eight feet and then the ground was lined with stones in a regular pattern, suggesting that there was an ancient passageway below.

"I've no idea how I'm going to get back up!" he muttered and let himself down into the cavity. He found that the ceiling was just high enough for him to stand and he shone his torch one way down the passage and then the opposite direction. "Adam, can you hear me?"

He couldn't be certain but he again thought that he heard a weak moan and he headed down the passage towards the sound. He had travelled about ten yards when he was brought up short by a wall of rubbish; there had clearly been a roof fall and the passage was blocked. He shone his torch through a gap in the obstruction; he could see nothing initially but, as he peered through the debris, he was able to make out an arm and then a head amongst the rubble.

He tried to speak to him but Adam was clearly not conscious so he turned his attention to the roof fall to see if he could remove the obstruction. His eye was drawn to the loose material at the top of the pile and he realised that if he tried to move anything it would precipitate a further massive fall of rubbish into his path and probably on top of Adam.

He made his way back along the passage to the hole he had entered by and shouted up.

"He's down here but he's trapped and I think he's hurt. Sue, there's a ladder leaning up against the side of the barn. Please could you go and fetch it. Rowan, if I pass my mobile up to you, please would you call the emergency services. We're going to need an ambulance and we need the fire brigade rescue service; ask them if they've got any equipment for shoring up a crumbling roof." And he listened while Rowan very confidently made the calls.

Susan returned with the ladder and, on Jim's instructions, fed it down into the cavity. Rather than climbing out immediately, Jim went back to the roof fall to have another look at Adam. There was still no obvious sign of movement.

It took just over half an hour for the emergency services to reach the castle. Jim briefed the firemen and two of them descended the ladder to appraise the problem for themselves. They were back at the entrance within a few minutes, having decided that the equipment they had brought would not do the job. The chief shouted up some instructions to one of the crew, naming the piece of equipment they would need. He radioed back to the station and another vehicle was despatched to bring the requisite item. Another half hour of waiting and, in the meantime, the fire crew set up floodlights to illuminate the scene above ground with cables to provide light in the tunnel. Jim took the opportunity to go down the tunnel again to have another look at Adam; there was still no sign of movement.

Jim was anxious to keep Susan occupied as she looked as though she was about to throw herself down the hole at any moment. He asked Rowan and Susan to go back to the office and get tea and biscuits for all the crew, while they waited. The women produced the tea and the emergency crews drank it gratefully as they stood round chatting.

The replacement equipment finally arrived and the team went into action with a sense of urgency. Jim was conscious that they knew their job and he kept out of their way as they worked. But time passed slowly. An hour, two hours, three hours and still they worked on as the estate team stood anxiously around the keep in the middle of the night. Finally, the crew below ground called for the stretcher to be let down the hole and the ambulance crew went down with it. If Adam was badly injured, they were the ones who knew how to move him onto the stretcher.

It was nearly another hour before there was movement below the hole and the stretcher was manhandled back up to the waiting crew with Adam strapped firmly in it. There was no sign of consciousness and Susan was almost hysterical.

"It's alright love," said one of the paramedics. "He's alive and breathing naturally; he's quite badly hurt but he'll be alright. Do you want to come down to the hospital in the ambulance with him?" Susan nodded and thanked him.

"I'll follow you down in the van later, Sue," Jim added as Adam was placed in the ambulance and Susan climbed in beside him before it set off towards Carlisle with sirens blaring.

Jim asked Rowan to prepare a few sandwiches for Susan and himself and then stood around for a little while as the fire service crew recovered their equipment and stored it back in their vehicles. He thanked them and watched as they drove away then gathered a few items he needed from home and set off towards the hospital at a more leisurely pace.

By the time he arrived, Adam had been admitted and was in the operating theatre whilst Susan paced up and down the corridors and the waiting room like a caged tiger.

"Come on Sue; you didn't get to eat your dinner tonight. I've brought some sandwiches for us both." It took some coaxing but he eventually got her to sit down and eat.

It was seven o'clock in the morning when one of the hospital staff came to give them an update.

"He has been hit on the head and lost some blood and is still unconscious but there does not seem to be any permanent damage. However, he has also broken his leg in three places and that is going to take a month or two to heal. Would you like to see him?"

They were led through to one of the wards and found Adam sleeping with his leg in traction. "Can I stay here with him until he comes round?" Susan asked. Somewhat reluctantly, the request was approved.

"Right," said Jim. "You've got your mobile. When you need a lift home, give me a call and either Rowan or I will come and rescue you. Have you got some money to get breakfast?" Susan assured him she had.

Not surprisingly, Rowan was in bed fast asleep when he got home. Rather than waking her, he sat in an easy chair and dozed fitfully for a couple of hours. He had a bad feeling about Adam's accident. He felt that he should have known that Adam would attempt to find a way into the dungeons and he should have pre-empted the move and forbidden it. Too late!

It was early evening when Susan called from the hospital. Adam had recovered consciousness and they had talked together. Please could someone rescue her. Rowan drove the Range Rover down to the hospital to pick her up. It was a good move; Susan was highly stressed after the events of last night and it enabled her to have a good cry with Rowan without feeling embarrassed.

"Oh Rowan! I thought I'd lost him," she sobbed. "I don't know what I'd have done without him. I love the stupid man. I've just told him he's going to marry me whether he likes it or not; do you think I did right?"

Rowan gave her every assurance that she thought she'd done the right thing.

Susan visited the hospital every evening on her way home from work. Adam was quickly impatient with being stuck there but, knowing that it was entirely his own fault, suffered in silence for the most part.

Jim visited him and sympathised and then chalked him off severely for attempting to gain access to the dungeons without consulting and made it quite clear that he forbade any further attempt.

"Oh, but James, it was brilliant. There's a whole labyrinth down there; I even found a locked door and I'm dying to know what's inside."

"You heard me; the answer is no, not until we have the experts on site," was Jim's final word on the subject.

In the event, Adam was stuck in the hospital for over a month. He was eventually discharged on crutches with his leg still in plaster and was a thorough pain to himself and to everyone else. With Susan out at work, he hated being stuck in the cottage by himself all day and made full use of his crutches to hobble up to the estate office each day and plague Jim and Rowan. Everyone was relieved when the plaster was finally removed and he could start to live a normal life again.

Susan was totally determined to ensure he did not escape her clutches and dragged him down to the Registry Office at the first convenient opportunity: Jim and Rowan accompanied them as witnesses to the marriage. Although Bramble Cottage had been included in the refurbishment a couple of years before, the kitchen and bathroom were still furnished with pre-war fittings. Jim's wedding present to them was to have the two rooms gutted and brought up to twenty-first century standards. He also put Adam on the estate payroll although it was difficult to define a job title for him and he was simply entered as 'handyman'.

Chapter 23

Being stuck in hospital for a month, unable to move or go anywhere, was probably Adam's worst nightmare. He was furious with himself for ending in this predicament; it was his own fault but, given the same choices, he would still have wanted to explore the castle dungeons again.

He had never been much of a reader and spent the long days lying disconsolate on his hospital bed, thinking back over his life. He had never known his father and had been brought up by his mother in a high-rise tenement block where one never met one's neighbours. She had worked long hours to earn enough to keep them both but she had insisted on high standards of decency and honesty and had drilled them into him as he grew. He had hated school; it was only towards the end of his time there that one teacher had submitted him to tests which had shown that he was badly dyslectic. That neatly explained why he had such difficulty in learning but did little to help his progress. The only areas in which he did excel were practical subjects such as woodwork and metalwork, although he was also pretty good at most sports.

He left school at the earliest possible opportunity and without any academic qualifications and signed on at the Job Centre. At their insistence, he applied for various unskilled jobs although, even when he landed one, he somehow had difficulty holding on to it: he was too slow to learn or couldn't understand the instructions or hopelessly miscalculated the numbers. But at least he earned a little money or received unemployment pay in between and was able to give some to his mother to help with the household bills.

It was at about this time that his mother was taken ill and eventually diagnosed with thyroid cancer. She had died on his eighteenth birthday and he had been in tears as he travelled back from the hospital to his flat on the bus. A pretty young girl sitting next to him had pushed him to tell her the reason and had comforted him when he explained. She got off the bus when he did and treated him to a coke and burger at a local burger bar and they had chatted together for ages. Her name was Susan and, before they parted, she had agreed to a date at the cinema, later that week.

Susan lived in a posh part of Bromley and Adam quickly became a regular visitor. Her widowed father had been killed in an accident a few months earlier and her brother, who had recently graduated from Cambridge, was currently bumming around Europe, so she had the house to herself. Their friendship developed strongly and Adam was able to help her with little projects, repairs and decorating around the house and he became a regular visitor. Over the months that followed, their relationship often became more intimate. Adam asked her to marry him but she refused, "not until you've got a regular job" she told him and she wouldn't allow him to move in. That was a problem, he could never hold onto a job for more than a few months and so the relationship had staggered on for five or six years when sometimes they would not see each other for weeks on end.

He had called round to see her one Sunday evening to be told that he had just missed meeting her brother and Susan had gone on to tell him about the letters Jim had received and they had speculated together on the possible outcome. It was just a few days after that when he had received the surprise text from her. Jim had asked if he would be interested in joining him in north Cumbria for a working holiday with no pay. He had just lost his latest job and jumped at the opportunity although he recognised that he would probably need to sign-on at a local Job Centre so that he could continue to get his unemployment allowance. Susan had paid for his fare and helped him to carry all the luggage Jim had requested up to the bus terminal at Victoria Station. "You'll recognise him easily,"

Susan had told him. "He's over six and a half feet tall and has a mass of red hair and a beard." "Yes, no mistaking you," he thought to himself as a great giant of a man with flame-red hair came lumbering towards him at the bus stop.

He had liked Jim immediately; he was open and easy in his manners as well as being good company. He had liked the way that Jim had fought manfully as they cycled up towards Dunkield that first morning. He was clearly struggling with a clapped-out bike and the weight of the baby buggy but had refused to give up and, although he did finally agree to swap bikes for a period, insisted on each of them taking turns on the two bikes.

When they finally reached the estate, he felt for Jim: gates twisted and hanging off the posts, pot holes everywhere in the driveway, fields and cottages in an appalling state of decay, the castle a burnt-out ruin and the stable block with the caved-in roof. Yes, where would one start.

The two of them discussed that subject over lunch and afterwards, went straight back to the stables to have a closer look at the roof. Jim had introduced him to Rowan and Adam had seen the smouldering look which passed between the two of them as they looked at each other and had seen the longing in their eyes. He had left them to it and found his way into the adjoining building which turned out to be a barn, not more stables. Adam had immediately identified the problem with the roof. It was glaringly obvious and it seemed incredible that no one had bothered to do anything about it for twenty years. With the help of the joiner/handymen that Jim recruited, they had fixed the problem in a few hours.

In the brief time he had known Jim, he had already worked out that he was sincere in his wish to put the estate back on its feet and, on that Sunday when he had addressed the tenants, he had seen the strength of the man as he unfolded his plan to them. It was a brilliant political speech which included the tenants in the plan and gave them the opportunity to redeem themselves. He had won them to his side and, when Jim left shortly afterwards, Adam had remained and listened to the chorus of support for Jim's proposals.

In the following weeks, Adam had identified a host of little projects for himself which would help to achieve the objective of rebuilding the estate and generating pride in the place. What did surprise him, however, was how much he was enjoying himself. He had spent his whole life to date in an urban environment and quickly realised that he was a country boy at heart. He loved the life on the farm and the openness of the countryside around him and felt that this was what he was born for. The only downside was that he missed Susan and he was pleased when she suggested that she might visit. He certainly had no wish to return to London.

When she did visit, he encouraged her to work with him in the fields or wherever he was at the time and he knew that she enjoyed it as much as he did. He tried to persuade her to sell-up down south and come and join him; she wasn't ready yet.

Susan came again at Christmas and they had a fabulous time together, cosy in Bramble Cottage. She was over the moon at her big brother's engagement to Rowan, who she thought was absolutely right for him but she was still not ready to make her own commitment to move to Dunkield although Adam detected that she was weakening.

Jim had invited her up for his wedding in May and, when Adam found out about the estate's financial problems shortly before the wedding, he told her about it. That finally galvanised her into action. Within days, she had sold the family home in Bromley and arrived for the wedding with the good news of financial rescue and her permanent relocation. She found a job in Carlisle and settled into Bramble Cottage with Adam. Adam felt a wonderful sense of completeness in her presence and he loved the intimacy they were finally able to share there.

Gregory Price's suggestion that there could be underground rooms and dungeons below the level of the ground inside the keep, whet Adam's appetite and he wanted to explore. He admired and respected Jim but he knew that, if he asked him for permission to explore, he would refuse on the grounds of safety. At every available opportunity he stole into the keep, trying to find a way in. Late one afternoon, he was carefully combing round the inside perimeter of the keep when he saw a likely spot. He explored the area and found that he was able to extract several loose timbers and other rubbish and gradually uncovered a hole. He had a torch in his pocket and shone it into the abys, revealing an underground passageway below. With little thought on how he was going to get back up, he squirmed through the hole and dropped to the ground below.

It was exciting and his pulse raced as he set off to explore by the light of his torch. He had entered a labyrinth of passages and rooms and he explored them, one by one. At one point he had to squeeze past an obstruction and it seemed to shift slightly as he eased himself past it. He found an assortment of rooms and inspected each until he came to a room which was locked. At this point, it was obvious that the battery on his torch was fading and he quickly made his way back towards the place where he had entered. He came to the obstruction and was just starting to squeeze back past it when the whole structure shifted violently and collapsed and rubbish cascaded down towards him. He remembered nothing more.

He leaned forward on the hospital bed to scratch an itch on his leg, then realised that it was inside the plaster. He would have to suffer. Yes, he thought to himself, given the same choices, he would still have wanted to explore the castle dungeons again. Susan had been pretty uncompromising in her admonishment of him. She had insisted that, whether he liked it or not, he was going to have to marry her whilst he was still alive. "You've held this job down with Jim for four years, so you've passed the test". The fact that he wasn't formally employed and received no wages did not seem to be part of the discussion.

Oh well! If marrying Susan was the worst punishment he had to endure, he felt that he might possibly survive, and he smiled to himself. Yes, he liked life in the country.

Chapter 24

Gregory Price telephoned to say that Historic England had accepted the technical proposals to restore the castle keep but had again confirmed that there were no grants available for the work. He had been in touch with the Lottery Fund and had received the same response. He arranged to visit the estate to discuss the next steps.

When he arrived, he told Jim that the estimated costs for the next phases of the work, the first of which was for a significant sum for ground clearance by a firm of contractors.

Jim had a word with a few of the retired tenants who were not currently engaged on farm work. Would they be interested in earning some pin-money, clearing the site. He got half a dozen acceptances, hired some dumper trucks and small, tracked diggers and set them to work. Adam still had his leg in plaster and they placed a comfortable chair at a point where he could sit and act as clerk of works and keep an eye on progress and also look out for any objects of significance or value. There was a worked-out quarry at one point on the estate and all the rubbish from the site was transported to there and dumped. Adam sat there looking very important and no one was allowed to slack. Gradually, the basements, dungeons and passageways were revealed, including the locked room that Adam had discovered.

Price had estimated five months for this phase. Adam had it completed in four weeks.

It is possible that some archaeological gems were missed in the process; but the job was done.

The keyhole to the locked door was squirted with penetrating oil for several days in succession and then a locksmith was brought to site to unlock the door. This was no easy task as the lock mechanism was heavily rusted and he had to work on it patiently for several hours.

Jim, Adam, Price and several others stood around excitedly while the locksmith worked on the mechanism, speculating on what treasures the room might hold. Price told them of an hotel in Windermere which had opened a cellar door which had been locked for over one hundred years. It had been found to hold an absolute fortune in silverware; what would they find?

Finally, the locksmith was able to trigger the strike plate in the lock and open the huge oak door.

Jim gave Adam the honour of being the first one into the room although he followed close behind. It was festooned with spider's webs like something out of a film-set for an Indiana Jones movie and they clawed their way through. The room was huge with a high domed vaulted stone ceiling, beneath one of the clasping towers and it was absolutely dry.

Both of them had torches, they flashed them around the room, looking for the expected treasure. but, disappointingly, the room was almost completely empty. At one end there was a small table with a cross on it and two pewter goblets and a pewter plate indicating that it had obviously been the chapel of the castle at one stage.

One corner was crowded with an untidy pile of armaments from the middle ages; pike staffs, battle axes and shields. For Jim, however, the *pièce-de-resistance* stood in another corner. It had to be his forebear's second-best suit of armour that he had fantasised about when he first heard about Dunkield. Apart from that, there was nothing of obvious value. They were disappointed and the party felt deflated.

Jim had invited Gregory Price to join them for the opening of the room. He was standing behind him and appeared to be in a state of agitation.

"James, James, can I borrow your torch?" Jim handed it over and, instead of shining it on the contents of the room,

Price was pointing it at the walls. Adam pointed his torch in the same direction.

"Wow!" said Price, rather enigmatically. And then, again, "Wow".

They all looked at where the torches were pointing and then around the room as the beam moved. All around the room were paintings on the plaster, ancient paintings which to the modern eye appeared childish and unreal but there must have been more than twenty of them decorating the walls of this ancient chapel.

There were paintings of knights in armour, there were scenes obviously taken from the crusades. There were biblical illustrations and there were also later paintings which appeared to portray images of the Border Reivers and their raids.

"Here's your treasure trove", Price mused.

"I'm not sure I follow," Jim countered, retrieving his torch.

"These wall paintings are unique," Price told him. "Not only do they portray scenes. never seen before, they are a fantastic record of middle England in the centuries following the Norman invasion. The experts will be desperate to preserve these images for the nation. This is your ticket to funding the restoration of the keep."

Gregory suggested that they should get someone from the Courtauld Institute in London to authenticate the paintings as a matter of urgency and advise on their preservation and conservation. "They are the leading expert authority on the history of art and on art conservation," he told them. "If they confirm their dating and history of these paintings, you may well find that the attitude to supporting funding to ensure their preservation, suddenly comes alive."

Jim slept badly that night as the paintings in the storeroom weighed on his mind.

He had described the find to Rowan but the following day, suggested that she came to see it for herself.

"I quite like the idea of displaying the suit of armour and some of the armaments inside the keep when its finished, but frankly, even if they were moveable, I can't see us wanting to have some of these paintings in the lounge, can you?"

As promised, Gregory contacted the Courtauld Institute to tell them about the paintings. Two of their team arrived on site within twenty-four hours to examine the paintings and promptly declared them to be of major national historical interest. The paintings of scenes from the Border Reivers were probably the work of George Gower or John Bettes the elder but identifying the artists of some of the earlier works was going to require a great deal of study and research.

This was the response Price was hoping for and he re-submitted applications for grants to protect these national treasures to the National Lottery Heritage Fund, Historic England and every other source he could think of. It worked; these treasures must be saved for the nation and the keep must have a proper roof to protect them. One of the major stipulations for grants was that the paintings should be accessible to the public. Rowan worked out that a thirty-minute slot, every first Wednesday of the month, probably fulfilled that obligation.

With the excitement of the locked door over, and funding now available, the work on the keep moved into its next phase. This time, contractors were brought in and they scaffolded the entire inside of the building to give the work team access to every level inside. Adam's leg had healed by now and he was walking more or less normally. He and Jim could not resist the temptation to take advantage of the scaffolding at weekends when there were no workmen around. They explored the upper levels of the keep and followed the walkways and winding staircases built into the clasping towers on the sides of the main keep. It helped them to envisage how the building would work when the internal floors were finally installed.

They were walking back to the estate office when Caleb caught up with them.

"Could you spare a moment, your lordship?" Relationships between them had been warm and friendly since Jim's marriage to Rowan but Caleb still insisted on calling him 'your lordship'.

"I wanted to talk to you about pheasants. I've had a lot of success breeding them over the past couple of seasons. You've probably noticed they're getting thick on the ground. I think it's probably time to organise a shoot or two, if you've a mind to."

"Come and have a coffee in the office and we'll talk it through," Jim suggested.

Jim made the coffee and handed Caleb a mug then said "Yes, I'd like to organise some shoots but I've no idea where to begin. I've never even fired a shotgun."

"Oh, we can soon sort that," Caleb told him. "I've got a spare gun. It used to be my favourite but it's got a bit heavy for me now. It'd be perfect for you. We'll have a few sessions up in the woods and you'll soon get the hang of it. Now, in the days of your namesake, the 12th Duke, he used to invite the landed gentry from miles around and the shoots often lasted two or three days. But, the entertainment and fine dining in the castle were a key part of the event and, until you've completed the rebuilding of the castle, it may be pushing ahead too quickly to contemplate trying to revive that type of event. What I was going to suggest for your consideration was to organise a shoot for farmers in the area to sort of run ourselves in slowly, if you get my meaning. They will still want a good lunch; its regarded as a fundamental part of the shoot."

Jim thought that was an excellent plan and would help build relationships with local farmers. They arranged to visit the woods together the following morning for his first lesson with the shotgun.

Caleb called for him at first light and they took the Range Rover up to the edge of the forest. From there, Caleb led the way into the woods. Jim had had little occasion to visit this area and he was amazed at just how extensive and dense the forest was. Without Caleb's guidance, he would quickly have been lost.

They reached a clearing and Caleb started his instruction on the use of the twelve-bore; he was fanatical about safety and spent the first half hour telling and demonstrating how to hold the gun and break the barrel when not in use. From there, he got Jim to follow birds with the gun, again and again, with no cartridge inside. "Aim just ahead of your target."

Finally, after over an hour he handed Jim half a dozen cartridges and allowed him to fire live at pheasants they disturbed. He missed the first three entirely but then downed the next two in quick succession. Caleb congratulated him. Later, Rowan was slightly less enthusiastic when asked to clean them.

"You can hang onto this shotgun, until you get your own and make your way up here and practice over the next few weeks," Caleb told him. "But remember that you need to apply for a gun licence and the police will want to see that you have a secure place to lock it away, when not in use."

Over the next few weeks, Jim made several trips up to the forest to practice with the shotgun and increased in competence each time. He was perhaps not quite up to Olympic standard but gave a good account of himself.

Jim mentioned to Doug the idea of a shoot for local farmers. He didn't shoot himself but said he would be very happy to accompany the shoot. He had built up a good relationship with a good number of farmers in the area and thought that a shoot would be an excellent way to consolidate friendships.

Chapter 25

While all the work and disruption continued on the keep, the time arrived for Rowan and Jim to take their long-awaited honeymoon trip. Rowan had worked hard on the plans and Jim's role was really only to be available to travel on the appointed day.

She had decided that, as this was a once in a lifetime holiday, it should be the best possible and she had chosen the Seychelles as her destination although this was immediately complicated by the fact that they comprised one hundred and fifteen separate islands.

She had taken advice from the travel agent and decided to stay on the main island of Mahé and booked in at one of the most exclusive beach hotels on the Beau Vallon white powder beach. The resort was just 30 minutes' drive away from Seychelles International Airport and 15 minutes away from the capital, Victoria. She was determined that it was going to be a relaxing holiday and, on arrival, she confiscated Jim's mobile telephone, locked it in the safe in the bedroom and refused to tell him the combination number, despite being tickled almost to the limit of her endurance. But it worked. They did nothing, and they did it well.

The climate was hot, but dry. The difference in temperature between the shade and being out in the direct sunlight was striking, described by one visitor as walking from an oven in to a furnace. Sun bathing is always done in the shade.

Their chalet was only yards from the sea and the brilliant beach and they quickly adopted the local custom of taking a siesta during the hottest part of the day, emerging later in the afternoon to take cocktails on the terrace, overlooking the beach. Later they would wander down to the sea and buy food from the beach barbeque.

The sea was deliciously warm and each day they swam or snorkelled in the warm clear waters of the bay with myriads of tiny fish swarming before their face masks or they lay on sunbeds reading. By the fourth day, even Jim was starting to relax.

The meals were unbelievable, the food was subtly different from that they ate at home, but an absolutely delicious riot of flavours, much of it Creole inspired. At night they lay together in their bed with the overhead fan gently cooling their bodies, and they made love. It was beautiful.

For the first fortnight they never moved from the hotel. After that, they took occasional trips in the hotel's minibus to the tiny capital, Victoria where they discovered that most of the islanders were trilingual, speaking English, French and Creole.

They took trips to the Morne National Park and other beauty spots, amazed at the lush, green vegetation, so prolific that one had the impression it grew as you stood and looked at it. They took a boat trip to Curieuse Island, the only place in the world where the Coco de Mer tree grows. It's very rude-looking fruit has the record of being the largest seed on earth.

They went on an organised fishing trip with others and fished for marlin, sailfish and barracuda. They visited the Vallée de Mai, so beautiful and luxuriant that it was claimed by some to have been the site of the original Garden of Eden. Elsewhere, they saw the giant Aldabra tortoises and other sights but they eventually returned to their hotel, happy to chill out on the beach. One day they met up with another couple of about their own age and sat chatting with them for several hours. They had two small children who were playing happily in the sand.

As they were lying in bed that evening Jim said, "Those two kids on the beach were really cute. You know, one thing we have never discussed in all the time we have been together is whether we want to have children. What's your view?"

"Before we got married, I hated the thought but, since then, I've come to quite like the idea. How do you feel about it?" Rowan asked him.

"Now that things have settled down at home, the idea of tiny feet pattering about sounds quite appealing and besides, we need to create the 14th Duke at some stage."

"I'm glad you feel like that," Rowan told him. "Because there's something I've been meaning to mention to you. You remember how busy it was at lambing time, absolutely hectic. I ran out of pills and I've not got around to renewing the prescription since. By my calculations, I'm now three months pregnant."

Jim went very quiet then pulled her towards him and held her tight for a very long time. When she looked up, she saw that he had tears in his eyes.

"Well, your ladyship, there's an announcement that will help to make our honeymoon memorable." And he kissed her again and again. "If it's a girl, we'll have to call her Victoria after the capital here. I'm not sure what we should call it if it's a boy although there's an island just off the west coast called 'Conception' but that doesn't really have the right ring to it."

For Jim, Rowan's surprise announcement put the cap on the entire holiday; it was brilliant. He was more than ready to return home, simply so he could tell everyone about the next generation of Mountjoy's.

The first person he wanted to tell was his sister, Susan. When he told her, she stuck her stomach out and said "So?" She was obviously expecting as well. That was lovely and the two women were able to share their experiences as the months progressed.

Paradoxically, he was approached by Doug a few days after his return on yet another matrimonial issue.

"Your lordship. I, er! I wanted to ask your permission to get married. I know that it sounds a bit old fashioned and feudal but, if we get married, Lisa will be moving into the tied cottage with me; so, it seems only right to ask your approval.

"You have my whole-hearted approval and my congratulations, Doug," Jim replied. "And, as a present from me and the estate, we'll make a sum available for you both to have the kitchen and bathroom of your cottage brought up to date so that your bride can live in twenty-first century comfort. That should please her." And he told Doug the sum he had at his disposal to do the work. He suspected that the old-fashioned nature of the cottage would have rankled with Lisa and Doug was delighted. The wedding was to be in the village church a few weeks hence and Jim and Rowan were invited as guests of honour. Jim was pleased to be included. The marriage would give stability to Doug's future and he awarded him a substantial increase in salary as he thoroughly deserved it. He had taken full control of the estate's farming activity and relieved Jim of all the day-to-day problems and queries. It was working well; besides, Jim had already noticed that the presence of a women in the home, tended for some reason to increase costs. There was clearly some unknown Keynesian theory of economics which had not been covered in his university course.

Of equal puzzlement was the apparent lack of progress on the renovation of the keep. He was certain that something must have changed but, for the life of him, he couldn't spot the difference. He made a point of catching up with Gregory Price and complained that, since the ground had been cleared, nothing seemed to be moving forward.

"You've got to remember that this work is being monitored by Historic England and, so far as they are concerned, this is an archaeological study to learn more about building practices and design in the immediately post-Norman period. Everything that is taking place is being carefully recorded and catalogued for future reference."

"So, when will we start to see reconstruction work begin and when will the place be habitable?" Jim wanted to know.

Price sucked through his teeth and shook his head as he pondered the question. "Well, the current investigation phase will probably last another three or four months; but remember that some repair work is already being done as the stonemasons come across any particularly crumbling stonework. As for when it will be habitable, that will be at least another year."

"Is there anything we can do to accelerate the process?" Jim asked. The answer was no! Things just had to take their course.

Patience had never been one of Jim's most outstanding virtues.

He was not comfortable with the idea that nothing could be done to accelerate progress and thought about this for several days. He read a story in the local paper of some new houses which had been completed for over nine months but could not be occupied because they were still awaiting services. That gave him an idea. He already knew that the water pressure on the estate was rather low at some of the cottages higher up the hill. That was likely to be particularly noticeable on the upper floors of the keep, when completed. The Electricity Board had also cavilled at the level of supply required in the new cow barn and would almost certainly want a larger substation before they provided a supply to the renovated castle. These were things that he could start to action way ahead of the completion of the renovations in the hope that they would be completed by the time they were required.

He put in his application for the provision of a larger substation, to be sited near the cow barn. Yes, that would probably take six months, or more. Well, at least he had started the process.

Repairs to the water supply were largely in their own hands. By a process of elimination, they identified the approximate area where the water pressure fell sharply and Jim sent Adam off with a spade to follow the course of the supply pipework and find where the blockage occurred. It took him the best part of a week but he eventually exposed a length of pipework that was buckled and was badly corroded and leaking copiously. They hired a piece of equipment which cut a narrow channel for a new plastic waterpipe and buried it underground. They bypassed a significant length of the old pipe and connected the new pipe into the system at each end. It was like a miracle; the problems with the water pressure disappeared immediately.

It was getting on for three years since Adam had completed the repairs to the drive from the gateway and, with the increasing volume of traffic from those working on the keep, the road had started to deteriorate again with many potholes reappearing. Jim asked Adam if he would revisit that problem so that it did not become an impediment during the latter stages of renovating the castle. Adam took it as almost a personal affront that the holes had dared to reappear after his previous work and developed a method of applying a tar product into each hole, before refilling it. He also dug stones from the earthworks surrounding the castle and used them to reinforce the edges of the drive where they showed signs of collapse. The final section of the roadway up to the keep had pretty well disappeared over the years and Adam completed his work by relining the edges and bringing in huge loads of small stones and shale to provide a surface. It would, no doubt, require some further attention and better surfacing when all the rebuilding work was completed but it was a significant improvement for the present.

Doug kept Jim informed as to when the local farmers were likely to complete their harvests and they sent out invitations to the shoot to a dozen farmers, carefully avoiding market days and planned auctions. Caleb had lined up Elizabeth and Rowan to organise the luncheon and, under his direction, they created a magnificent feast for their guests. Jim, received his instructions on how much beer, wine and spirits to order. Caleb asked Adam to work with half a dozen of the retired estate tenants as beaters who would approach from the forest and drive the birds towards the guns in the area which had been planned for the shoot

All but one of the farmers invited, accepted the invitation and they arrived at the estate office in their four-wheel drive vehicles just before eight o'clock on the appointed day. It was a beautiful morning and the forecast was for the day to continue fair.

Jim knew most of the farmers by now and welcomed them before leading them up to the shoot. They spread out across the heath as the beaters started their drive from the woods and the air was full of pheasants flying in every direction. Caleb had been right, there was no shortage of game. Some of the guns were good and brought down an excellent bag of game. Others were clearly not experienced and could probably not have hit the side of a house at point-blank range. Regardless, there was a great deal of hilarity and leg-pulling and they were having lots of fun.

Rowan and Elizabeth arrived in the Range Rover at about half past eleven, bringing the feast. The guns had worked up a thirst and concentrated on the drinks first, before tucking in to the excellent repast. A separate feast had been prepared for the beaters and they stood around in a little group enjoying their 'baggins' and a drink before Caleb ordered them to regroup and sent them back into the woods, ready to launch a second drive when the guns had satisfied their hunger and thirst. That took a surprising length of time as the farmers were thoroughly enjoying their feast and the chance to stand and chin-wag together. Finally, all the dishes were empty, they paused for one last drink and then dragged themselves back to the shoot. The drink had worked well and many a pheasant survived that afternoon as a result of less than sober aim.

Despite the forecast, it started to drizzle, mid-afternoon and the guns were happy to give up the fight and they all drifted back down to their vehicles near the estate office. Jim offered to let the farmers take their bag with them if they wished. Some did so but there were plenty of birds left to share amongst the beaters. Jim was impressed to see that the farmers were very generous with their tips for the beaters and the gamekeeper.

The day had been successful and had been really good fun. Best of all, it had established Jim's reputation among the farming community and he received many return invitations to a variety of events on other farms.

Chapter 26

Jim borrowed the quadbike from Adam one day and drove it down to the bottom of the estate near where he had sold the land for housing. He wanted to ensure that the wall sealing-off the estate from the new housing development had been completed properly. It had, and he was pleased with the quality of the work. The old bridleway was on the other side of the wall so that it no longer passed through the estate. Peering over the wall, he could see that building work had already commenced on the erection of housing. He turned the quadbike around and drove up to the highest part of the estate. He was not complacent but each time he came up here he felt that he could see progress and advancement all around him.

Back at the centre, archaeological prodding within the castle keep had finally come to an end and work had started on restoring the building. It was painstakingly slow and Jim was of the opinion that watching paint dry would have been much more exciting.
This time, the entire exterior of the building was encased in scaffolding from the ground to the battlements and a team of workmen started the process of re-pointing every inch of the stonework. They were skilled and tidy workers and made a very neat job of the exercise but it took nearly five months to complete. At the same time, a team of stone masons took advantage of the scaffolding and cleaned and dressed the window surrounds in preparation for fitting glazing at a later stage.

There had been long discussions about replacing the floors inside the keep which had been destroyed in the fire. When the castle was built in the twelfth century, England had been covered in ancient forests of huge oak trees, big enough to span the enormous width inside the keep. After nearly a millennium of industrialisation, building war ships and deforestation, those forests no longer existed and finding trees large enough to replace the originals proved close to impossible. After much heart-searching it was agreed that the floor structures should be formed of steel girders although these would be disguised by cladding them from both above and below by traditional materials.

The steelwork was prefabricated off site and delivered to site on huge lorries. It was then assembled, bolted and welded into complete frameworks, one for each floor level. Inside the keep, stone and steel brackets had been built into the side walls for the assemblies to rest on. When everything was ready, a huge crane was brought to site and it lifted each section into place over the tops of the walls, starting with the ground floor and slowly working up to the roofing assembly. Once all the assemblies were in place, they were covered with temporary boarding so that the floors could be used and the roofing was quickly completed to weatherproof the building and enable the detailed work to proceed inside.

Jim and Rowan had agreed that the main internal walls of the keep should be maintained as the original stone walls to preserve the authenticity of the building. These were badly blackened from the fire and experts were brought in to sand-blast them and clean them to the original stone appearance. The circular staircases in the side towers were also blackened but there was very little natural light there and it was decided that those walls should be painted white, substantial handrails fitted and any heavily worn treads replaced.

Unsurprisingly, the twelfth century builders had given very little thought to the need for services such as electricity, water and drainage and concealing these presented some interesting challenges. Lighting experts were brought in to advise on providing the maximum possible lighting conditions from concealed lighting and wiring.

Under-floor heating was to be installed on each level but it was planned that the huge open fireplace should be retained on the main floor but with a new lined flue to maximise efficiency. With the walls being up to five feet thick, they had been advised that, once the keep was warm, it would retain the heat and additional insulation should not be needed. Everything took time and the possible end-date drifted backwards, week by week.

Meanwhile, Christmas was fast approaching and the Christmas Eve party in the barn had already become an expected tradition. A very rotund Rowan and an equally rotund Susan willingly volunteered to organise it once more. It transpired that Doug's new wife, Lisa, had quickly joined the pudding-club and, although she was nowhere near as far advanced, she offered to help in arranging the party. Jim offered the option for them to bring in outside caterers to provide the meal but the ladies believed that the party was a private party for the estate and insisted on doing the catering themselves. However, a few months earlier, he had asked Adam to build a detached shed a few yards from the barn with an oven and half a dozen gas rings, fed from gas bottles. This greatly increased their scope for creativity.

With the completion of the cow barn, Adam had moved all surplus equipment into there, out of the old barn and this helped to increase the space available inside. Hay bales were arranged around the perimeter giving somewhere for everyone to sit, while they ate and still leaving plenty of space for the dancing afterwards. The old workbench had been removed and replaced with a make-shift bar. That was popular.

The number of people on the estate was gradually increasing and everyone was there on Christmas Eve; no one was going to miss the party. Talking to some of the old-stagers, Jim was pleased to find that their sense of pride in the estate was continuing to grow. They remembered the depths that it had sunk to following the departure of Lord Frederick but they also recognised how things had improved since Lord James arrived and, very important to them, they remembered how Jim had given them the opportunity to help in the process of restoring the estate and be part of that improvement. Yes, of course they were proud and they were grateful to him for the way he had helped them to restore their own self-respect. Best of all, there was a sense of belonging, of being part of a successful team.

The women had laid on an excellent meal and desserts had again been provided by the wives and widows. Rowan had organised plates of nibbles and chocolates and there was ample drink for everyone. Even some of the older, more strait-laced matrons among them were quite tipsy as they sat giggling in their corners. It was a good party and the accordion player soon had them all up on their feet for the now traditional barn dance. They had a great old time.

Whether it was the barn dance or the natural course of events, Jim was never quite certain but, early on Christmas Day, Rowan went into labour in the middle of the night. He helped her out to the Range Rover and lifted her carefully inside before driving to the hospital in Carlisle. Hospital staff helped her out of the car and into a wheelchair and she was taken to the labour ward. Jim said that he would like to be present at the birth and was given a surgical gown and sent to scrub-up. After the panic of getting to the hospital on time, things seemed to slow down and, although both Rowan and Jim were ready, it appeared that the baby was in no particular hurry to get born and it was mid-afternoon when the little one arrived; a bouncing baby boy.

The birth of the first child is a special moment in the life of any parent and it was no less so for Lord and Lady Mountjoy. Rowan was tired but overjoyed as she bonded with her new baby. Jim was so ecstatic as he sat beside his wife and son that words were meaningless. Life was simply perfect.

"Are you sure he's mine?" Jim asked.

"What? With that great shock of red hair? You're joking."

Jim stated the obvious. "Yes, but he hasn't got a beard."

"Give him a week or two," Rowan suggested. "What shall we call him? And don't tell me Wenceslas or Claus, just because its Christmas Day."

"Our common ancestor was Edward, the 9th Duke. How about calling him Edward?" Jim suggested. Rowan said she liked the name and was happy with that so long as it didn't get shortened to 'Ted'. So, Edward it was.

A very proud father left later that evening to go and announce to the world that the future 14th Duke had arrived; Mother and baby remained at the hospital for two days to gather strength. Jim drove to the hospital to collect them and drove home as gently as if he were carrying a live bomb with a dodgy detonator.

Back home, the detonator went off every four hours throughout the night as Edward strove to train his new parents to respond to his needs. But, for the most part, he was a placid baby and, having been fed and changed, gurgled briefly before going back to sleep again.

For Jim and Rowan, his presence changed their lives completely and he became the centre of their universe.

Susan's baby was not yet due, so she was very happy to help Rowan to keep on top of the feeding, changing, washing and finding out which way up to hold her new charge. Jim doted on his new son and did his bit to help with all Edward's demands; but there were some things that only a mother could do.

While there had been just the two of them, converting one bedroom of the static caravan home into an office, leaving just one bedroom, had been ideal. Suddenly, with Edward's arrival, it was no longer quite so convenient to have just one bedroom as every sigh and snuffle throughout the night had them both awake. After the first couple of nights, Edward was given the sole use of the office at night times and Jim increased the level of heating in there, although Rowan accused him of attempting to boil the baby. Gradually, they got it right and it was quite convenient for Rowan to have the baby in the office while she worked in there and she could also leave him there while she got on with other tasks in the remainder of their home. However, they both looked forward to the completion of work on the keep.

Adam was complaining loudly; what was Susan playing at? Rowan's baby was already a month old and there appeared to be no sign of Susan producing. He threatened her with a five-mile run if she didn't get a move on and produce by the weekend. The threat seemed to work and she went into labour a couple of nights later and Adam ran her down to the hospital in the van.

The birth was reasonably straight forward and she delivered a lovely baby girl who they called Lucy. However, the baby was seriously anaemic and she was kept in hospital for a week while they did blood transfusions and normalised her blood condition. Adam was the epitome of the anxious father and became a leading expert on blood conditions, monitoring the charts at the end of the cot and entering into long conversations with the hospital staff on the next moves. Fortunately, the baby recovered before he had to take his final medical examinations.

Mother and baby were allowed home and Adam was the proudest father ever. After every feed he could be seen wheeling Lucy round in her pram to get her to sleep. It was best not to ask him how she was getting on; he would tell you – at length.

Work on the keep appeared to continue to rush forward with all the urgency and pent-up energy of a dead snail. In fairness, the work was progressing, if rather more slowly than they would have liked. As their third wedding anniversary approached, Rowan announced that, ready or not, she was moving into the keep on that day, the first of May, whether it was finished or not. She started to order items for the keep, in earnest. Every day there were deliveries of furniture or other items she had ordered and they started to pile up to the extent that the workmen had to work around them.

Jim went to have a chat with the clerk of works.
"What do we have to do to get the work completed by 30th April," he enquired.
He was told that it was impossible.
"How big a bonus would it take for your team to make it possible?"
The clerk of works thought he wasn't serious and named a sum.
"OK!" Jim told him. "There's that for everyone in your team and double that for you if everything is finished by that date and all your tools, equipment and bits and pieces are off-site."

Suddenly, the impossible became possible. The men worked long hours and weekends and gradually, the proper floors were fitted, as were ceilings, doors and windows. The kitchen and the bathrooms and toilets all started to take shape. Bedrooms were partitioned off on the top floor although they had decided to leave the main floor open-plan to see how it worked, before dividing that up.
The services were connected up, including the electricity which had been upgraded at Jim's request. As feared, that had taken significantly longer than the promised six months but so had the restoration work; it was now completed and Jim was highly relieved that he had ordered the supply upgrade so long ago.
On the last day of April, a string of lorries arrived to cart away the last of the builder's materials and equipment. Jim hired some of the lads to help unpack all the furniture

and effects Rowan had ordered and carry them up to their appointed destinations.

When all the men had left, Jim had a last look around the keep to ensure that everything was clean and tidy. He checked the nursery; that was in order and ready to receive Edward.

He went back to the static caravan to collect Rowan who had Edward in her arms and led the two of them across the keep and then carried the two of them across the threshold into the keep.

"Welcome to your new castle, Lady Mountjoy. I thought that it would be rather nice if you could actually wake in your new home on your anniversary."

Although they had been monitoring the progress as the restoration had proceeded, it was wonderful to be able to wander freely throughout their completed home. Most of the services were on the ground floor. There was a smart, modern kitchen with a separate breakfast dining area as well as a laundry room and a walk-in larder and store room and a separate washroom. There was also a small area which was to serve as the estate office.

The first floor was a vast, round open room with the main dining area which had a long refectory table at one side and a comfortable sitting area close to the open fire at the other. The Duke's second-best suit of armour which they had found in the basement strong room had been professionally cleaned and stood shining, near to one of the windows close to a display of pikestaffs, battle-axes and shields from the middle-ages. Tucked away in one of the side towers was a convenient washroom.

The top floor held the bedrooms with en-suite bathrooms and, of course, the nursery. Edward had just been fed and changed so Rowan deposited him in his new cot, while they completed their tour of the bedrooms. The whole place was magnificent and lived up to their hopes and dreams in every way.

Jim had purposely purchased a supermarket warm-in-the-oven meal and went down to organise that while Rowan made up their bed, ready for later. He opened a bottle of champagne to celebrate their new home and the two of them sat at the refectory table and toasted each other, Edward and anything else they could think of; it was a very special evening. By now, Edward was sleeping through the night but would require one more feed before he settled for the night. Rowan went up to feed him while Jim tidied up and washed the dishes then, both still fairly merry from the fizz, they retired to bed early.

"It's a bit early to be in bed," said Rowan. "what shall we do now? How about 'I Spy'?"
"OK," Jim replied. "Bags I start; I spy, with my little eye, a very beautiful young lady who doesn't know what I'm about to do to her."

Rowan was fairly certain that his next moves were not in the rules and it completely changed the game.

Chapter 27

It was a lovely feeling to wake in their new home on the morning of their third wedding anniversary. Rowan lay there luxuriating in the whole ambience of the place as she stretched and yawned sleepily and took in her surroundings.

She loved the Dunkield estate, it had been her home throughout her life. In her student days she had feared that growing up and finding work would take her away from it and she had hated the thought; it was her home. All her life she had dreamed that the castle would one day be rebuilt and here it was, complete. The tall red-haired gentleman of her dreams had become real and he had come to fetch her and carried her into the castle. As a child, she had never thought to wonder what he would do to her when he got her inside. Now she knew, and she had certainly enjoyed his unorthodox version of 'I Spy' last night. Her loving husband, so gentle and caring, fulfilling her every dream. And now they had a beautiful baby son to make their family complete in their majestic surroundings. She felt incredibly lucky: it seemed that dreams did come true.

Edward, however, less captivated by his new surroundings, knew only that it was breakfast time and demanded his parent's attention, vocalising his needs, just in case they had forgotten his presence.

"You bring Edward down and I'll go and warm his bottle and make the breakfast," Jim suggested as he rolled, rather reluctantly, out of bed, his feet immediately registering the luxury of the under-floor heating.

As he opened the door into the clasping tower, the lights on the winding staircase came on automatically. However, the stone steps were cold and he wished he had brought his slippers across from the estate office. He must remember to get those today.

He paused briefly in the kitchen to admire the place. Like the rest of the keep, it was lovely; so clean and gleaming and worthy of the castle. The restoration may have taken an incredibly long time, but the final result was outstanding. He may have done absolutely nothing to deserve the Dunkield estate but he had worked hard to improve it since he arrived and he felt a sense of pride in the achievement. The restored keep was a bold statement proclaiming the regeneration of the estate and its role for future generations.

He shook his head to get back to reality, prepared a bottle for Edward and made breakfast for the two of them.

Over the next few days they gradually moved the remainder of their possessions from the estate office static caravan, into the keep.

"What are you planning to do with the van, now that we no longer need it?" Rowan asked as she carried the last of their bits and pieces across.

"I had thought of moving it elsewhere on the estate to act as a spare cottage," Jim told her. "But the planning guy was up here the other day and pointed out that we don't have planning permission for it. In any case, its nearly four years since I bought it and it was a reject even then. I think I'll let Adam scavenge anything he wants from it and then break it up for scrap. We've done a lot over the last few years to smarten up the estate and I want to continue that process. Aiming at being a model farm is perhaps a bit ambitious, but I'd like the whole place to be immaculate so that our work team and the retired tenants can continue to be really proud to be part of it all."

Before Adam could get to it, however, Doug put in a claim for the van.

"I'd like to site it behind the cow barn. With your permission, I'd like to offer work experience courses to youngsters from the agricultural college as a way of putting something back into the community. Its self-financing; the college pays us for training them although some of that will be spent on retired tenants who will be needed to shadow the youngsters and teach them about farming. I'll turn the former estate office back into a second bedroom with bunk beds for the students to sleep in." James felt that was a project which was worth supporting.

"It would also mean that we've got a loo there as well as somewhere to make a cuppa and I could also keep the cattle movement records in there," Doug added.

Jim was fairly relaxed. "OK, get Adam to help you relocate it but I'll leave it to you to put in an application for temporary planning permission."

Adam did a deal with the caravan park to borrow their trailer again and the van was duly relocated, well out of sight.

Now that all the heavy vehicles had left site, Jim asked Adam to have yet another go at the estate driveway. He had continued to keep on top of the task and most of it was not in bad condition. What did need some work was the final approach to the keep. The temporary work he had done earlier had served its purpose but it now needed a more permanent solution. He neatly concreted in some proper kerbstones and contractors were brought in to lay a tarmac surface and then continue resurfacing the entire driveway back to the estate gates. Adam completed his work by landscaping the area around the entrance to the keep. Now it did look smart.

The time arrived for Lisa's baby. Her mother came up from the village and the baby was delivered in her own cottage although the midwife did turn up after all the excitement was over. It was a bouncing baby boy and Lisa and the proud father named him George.

About a month after George arrived, Rowan invited Susan and Lisa and their babies to morning coffee at the keep. Edward and Lucy were several months older than George but it was a good opportunity to get together and allow the babies to play in each other's company. While they were chatting, Susan asked Lisa if she was planning to go back to work when George was old enough. She said that she had talked it over with Doug and her intention was to stay at home to look after George.

"Would you be interested in looking after Lucy on day care at the same time, so that I could go back to work? asked Susan. "Obviously, I'd pay you but I think I would go potty if I had to stay around all day watching Adam coo at Lucy."

Lisa said she hadn't thought about it but she would be quite happy, so long as Doug agreed.

The idea seemed to work from both sides and Susan was back at work within six months of Lucy's arrival and Lisa was very happy to be able to earn a little pin-money. The arrangement worked well for both of them.

Jim asked Rowan if she would be prepared to host a dinner. He wanted to thank Peter Longfellow for all his help and to invite him and his wife, Ann. It would obviously be essential to invite Doug, so Lisa would also be invited and in that case, inviting Susan and Adam would complete the party. Rowan was exceedingly proud of her new home and wanted to show it off and she happily agreed to organising the dinner.

It was planned that Peter and Ann would arrive a couple of hours before the proposed dinner and would take a tour of the estate with Jim and Doug. On this occasion, Jim drove them in his Range Rover with Peter in the passenger seat and Ann and Doug on the back seat.

They started at the bottom of the estate although it was now sealed off from the poor-quality fields which had been sold for housing. From there, they headed slowly uphill, pausing every few hundred yards. Without exception, the quality of the fields had been transformed. They were green and lush. Every field was in use, either for sheep or cattle or for hay or winter feed crops. Hedges were neat and tidy and tightly woven to prevent livestock escaping and all the gates were properly closed and latched. There was no sign of weeds, briars, gorse or broom. It was an impressive transformation from when they had started.

"Are you using much fertiliser?" Peter asked.

"Not really," Doug told him. "We use a little, where necessary and also a small amount of spray. The main treatment is slurry. With that number of cattle, we generate quite a lot of slurry. I bought a muck-spreader at auction a couple of years back and we've been able to spread on every field at least once each year. As you can see, it's had a pretty good effect.

They stopped off at the cow barn. Peter had already seen it on previous occasions but it was a natural place to stop and they got out and looked at the cattle. Peter and Doug went into the static caravan and Peter had a quick look at the cattle movement records.

"I see that you're majoring on Aberdeen Angus and Charolais," Peter commented. "That's a good plan; they tend to put on more weight per pound of feed than many of the other breeds. How many have you got in at the moment?"

"There's just over three hundred and eighty," Doug told him. "As you can see, we're getting fairly close to capacity."

"That reminds me," Peter interjected. "There is some serious organised cattle rustling going on in the area at the moment; there have been at least half a dozen thefts in the last couple of months. You might care to think about mounting a guard for the next few weeks."

Doug thanked him and said that he would.

The inspection completed, they returned to the keep and got there just as Susan, Adam and Lisa arrived. Jim made the introductions all round, and then led them up to the middle floor of the keep where the refectory table was laid for the dinner. First, he invited them to sit in the easy chairs around the fire and served an aperitif of prosecco to the women and beer to the men.

"You really do seem to have a golden touch," Peter said to Jim. "From a disaster area, you have transformed the farm into a very respectable and productive unit. And here, you have taken a ruined castle and made it into a delightful home. What's your secret?"

"Well, the state of the farm is entirely down to a recalcitrant farmer's son you introduced me to. It's all Doug's work and I'm hugely grateful for that introduction as well as all the help you have given me since. I remember walking into your office that first day knowing absolutely nothing about farming, I couldn't even tell one end of a sheep from the other. You listened to me and gave me simple but sound advice which helped me to see where I had to start.

"As for the castle, I felt honour bound to restore it as part of my stewardship of the estate for future generations and I'm pleased with the result." Jim confessed.

Doug chipped in at this point. "The real secret on the farm is that James allowed me to get on with the job and didn't interfere. After the constant battles I had with my father to alter anything, it was so refreshing and fulfilling. By the way though, James; Peter tells me there's some organised cattle rustling in the area at the moment. I'm going to sleep in the static van behind the cow barn for a few nights. Leave your mobile on and, if anything happens, I'll call you and you bring the Range Rover down and block the main gateway to stop them getting away." Lisa looked a little unhappy at the plan but said nothing.

The three babies had been consigned to the nursery upstairs for the duration of the dinner party and there was a baby alarm monitoring them; all was quiet for the moment. The party moved to the table and Jim helped Rowan to serve the dinner. It was an excellent dinner party; the food and wine were perfect and the conversation flowed, throughout. Longfellow turned out to be the ideal guest with a never-ending stream of anecdotes and jokes. It was great fun and there was not a squeak from any of the babies throughout.

It was late when the party eventually broke up. Retrieving George and Lucy from the nursery woke Edward and Rowan gave him a quick feed and settled him down again while Jim cleared away the debris, filled the dishwasher and washed the pans. He made his way upstairs just as Rowan emerged from the nursery and thanked her for an excellent dinner party.

Both Jim and Doug took seriously the threat of a possible cattle theft. Doug had slept in the static van with the windows open to ensure that he heard any movement in the night. The following morning, Jim moved the Massey Ferguson tractor to just inside the entrance to the estate. The tractor was not being used currently and he preferred the thought of the tractor being used as a first line of defence, rather than rustlers driving into the side of his Range Rover in an attempt to escape.

Nothing happened for several nights and he was starting to wonder if they were over-reacting. Then, about a week after the dinner party, his mobile rang just after two o'clock in the morning.
"They're here!" Doug reported. "A cattle truck has just driven down North Lane."
Jim acknowledged and was out of bed in a flash. He pulled on some clothes, made his way out to the Range Rover and drove to the estate gates. He parked the car across the roadway, just outside the gates and then made his way back to where the tractor was parked. He drove that back and parked it just inside the entrance, pointing back into the estate where the rustlers would come from as they attempted to leave. He collected his twelve-bore from the back of the Range Rover, and waited in the moonlight.

His mobile rang again and Doug reported that they were on their way back out; he would follow on the quadbike. A few moments later Jim heard the sound of a lorry approaching. It had no lights on but he could see it clearly by the light of the moon. It halted about an hundred yards from the entrance having obviously spotted the blockage in its way. Then the driver must have made a decision to charge at the road block in an effort to force an escape route. He miscalculated; the grey Massey Ferguson stood there, solid and immovable and hardly trembled as the cattle truck drove into it at full speed. The engine of the tractor buried itself in the engine of the truck which stalled immediately; the vehicle stopped dead as though it had hit a brick wall. If the vehicle had air bags, they failed to inflate and the driver and his companion were catapulted into the windscreen.

Just as Jim heard Doug drive up behind the cattle truck, he saw that a fire had started in the van's engine. He shouted to Doug to help him drag the occupants from the truck and they did that in double-quick time having to ignore any injuries the men may have sustained. They dumped them on the grass verge a little way from the vehicle and then rushed round to the rear to open the back doors to release the cattle. The animals were terrified, both by the impact and by the smell of fire and Doug was lucky to avoid being crushed to death in their rush to escape.

"Just let them go," Jim shouted. "We can round them up in the morning." At that, he pulled out his mobile and called the emergency services and asked for fire, police and ambulance services as he walked back to where the driver and his accomplice lay. The fire had taken a real hold and the vehicle was blazing and the fire had even ignited the diesel in the tractor and between them they pulled the rustlers a little further back from the fire.

Jim put his shotgun back in the Range Rover out of sight under some sacks and then moved the car further away from the gateway both to get it away from the danger of the fire and also to give the emergency services access to the fire.

Doug was peering at the miscreants, neither of whom was conscious. "I know these two. This one works for the agricultural wholesalers and this guy is always hanging around at auctions. I've always thought he was a fairly unsavoury character."

They heard the emergency vehicles almost as soon as they left Carlisle although Jim did wonder if it was really necessary to have their sirens blaring at half past two in the morning. The fire brigade quickly tackled the vehicle fire although, with the diesel burning furiously, they were having difficulty getting it under control. The paramedics from the ambulance service had to squeeze past the burning tractor to reach the injured men. They were extremely cautious as to how to handle them; they were both still unconscious and unable to respond and it was difficult to know what injuries they had sustained.

The police took statements from Jim and from Doug who did his best to identify where each of the men was known from.

It took over half an hour to bring the fire under control and a further half an hour before it was finally extinguished. The paramedics had the injured men strapped into stretchers but were unwilling to carry them past the tractor until the fire was fully out. They then carried them through the blockage and into the waiting ambulance and set off for Carlisle, closely followed by the police car.

"That should put an end to the rustling for a while," Jim suggested.

"Yes, and we've not lost any cattle but that's the end of our poor old Massey Ferguson." Doug commented.

"Don't fret too much. I had it insured for a high value as a classic antique. It won't be sufficient to buy us a brand-new tractor, but it should go part of the way towards it. We'll get a machine with a cab and with all the kit to cut hedges for ourselves as well." Jim told him, looking quite pleased with himself. "Unfortunately, the fire has melted the tarmac on our beautiful new drive and my car is marooned outside the gates by these burnt-out shells and I'm going to have to walk home. Come on; that's enough excitement for one night." And he started his long trek back towards the keep.

The following morning, he spent a long time on the telephone trying to find an outfit capable of removing the burnt-out hulks of the cattle truck and the tractor. He finally succeeded and the vehicles were gone by the end of the day and Jim was able to retrieve his Range Rover and drive it back to the keep. He contacted the insurance company to notify them of the loss of the tractor and the damage to the driveway and, a couple of days later, took Doug down to Carlisle to choose a brand-new tractor.

Unfortunately, that was not quite the end of the affair. One of the rustlers recovered quite quickly from his injuries but the other was permanently incapacitated. His family briefed lawyers who obtained legal aid to construct a case against the Dunkield estate, holding them responsible for his injuries. Fortunately, the court threw the action out at the first hearing as vexatious and mischievous. The local newspaper ran an article on the incident and, for a period, Jim was the hero of the farming community in north Cumbria for having rid them of the rustling scourge.

The estate was also gradually earning a reputation for the quality of the cattle it sent to market. They were consistently good and Dunkield beef cattle increasingly attracted a premium at auction. Margins on farming were never stellar but this helped to make the farm profitable and Doug jealously guarded that reputation, refusing to release animals for sale which he did not consider were ready. Jim maintained a close eye on the accounts for the estate and this premium was making a useful contribution to generating a profit for the estate.

Chapter 28

Jim enjoyed the kudos that his posh title gave him and the automatic and immediate admission it provided, opening doors into any situation. However, he had no great pretension that he was in any way superior to, or better than others. His elevation had resulted from a random spin of the fickle wheel of fortune and he tried hard to avoid putting on airs and graces. However, he did enquire whether his status required him to attend and to sit in the House of Lords and was quite relieved when he discovered that a hereditary title no longer automatically afforded entry to that august body.

He thought about his original plan to generate income from organising shoots on the estate for the local landed gentry. Caleb had continued to breed pheasants to the extent that they were now thick on the ground and, in some places, one was almost in danger of falling over them. The alacrity with which the local farmers had accepted invitations to the free shoot last year demonstrated how popular they were. What was less obvious was how one could actually generate income from them although, with the windfall from the sale of the housing land, the urgency for that had diminished. Besides, neither he nor Rowan felt any great desire to attempt to barge into high society. He decided to let the idea drop for the moment and repeat the exercise with the local farmers, instead. He asked Caleb to organise the detail of the day once more and involved Doug in deciding who to invite and fixing a date when there were no other fixtures.

Several additional farmers who had heard about last year's event, asked to be invited this year and at least another half dozen who had not been invited, turned up on the day. They met at the barn, as before but the number who advanced from there was quite ridiculous and put Jim in mind of a scene from the Charge of the Light Brigade.

He concluded that, if the party grew any further, it would be advisable to split the numbers over two days, in future. On their signal, the beaters advanced from the woods and the air was thick with game and with flying shot; it was a miracle that none of the beaters were injured.

The quantity of food and drink required for lunch for the numbers involved was so large that Rowan drove the tractor up to the meeting point with the lunch laid out on the trailer. Guns and beaters gathered round the trailer and the pheasants were left in peace for an hour or so as they tucked into a fine repast and boasted about how many birds they had brought down.

As on the previous year, it took a great deal of encouragement to persuade them to part from the food and drink and head back towards the shoot. Caleb had organised the beaters back into the woods and they drove another batch of pheasants down towards the guns.

The bag for the day was enormous although it was rather lower than the total number of hits claimed by the guns. There were plenty of pheasants for each gun who wanted to take some home and still ample to reward the beaters. The day was declared an outstanding success and Jim was again impressed with the generosity of the farmers towards the beaters and the gamekeeper. No wonder Caleb was in favour of increasing the number of shoots.

Out of the blue, Jim received an invitation to the Cumberland Show from the company he had brought the new tractor from, as a thank you for his custom. He had not previously attended the show although he knew that Doug went each year so he wrote to accept the invitation and asked if he could have an invitation for his farm manager. This duly arrived and the two of them went off together. The tractor supplier had taken a hospitality tent and the entertainment was lavish, throughout the day.

Tempting as it was to spend the entire day eating and drinking, Jim wanted to see the rest of the show. Initially he walked round with Doug who was a mine of information and explained much of the show and the animal-judging to him. He then wandered around on his own, looking at machinery and all the various exhibits; it was fascinating.

He was just passing a small booth belonging to the Agricultural Advisory Service when Peter Longfellow called out to him.

"James, come and join me; there's someone here I'd like you to meet." And he pointed towards a young man, probably a few years younger than Jim, who was sitting beside him.

"James, this is Lord Andrew Meydrew. Andrew, meet Lord James Mountjoy."

The two men solemnly shook hands while Peter continued.

"Andrew has just succeeded to his family seat and estate. His place is in nowhere near as bad a state as yours was but it does need some work and I was telling him about what you have managed to achieve in just a few years."

Andrew joined in the conversation. "Yes, Peter seems to think you have a magic wand. Like you, I'm not from a farming background and I'd welcome any advice you can give me."

"Would you like to come over and see the place?" Jim enquired. Andrew was keen to do so and they agreed a date between them.

On an impulse, Jim asked if he was married? It transpired that he had married just a month before to a young lady called Nicola.

"Why don't you bring her over at the same time? She can meet my wife while we're talking and then we can have lunch together." Andrew was happy to agree and they chatted for a few minutes more until Jim excused himself to return to his hosts for the day.

Andrew and Nicola Meydrew arrived on the appointed day in a rather smart Rolls Royce: Jim introduced them to Rowan and they sat and drank coffee together. Nicola was still rather shy but it was obvious that the two ladies related to each other immediately. The men left them in the keep and went out to view the estate in Jim's Range Rover.

They drove up to the highest point on the estate where they could view most of the land and Jim talked about his experience as they drove.

"My problem was that the place had not been farmed for twenty years and everywhere was in a dreadful state of neglect. The fields, hedges, cottages and roadways – everything was in a state of decay and the castle was a burned-out ruin. No one on the estate was working, nor had been for years, they were all retired. My first task was to get them off their posteriors and helping. I was able to challenge them and get them involved in the process of improving things. At Peter Longfellow's suggestion we let some of the fields for grazing and also made a modest investment in some beef cattle for fattening. One of the best things we did was to set a programme to refurbish all the cottages. That helped them to feel that they were appreciated and cared for. My luckiest break was that Peter recommended a young farmer's lad to me. He has been absolutely brilliant and is now my farm manager. I'd be lost without him."

"You make it sound very easy," Andrew said. "I think you are just being modest."

"The very first day I came here I met Rowan who is now my wife. I was absolutely lost as to where to begin and she said something amazingly wise. She said 'the estate isn't land or buildings, its people'. I took that on board and have tried to work with the people on the estate, throughout. It's worked for me and it would probably work for you."

A pheasant flew up in front of the car as they drove back to the keep. On an inspiration, Jim asked "Do you shoot?"

"That's one of the few things my father did teach me," Andrew replied.

"Good! Let's fix a date for you to come over and help me to thin these birds out." Jim suggested.

Back in the keep, Rowan had the lunch on the table and it was obvious that she and Nicola had hit it off; Nicola was sitting there feeding Edward.

"Andrew," she called as they entered. "I want one of these."

"Are you sure?" Jim asked. "They can get very noisy." Andrew's response was that she would just have to save up enough to buy one but, in reality, he too was quite taken with Edward.

They sat down to lunch together. Rowan had laid on a good repast and it was easy to sit round the table chatting. Some genuine friendships were forged that day and it was quite late when their guests finally rose to leave.

Jim and Andrew had fixed the date for their shoot; Nicola was to join him and spend the afternoon with Rowan and they would then have dinner together afterwards.

In the interim, however, Jim and Rowan had been invited back to their estate to attend a Hunt Ball.

"It's quite a distance and the Hunt Ball tends to finish very late, so come prepared to spend the night with us." Andrew suggested as they were walking back towards their car.

"She's nice," Rowan commented as they waved their visitors off. "She's incredibly shy but very sweet, I liked them both enormously."

Rowan was excited at the prospect of the Hunt Ball. Discovering that she rode, Andrew had invited her to ride with the hunt if she wished; she declined as she was not much in favour of fox hunting but the ball was an entirely different matter. Naturally, it would require a new dress and she made several visits to shops in Carlisle before she eventually found the one she wanted. She would have liked to have had her hair done for the occasion but she had learnt over the years that whatever she did to her unruly mop of curly red hair, it always ended up as an unruly mop of curly red hair. In truth, however, her hair suited her face perfectly and she always looked lovely.

Jim felt that his sartorial requirements were no less arduous as he submitted to the indignity of being measured for a formal evening suit.

They decided against taking Edward with them and Rowan arranged with Lisa to leave Edward with her, for the twenty-four hours that they would be away.

The Meydrew stately home was about an hour and a half to the south-west of Dunkield, towards the Solway Firth. It dated from the early eighteenth century but was no less impressive. Andrew was out with the hunt when they arrived but Nicola was there and she greeted them warmly although she expressed disappointment that they had not brought Edward with them. They were shown to one of the guest suites and then joined her and other non-riding members of the party for afternoon tea. It was immediately clear that most of the landed gentry of Cumbria had been invited to the hunt and they were introduced to Lady this, Lord that and Viscount something else.

Jim smiled to himself. He had deliberately shunned the idea of imposing himself on high society and yet, through his chance meeting with Andrew, he was now being thrust head-first, into that very situation.

The hunt returned shortly before five o'clock. They were in high spirits having had what they regarded as a successful day. Light refreshments were laid on and all the guests stood around eating, drinking and talking before they started gradually to drift to their rooms to wash and dress in preparation for the evening.

Jim quickly donned his tuxedo and then spent nearly an hour struggling with his bow tie; he had just mastered it when Rowan emerged from the bathroom. She was wearing her new gown of emerald green which complemented her red hair and she looked absolutely beautiful. Jim's suggestion that they should skip the dinner and find some other way to pass the evening, did not go down well.

In the dining room, long tables had been set for about three dozen guests and there were place names at each setting. Jim and Rowan found themselves seated beside two other couples of roughly similar ages to themselves. Andrew and Nicola had obviously thought very carefully about the seating plan and, by the end of the evening, the Mountjoy's had two new sets of aristocratic friends; David and Marjory Butterfield and William and Felicity Fieldon-Wright.

Jim established that both David and William enjoyed shooting and they were all invited to the shoot which Jim had arranged with Andrew.

The meal was sumptuous and there was course after course; all of them superb. The ball was due to commence at ten o'clock and as that time approached, more visitors arrived to join in the dancing. Andrew stood and proposed the traditional toasts of the evening and the dinner guests then processed through to the ballroom where a small orchestra was tuning up in readiness.

Rowan was agog at all the beautiful ball gowns but she had no reason to be envious; she was almost certainly the loveliest young woman there and Jim was proud of her. They danced on and on until more light refreshments were served at midnight and the ball continued again afterwards. Over the next couple of hours, guests gradually drifted off to their carriages or to bed but the two of them were still on the dance floor when the orchestra finally decided that they had earned their corn and stopped playing, just before three o'clock. They were both footsore and weary but they had enjoyed themselves immensely.

After such a late night, they slept until nine o'clock that morning and apologised to their hosts for their late arrival at breakfast. Apparently, Andrew and Nicola had also overslept so they sat and chatted and eulogised about how well the ball had gone, it had been a great success. Just before midday, they made their final farewells and thanks for a great evening, and left to motor back to Dunkield where Edward seemed quite pleased to see them.

Chapter 29

The Hunt Ball had been doubly beneficial for Rowan; not only had she thoroughly enjoyed herself, she also felt that she had picked up some useful tips on entertaining and she applied them assiduously in planning for the shoot visit by their new-found friends.

The plan was that Andrew and Nicola Meydrew, David and Marjory Butterfield and William and Felicity Fieldon-Wright would arrive mid-morning. The men would go off to their shoot and the traditional shoot luncheon would be sent up to them in the Range Rover just after midday; after which the shoot would continue through the afternoon. Caleb had organised a small bevy of beaters and the men had plenty of sport and enjoyed their outing.

Meanwhile, the wives would take coffee in the keep, followed by a light luncheon. For the afternoon, Rowan had hired a local beauty parlour to visit the castle and provide a wide range of beauty treatment for all the women as well as a pedicure and a nail manicure service. It was a total extravagance but the women loved it as they sat there with a glass of champagne in one hand while they were pampered to their heart's content and they chatted happily while soft music played in the background.

Rowan timed her programme to ensure that, by the time the men returned from their shoot, all evidence of their hedonistic, self-indulgent afternoon had been cleared from the lounge. She announced that cocktails would be served at seven o'clock, dinner was set for eight. At that point, all the party disappeared to their rooms to wash and dress for dinner.

Knowing that it is difficult to be an attentive hostess at the same time as preparing and serving a meal, Rowan had hired four young women from the village for the evening to prepare and serve the meal. She had also planned the courses and the recipes to be fairly simple to minimise the chances of anything going disastrously wrong. She dashed up to her room and changed in double-quick time then went down to the kitchen to supervise the work. Everything seemed to be under control.

At around seven, the guests slowly reappeared and were served cocktails and canapes by two of the girls before they retreated back down to the kitchen to finalise the meal.

At eight, she quickly checked that all was ready below stairs and then invited her guests to the table.

Her hired team did well. They served each course without mishap, cleared the dishes at the end of the course and promptly brought the next course. Rowan had arranged the seating plan so that no one sat next to their spouse and that too worked well with the conversation never flagging. Part of the talk was about shoots, hunts, balls and parties amongst the 'in' crowd and Rowan and Jim found themselves invited to a succession of events throughout the county over the coming months. Almost by accident, they had become part of the movers and shakers set.

They had arranged for Adam to drive the girls back down to the village when they had finished serving the meal and tidying up the kitchen and Jim popped down to pay them and to thank them for their work. He returned to join the rest of the party, still at the table, working their way through an excellent Cognac and a vintage Port.

They finally rose from the table at around eleven o'clock and all drifted off to their separate rooms. Jim and Rowan completed the tidying up downstairs and got themselves organised for breakfast before they too retired to bed feeling that it had been a most successful day.

They were up early next morning and prepared the breakfast which again turned out to be a long and leisurely meal with no one in any great hurry to depart. When they did finally drift off it was clear that they had all enjoyed their stay as they discussed and looked forward to the next event, they had diarised.

Chapter 30

With life on the estate having settled down into an organised pattern, both Jim and Rowan had for some time been thinking that they should be putting something back into the community through supporting charitable work. They had both thrown their support behind Doug's project to offer work experience courses to youngsters from the agricultural college. Jim was happy to pay retired estate workers to nanny the youngsters and pass on their experience and to teach and train them. Rowan mothered the kids and regularly sent down food and other treats for them. It was working well but they both felt that they would like to do more.

Since his name had first appeared in Debrett's Peerage, Jim had been regularly bombarded with invitations to join the board of this, that or the other company as a director. What they wanted, of course, was to have his title on their letterhead to provide an aura of respectability, stature and stability. Some of them offered quite generous remuneration and other perks in return for the privilege.

Initially, Jim gave serious consideration to some of these approaches and even investigated a few of the companies involved thinking that it might provide an interesting diversion. He quickly realised that all the companies were looking for was to use his name; they did not require or expect any input from him. He was to be a 'sleeping partner' and he was sufficiently realistic to recognise that, although his degree might provide some basis of knowledge, he had no real business experience to offer beyond what he had learnt as he had fumbled through the problems of the Dunkield estate. He was also concerned that, as he would have no day-to-day involvement with the companies, he would have little insight into their corporate governance and scant visibility as to whether they were financially sound or if they were operating ethically. It was a recipe for disaster and he was not tempted.

He had also received a number of invitations from charities and non-profit organisations to act as a patron to their cause and, since their marriage, Rowan had also started to receive similar approaches. He was more drawn to this type of organisation and, over the Christmas break, they discussed the idea of accepting a few such appointments as a means of serving the community.

They made an early decision that, as they lived in north Cumbria, they would limit any involvements to that region. Neither of them was interested in trekking down to London or elsewhere for meetings or events. That significantly reduced the number of possible appointments and left a manageable pile of requests for consideration and they went through them together.

Patronage of the arts was mostly a thinly veiled request to cough up a donation in return for having one's name printed on a programme or elsewhere, as a sponsor. They were not necessarily against supporting such organisations but decided to limit them to causes they felt strongly in favour of supporting.

They were more interested in identifying small, local charities where, in addition to lending their name and possibly making donations, they might also be able to do a little hands-on work to help out, on occasions.

There were two charities which had approached them which particularly attracted their attention, both based in or around Carlisle. One was essentially linked to handicapped children, with spina bifida, providing them and their carers with a wide range of services, advice and support. These included access to medical facilities, help in locating appropriate schools and education facilities, assistance with claiming disability benefits and organising holidays, looking for employment opportunities as well as giving much-needed support to the carers. There was also a day-care centre for younger children which operated from a church hall and children were brought to there for games and creative sessions and to allow some respite to their carers for a few hours. Rowan and Jim visited the centre and were impressed with the work the charity was doing. As a mother, Rowan was particularly sympathetic to the work of this organisation and offered to work at the centre one day each week and also to work on their fund-raising committee.

The second charity they looked at was dedicated to helping the homeless, habitual drug takers, and other dropouts. It operated from a disused ex-army Nissan hut on the outskirts of town. Rows of beds which the council had been asked to collect as part of their refuse collection service, had been diverted to a second life and installed in the hut in long lines. Volunteers had upgraded the toilet facilities and the kitchen area and, each night, volunteers helped prepare food for those who came to claim a bed for the night. The meal usually consisted of a good, thick stew made from unsaleable off-cuts of meat donated by local butchers and supermarkets, and bread or rolls left over at bakeries at the end of the day. It was difficult to class those who ate as grateful but they turned up for their supper, night after night.

Having lived on the streets himself as a self-imposed drop-out, Jim felt particularly attracted to the work of this charity and a huge empathy with its 'customers'. He volunteered to help on a regular basis, at least one evening in the week. The session usually started with him driving the van round town to collect the meat and the bread contributions. Back at the Nissan hut, another of the volunteers would already have started preparing the stew and Jim would help to cut up the contributed off-cuts and add them to the pot. Whilst that was cooking, some of the team would clean out the hut and prepare the beds for the night. At nine o'clock the 'customers' would start to arrive for their supper of bread, stew and as many cups of tea as they could drink. At the end of the evening there would be a chain of washer-uppers to leave the place clean and tidy. One of the volunteers would stay for the night as a night-watchman to ensure that there were no emergencies and no untoward activities.

Jim was careful to ensure that he was known only as 'Jim' at the charity. There was no place for posh titles or airs and graces in this society and no one knew his true identity or where he lived. However, he did find ways to make a variety of anonymous contributions to the work in both money and in resources for the charity.

Because of his own experiences in life, he also found it very easy to relate to those who used the charity. Having been on the receiving end of similar benefits, he felt absolutely no sense of censure towards those who visited, rather an affinity that he had shared their hardships and deprivation. He was happily able to chat with many of them and understand their problems and he found the work enormously fulfilling and satisfying.

There was a tremendous sense of camaraderie, not simply amongst the volunteers but extending to embrace those who came to eat and to stay the night. Jim actually started to look forward to his weekly session and the anonymity it afforded him to be himself whilst helping others, less fortunate.

He had been working with the charity for about six months when, one evening, as he was doling out the stew onto plates as 'guests' passed, the person in front of him said "Hiya Jim; what are you doing here?" He looked up and into the face of Boots, the 'finder' from the archway under Charing Cross Station.

He was stunned for a moment but quickly recovered himself. "Boots! How brilliant to see you. You're looking great. Here, get yourself fed and I'll come over and we can

have a chat when I've finished dishing out the dinner."
And he dolloped a little extra onto Boots's plate.

The pause gave him an opportunity to think how to handle the chance encounter. He was delighted to see Boots and looked forward to talking with him but he was very glad that he had maintained his anonymity. Boots would hardly fit in with his life at Dunkield Castle.

Jim finished his tasks and then wandered over to where Boots was sitting.

"So, what brings you so far from Charing Cross?" he asked.

"I'm actually on the run," Boots confided quietly. "I seem to have upset the law a bit in London and I thought it might be a good idea to make myself scarce for a little while. I'm on me way up to Scotland to hide until things quieten down. But what about you, mate? Have you gone legit?"

"Sort of," Jim replied. "I've got involved in a few things locally and I enjoy helping here, particularly remembering how we had to struggle to get a good meal down in London. What's the news though? Is Big Lizzie as big as ever?"

"Nah! Bigger, she's huge," Boots told him. "She's going to end up in hospital – or dead."

"And what about Pretty Polly? Has she gone on the game yet?"

"No! Her parents traced her and they took her back home; baby 'n' all. That was kinda nice."

Jim was pleased to hear that bit of news. He had quite liked the kid.

They chatted on for fifteen or twenty minutes and Jim was very careful not to give any clues as to his identity or his changed fortunes. Eventually he excused himself because he had other duties to perform. He was not on duty as night watchman on that occasion and, at the end of the evening, he slipped quietly away, hopeful that his and Boots paths would not cross again.

On his next duty, a week later, there was no sign of Boots although one of the volunteers told him that someone answering to Boots description had been asking searching questions about Jim – which they were unable to answer. Jim was relieved.

About a couple of months later, Rowan was working in the estate office one morning when there was a knock at the door. She opened it to find a dishevelled tramp standing outside.

"I've come to see Jim; 'e knows me," said the untidy apparition.

"I'll get hold of him for you; who should I say is calling?" She responded, reaching for her mobile.

"Tell 'im its Boots."

"James," she said into the receiver, "A gentleman has arrived to see you. He says that his name is Mr Boots."

Jim's heart fell; this was something he had hoped would not happen and there was a slight hesitation before he replied. "I'm at the cattle shed with Doug. I'll be with you in five minutes. Don't let him inside."

It was less than five minutes before Jim roared up on his quad bike.

"Hi Boots. How did you know where to find me?"

"Oh, you knows me. Always had a nose for a good situation, didn't I." Boots told him.

"Come on up to the barn and we can have a chat," Jim told him as he led the way, away from the keep.

In the barn, they sat on hay bales and Jim asked. "So, what brings you up here?"

"Well, I 'eard as 'ow you'd fall'd on good times and I thought you'd want to share it with me, like we used to share everything. Y'know, for old times' sake."

"No," Jim told him. "the soup-kitchen and free handouts are down in town, not here."

"Oh! I figured as 'ow you wouldn't want all your posh friends round here finding out about your past; y'know, living on the streets of London, begging an' all that."

Jim was on his feet in an instant, towering over Boots. "Don't you dare threaten me or try to blackmail me or I'll have the police after you, faster than you can run. You can get out of here now, Go on!"

Boots cowered, realising that he had gone about it the wrong way. He changed tack and grovelled.

"Sorry Jim, I didn't mean to threaten you. It's just that I'm on me uppers and I thought you might give me a hand up, for old times' sake, like."

"This is a working farm, not a charity." Jim threw at him. He paused, then continued. "If you're prepared to do some farm work, I might be able to find you a job."

Work was not a concept with which Boots was particularly comfortable but he had already worked out that there were potentially some rich pickings here and he wanted to hang about to see if he could profit from them. "Yea. Yea Jim. That'd be great."

"Right; I'll take you down to meet the farm manager but Boots, I'll expect you to earn your living properly and honestly, no monkey-business."

Doug was still working at the cattle shed when they arrived and Jim made the introductions.

"Boots, this is Doug Midgley, the farm manager; Doug, this is Boots. Boots and I go back to a previous existence but he's currently in need of a job. Can you use him?"

Doug looked at Boots a little uncertainly, but nodded.

Jim continued "I expect him to earn his living, Doug; no favours. If you find him slacking, you have my full permission to send him packing, on the spot. Its holiday time and there are no students in the caravan. He can live in there for the moment."

"Boots, you do as Doug says, he's your boss. I'll send up some grub for you for this evening. There's a mobile shop calls at the barn at ten o'clock in the morning and I'll arrange for you to get food from there to look after yourself for the next week."

He left Boots in Doug's care to settle into the caravan and made his way back to the castle.

"You already know about my time slumming it on the streets of London," he told Rowan. "Boots was one of my unsavoury companions at that time. He turned up at the soup kitchen down in Carlisle a couple of months ago. I've no idea how he managed to find where I live but, just now, he tried to threaten me with my past and I put a flea in his ear. I should probably have chased him off the estate but, instead, I've given him to Doug as an additional farm worker. I think his chances of surviving are about as good as a snowball in a hot oven. I've promised to take some food down to him for this evening, if you can spare a little."

Jim took the food down to the caravan later that evening. Boots had clearly made himself at home there and grovelled his gratitude to Jim, again. The following morning, Jim told the shopkeeper in the mobile shop that he would pay for a week's food for Boots – but no alcohol.

He kept a careful eye on Boots over the next few days. It was clear that he knew absolutely nothing about farm work. Doug summed it up as "Doesn't know one end of a pitch-fork from the other," but he appeared to be willing enough and did what Doug asked him. Perhaps it was going to work out, after all.

It was Caleb who sounded the first alarm when Jim met him in passing, a couple of weeks later.

"Your Lordship, I'm not certain whether I should mention this or not. You know that I still do regular night patrols, keeping an eye on the game. A couple of times recently I've caught that new man of yours out in the middle of the night, snooping around some of the cottages. Each time he's seen me, he's headed off back to the caravan as though he was perfectly entitled to be wandering about in the middle of the night. It's probably just because he's a poor sleeper but I thought I should mention it to you."

Jim thanked him. "No, Caleb. Thank you for telling me and let me know if there are any more incidents."

Jim wandered out to the fields where Doug and some of the men were cutting silage for winter cattle feed.
"Hi James" Doug called. "I'm glad you've come. We're a bit short-handed since you sent Boots off."
"What do you mean?" Jim asked.
"He said that you'd sent him off on an errand and I've not seen him since mid-day." Doug replied.
"The lying toad," Jim responded. "I've not sent him anywhere, he's obviously slacking. I'll ball him out if you like but it might be better coming from you. If I need him for an errand at any time, I'll let you know."

Over the time Boots had been on the estate, there had been unexplained reports of items missing from various of the cottages; a purse here, a few trinkets there. As Rowan had said when he first arrived at the estate, no one ever locked their door and initially, the losses were put down to having misplaced items but Jim was starting to get suspicious.

Adam had been working alongside Boots and some of the others. He came to see Jim one evening. "Jim, that Boots guy you introduced is causing trouble. He's bad-mouthing you all the time and winding up some of the others. The men respect you and they're not paying too much attention to what he says but he's acting like a proper barrack-room lawyer and doing his best to stir them all up. You need to keep an eye on him."

Boots had no bank account and Jim had arranged with Rowan for him to be paid weekly, in cash. On his fourth week, he turned up at the office for his pay, as usual, and she handed him his money. He was just about to leave when he asked "Excuse me, Lady Mountjoy, I'm out of salt; could you possibly let me have a little until the shop arrives, next week." Rowan was perfectly happy to oblige and went through to the kitchen and brought some back in a small container. Boots thanked her profusely, and left.

Rowan settled back to her work. There had been a pile of bank notes on the desk and she suddenly realised that the pile was now much smaller and she did a quick check. She called Jim on his mobile and told him.

"I can't be absolutely certain that he took them and I can't prove it; but I'd just counted them before he came in and there's certainly about four hundred missing now."

For Jim, it was the final straw. He was already on his quad bike on his way down to the cattle shed and he caught up with Boots still walking back to there.

He stopped the bike beside Boots, held out his hand and simply said "Give!"

Boots feigned lack of understanding and Jim repeated more emphatically "Give; Now!"

Boots knew that the game was up. He put his hand in his pocket and pulled out the wad of notes and handed it over. "Sorry, Jim. I just needed to borrow it to ...."

His voice trailed off as he looked into Jim's eyes and saw a mixture of anger and utter disbelief.

Jim pointed down towards the entrance of the estate.

"You've got twenty minutes to disappear, before I report you to the police. Go! And don't ever, ever come back."

Chapter 31

Fortunately, Rowan's charitable work was proving less problematic. She was enjoying her involvement with the children's charity every bit as much as Jim had initially enjoyed his and she had no reason to remain incognito. She was proud to be Lady Mountjoy and did not mind a jot who knew her identity. However, like Jim, she had no problems in getting her hands dirty. On the days on which she attended the centre, she left Edward in the care of Lisa and she worked tirelessly in the day care centre, caring for the children. Saturday mornings often found her in the centre of Carlisle, shaking a tin to raise much needed funding for the charity, while Edward slept in his pushchair at her side. She was an inspiration to the mothers and to her fellow workers alike and quickly became popular as one of the key drivers of the organisation.

When necessary, the charity had the use of some council-owned, specially adapted coaches for carrying wheelchair-bound people. On several occasions, Rowan commandeered these and organised for children and parents to be carried up to Dunkield castle for a picnic. Rowan had always been popular with the wives and widows on the estate and she usually roped several of them in to help to organise the day. The event was always a well-attended trip and enjoyed by all.

In addition to her work with the charity, Rowan took seriously her relationship with the wives and widows on the estate. They had all known her since she was tiny and, if most of them had long since worked out her true parentage, none of them ever spoke a word about it. She was Caleb and Elizabeth's daughter and they honoured them for the way they had cared for her and brought her up. They all regarded themselves as her surrogate guardians; they had kept a parental eye on her over the years and each of them would happily go out of their way to care for her and protect her.

Without knowing the reason for their warmth and affection over the years, Rowan had basked in their affection and care as she grew up on the estate. With her marriage to James and her new title of Lady Mountjoy, it occurred to her that, in the spirit of *'noblesse oblige'* obligations were now placed on her as the Lady of the Manor, to return the courtesy and to start to care for her carers.

When she returned from university, she had picked up all the friendships of her childhood years and had ridden Beauty each day, visiting the wives and widows on the estate, always a welcome guest in their homes. She continued those visits after her marriage.

The arrival of Edward curtailed her horse riding but she still made regular visits around the estate. She learnt to drive the quad bikes and, with Edward in a papoose, regularly visited each home to show off her new son and to catch up on the news.

With the completion of the building work on the keep, she introduced a weekly coffee morning for all the women on the estate. It was a popular innovation and it was rare for any of the women to miss the event. It meant that, far from her marriage distancing her from the women, they became an increasingly closer-knit group and if Rowan needed help with a picnic for the handicapped children, refreshments for Christmas parties or anything else, she had a supportive army, ready to swing into action on her behalf. It was a great relationship and, in return, Rowan was hugely sensitive to the welfare of 'her ladies', lavishing special care on any of them when it became necessary.

Although she had married the 13th Duke of Dunkield, to them, she was still the lovely lass they had helped, cherished and cared for over the years; she was their Rowan.

Two of the widows, Enid and Rose were sisters who had each married one of the farm workers in their early twenties. They were now both in their eighties and their husbands had died years ago. Rose came to find Rowan one morning, in a great state of distress.

"Enid has had a fall. She's hurt her back and I can't get her up off the floor. I think she probably needs to go to hospital for a check-up. I don't have one of those telephone things; please could you call for an ambulance for her."

Rowan grabbed her mobile and followed Rose straight across to Enid's cottage. It was clear that Enid was in a great deal of pain and Rowan promptly called for an ambulance and then did her best to make Enid as comfortable as possible.

Rose wanted to go in the ambulance with Enid but Rowan suggested that they let Enid go by herself and she would then run Rose down a little later when Enid had been admitted, x-rayed and examined.

When they arrived at the hospital, Enid was lying in a bed, fairly well sedated but still able to converse. One of the hospital staff told them that the x-ray had shown that she had twisted her spine. The plan for the moment was for her to lie still in bed for a few days to see if it adjusted itself. In the meantime, she would be fed pain killers to cope with the pain level.

Over the course of the next month, Rowan ran Rose down to the hospital two or three times each week and Jim and Adam would also offer her a lift if they were going into town. Sadly, however, Enid was not making much progress and the hospital were starting to hint that they needed her bed. As they were driving back from the hospital one afternoon Rose said that it was such a pity each of them only had a one-bedroom cottage. If either of them had two bedrooms, they could move in together and Rose would be able to look after Enid.

Rowan passed this comment on to James over dinner that evening. He thought about it for a few moments and then suggested that Yew Tree Cottage was vacant and that had two bedrooms. He would take Rose to see it and, if she thought it would do the trick, he would ask Adam to do a bit of work to make it wheelchair-friendly and the two of them could move in there together.

He took Rose to see the cottage the following morning. She was thrilled with the idea and thought it would be perfect. Over the next few days, Adam widened some of the doorways to admit a wheelchair and built a ramp where there was a step and he helped Rose to move out of her cottage into Yew Tree, ready for when Enid was discharged from hospital a few days later.

Rowan went to visit Enid when she arrived home. It was clear that she was going to be largely wheelchair-bound but she was very grateful to Rowan and James for their care and consideration. She clearly could not cope on her own and she was very happy to be moving in with her sister.

Rowan checked on them again a few days later; everything was working well. The only problem Enid had not managed to conquer was bathing. Rowan mentioned that to Jim over lunch and he said that he would ask Adam to see if he could do something about a walk-in shower room to help her overcome the problem.

First, however, it was time for the now traditional Christmas Eve Party for the Dunkield estate and Rowan, Susan and Lisa got together to plan the event. The accordion player was booked, the meal planned and the only real departure from tradition was where to cordon-off a playpen of hay bales for the three babies. However, Rowan decided that they should also string-up dozens of Christmas fairy-lights throughout the barn this year as opposed to the fluorescent tube which had provided light in previous years. It certainly made the barn look particularly festive and created a wonderful atmosphere.

As always, everyone from the estate was present. Even the tenants who had long-since retired felt a great sense of pride in the estate which was now smart, productive and profitable. On his way there, Adam called on Rose and Enid and helped to wheel Enid up to the party.

The three women had arranged with the accordionist to introduce one other new feature this year. Before they started eating, they stood around the barn and sang Christmas Carols together for twenty minutes or so. It was a huge success and everyone joined in, making a lovely harmony. It seemed to embrace everyone, linking them together and identifying them as a member of the family of the Dunkield estate – a successful and caring family. Old and young alike were swept up in the magic of Christmas that evening as they celebrated the end of another successful year.

Mothers and babies did not last the entire evening but, as on previous years, many of the others were still there dancing as the clock announced Christmas Day.

For the Mountjoys this was a special Christmas. It was their first Christmas in their new home and they thoroughly enjoyed the luxury of the keep and spent a long time in front of the roaring log fire. Christmas Day was also Edward's first birthday and he received a great pile of presents. He was not really able to open them and, when mummy or daddy opened them for him, he largely ignored the contents and played instead with the lovely crinkly paper.

Whatever, all three were blissfully happy.

45992368R00137

Printed in Poland
by Amazon Fulfillment
Poland Sp. z o.o., Wrocław